Also by R.M. Clark
From Indigo Sea Press

The Right Hand Rule

Dizzy Miss Lizzie

indigoseapress.com

Center Point

by

R.M. Clark

Stiletto Books
Published by Indigo Sea Press
Winston-Salem

To Judy!

Thanks for
reading!

RM Clark

Stiletto Books
Indigo Sea Press
PO Box 67201
Winston-Salem, NC 27114

First Stiletto Books edition published
October, 2016
Stiletto Books, Moon Sailor and all production design are trademarks of Indigo Sea Press, used under license.

For information regarding bulk purchases of this book, digital purchase and special discounts, please contact the publisher at indigoseapress@gmail.com

Cover Concept by R.M. Clark
Cover Design by Pan Morelli
Manufactured in the United States of America
ISBN 978-1-63066-428-2

Dedication

Dedicated to Jan and Dot and the memory of Bill and Jim;
true center points.

Chapter One

I arrived at the sports bar perfectly sober, but I had no intention of staying that way. You only get one chance at turning twenty-five, and I was going to make the most of the opportunity. I waited in my car, cranking a great tune with the windows up. The bright O'Reardon's sign flickered above the front of the sports bar, the R barely hanging in there. Had this been any Saturday between September and May, the place would've been crawling with college kids—and lots of coeds—of legal drinking age, easy pickings most nights; but it was early August, and we had to settle for the local crowd, which was perfectly fine with me.

Two songs later, my friend Tom Richcreek rolled into the parking lot. He backed his small pickup into the space next to me. Jed Stormont was with him.

"Looks like it's just the three amigos," said Tom. "The others bailed." He used the remote to lock his car. "Hey, Koz, more beer for us."

My friends called me Koz, short for Kozma, my last name. Everyone else called me Dennis.

We entered O'Reardon's at just after 9 p.m., walked past the long bar with six kinds of beer on draft and several hi-def TVs and found a corner booth, our favorite during football season. A waitress arrived, mid-thirties, wearing a short dress that revealed a modest amount of cleavage. She wore heavy makeup and a nametag that read "STACY."

"I'm going to need to see some ID." Stacy placed a notepad back in her front pocket. It was a college town so everyone under thirty got carded whether they knew you or not. The manager was always watching.

Tom and Jed each handed over their driver's licenses, which Stacy examined and handed back. She glanced at me.

"What about you, sunshine?"

"It's his birthday!" Jed said. "Does he get a free drink?"

I gave her my license and flashed a wide grin. Stacy checked the date on her watch. She looked at the license, then at me again.

It happened all the time, so I guess it was the curse of being baby-faced. *Maybe it was time to grow some facial hairs*, I thought.

"To answer your question, yes, you get a free drink." Stacy handed me the license and took out her notebook. "What'll you have, boys?"

Tom took care of the ordering. "A Guinness Draft for me and the birthday boy, a Corona for Jed."

Stacy returned a short time later with the drinks and advice. "Don't go crazy tonight, Dennis. I don't want to read about you in the paper or anything, okay?"

"No problem, Stacy."

Jed raised his bottle. The lemon wedge was sticking out so he pushed it down with his palm. "Cheers."

"Cheers." Tom clinked his bottle with Jed's.

I put mine down to make a T with my hands. "Timeout. You're telling me that's all I get for turning twenty-five? Come on, you guys. We've been friends since kindergarten. I deserve a proper toast."

Tom cleared his throat. "To the first twenty-five years of your miserable life, Koz."

I shook my head. "Nope, that won't cut it either. Try again."

Jed held his bottle before me with the lemon stuck in its neck. "Here's to swimmin' with bow-legged women."

I couldn't believe what I was hearing. We'd been through everything for more years than I could remember. We'd shared good times, bad times and even coeds. "Sorry, you stole that from the movie *Jaws*. Unacceptable." I gave out an exaggerated sigh. "I guess I'm not worthy."

Tom leaned over to Jed, and they whispered something to each other. Tom raised his beer once again. "To Koz. We've known men wiser, we've known men humbler but I've never known a man more proud of his rock tumbler."

That was more like it. I laughed at the inside joke and tapped bottles with my two friends. Every year on my birthday, they reminded me of the unusual birthday presents my father used to give me.

"I still have that rock tumbler on the top shelf of my closet," I said, "along with the Erector Set he got me when I was eight."

"And the chemistry set?" Jed asked.

"Yup, it's there too."

I thought back fifteen years to the day, my tenth birthday. All I wanted was a Nintendo gaming system. I hinted about it for weeks and even pointed one out to my parents in the toy store. When I opened the presents at the end of the party, I saved the big one from Dad for last. It was the right size and everything. Dad was "the man" and he would take care of me. Come on, Nintendo! I ripped off the paper and there it was... an ant farm.

"The way I look at it, my dad just wanted to find something that interested me." I took a handful of popcorn and downed it. Sadly, I still haven't found it.

Jed lifted his bottle to clink it with mine, then repeated the act with Tom. "Here's to crappy birthday presents, then and now."

We turned our attention to the game on TV and cheered when the Red Sox pitcher struck out a batter. Stacy returned a short time later with three more drinks.

"Attention, people," Tom said. "What we thought was a rumor is, indeed, a fact. Our Stacy is a mind reader." His hands hovered above the table.

She leaned sideways and placed the drinks on the table. "I don't think so, slick." She used her elbow to point. "These are courtesy of that handsome gentleman over there."

We turned in the direction of a well-dressed man with a salt-and-pepper beard in a corner booth. He munched on popcorn as he watched the baseball game.

Jed dislodged the lemon and downed several more ounces, nearly knocking off his Yankee cap. "Anyone know who that guy is?"

Tom shook his head.

I squinted through the glare with one hand above my eyes to get a good view. "He looks... kind of familiar, but I can't place him."

"It's your birthday," Jed said. "He must have done it for you."

"Maybe it's a secret admirer, Koz. You are kinda cute."

"And you, sir, are a dick." I smacked Tom in the shoulder, then finished the contents of the first bottle. "Well, there's only one way to find out."

I walked to the corner booth, nearly running into Stacy along the way. The man clapped as the Red Sox scored a run.

3

"Excuse me. I wanted to thank you for buying us a round."

The man turned his attention from the game and looked up. "You're welcome, Dennis."

"May I ask why?" I couldn't decide where to put my hands so I folded them behind my back.

"Dennis, do you know who I am?"

He was wearing a dark suit with a red tie, making him slightly—okay, extremely—overdressed compared to the rest of the clientele. This was certainly no one I would hang around with.

"If I owe someone money, just let me know..."

"No, it's nothing like that. My name is Gene Clausen. I'm an attorney."

I looked carefully at his face. Then it came to me. "You were in our house once." I hooked my thumbs through my belt loops. "Yeah, just after my dad died, right?"

"That's right. I handled your parents' divorce, and I was the executor of your father's estate." He put his hand out and I gave it a firm shake. "Have a seat, Dennis. I have something that might interest you."

I looked back at the others, who watched from our booth. No way was I abandoning them tonight. "I'm kind of out with my friends. You're welcome to join us."

He took out his card and handed it to me. "I'm here on official business, Dennis. What I have to discuss concerns only you. I'll let you decide if you want your friends involved or not."

I checked him over and realized he was dead serious. *What the hell does my dad have to do with anything?* He'd been gone for fifteen years, so I was pretty much over it. Besides, lawyers always gave me the creeps.

"They're my buds," I said. "Tonight we're a package deal. Come join us, Gene the lawyer."

"Thank you. I'll do that." Gene slung a large canvas bag over his shoulder and slid out of the booth. "Lead the way."

Tom and Jed both stood as we arrived. "This is Gene Carlson. He's a lawyer—my dad's lawyer. Gene, this is Tom and Jed."

"Uh-oh, Koz," Tom said. "What did you do now?"

Jed raised the bottle and nodded. "Hey, man. Thanks for the brew."

"It's Gene Clausen. It's a pleasure to meet you both." He

shook their hands, then slid into the booth after me.

Gene took the bag and placed it on the seat. "Your father was a wonderful man, Dennis. He was truly one of my best friends."

"Thanks." With nothing more to say, I started on my second Guinness. It didn't taste nearly as good as the first one, thanks to the arrival of our unexpected guest.

Gene pulled out a package and placed it on the table. It was a leather satchel with string wrapped around it in both directions. "I promised your father I would personally hand this to you on your twenty-fifth birthday." He looked at his watch. "What do you know? I made it with a few hours to spare."

Stacy came by and removed the empties. Tom made no attempt to move as she leaned over him. She didn't seem to mind.

"Hey, Gene the lawyer, can I buy you a beer or something?" Tom asked.

"Just ginger ale, please. I'm still officially on the clock."

I turned the package over and examined it. It wasn't very heavy and had no markings. "What's in it?"

"I honestly don't know, Dennis. This is exactly the way your father handed it to me in my office fifteen years ago."

I shook it, but the contents didn't shift. "Does my mom know about this?"

Stacy returned and Tom sneaked a peek down her shirt as she placed the glass in front of Gene. Tom handed her two bills and winked. Stacy rolled her eyes as she walked away.

"I haven't told anyone, Dennis. I put this item in a safe about a month before your father passed away. A promise is a promise." Gene hoisted his ginger ale in my direction. "Happy birthday, Dennis."

We clinked glasses and I took a hearty drink. Any friend of my dad's was a friend of mine.

"Open it, Koz," said Jed.

"Is it just me, or does anyone else hear the 'Twilight Zone' music playing?" asked Tom. "I mean, we're talking about your dad and his crappy birthday presents when a mysterious stranger shows up." He mimicked the "Twilight Zone" theme while making weird movements with his fingers.

"C'mon, Koz," said Jed. "You're dying to know what's in it."

I took a small knife from my pocket and sliced off the strings

5

binding the package. I flipped open the top and pulled out two Manila folders. They smelled like my father's cologne—god, I missed that scent. I opened the thicker one, which contained photocopies of various documents and legal papers.

"What are these?" I asked Gene.

"I'm not sure, Dennis."

"Check out that one." Jed pointed to a page sticking out of the smaller folder.

I opened it and slid out what appeared to be a very old map. The poor light in the booth made it difficult to identify.

"I've seen old town maps before," said Tom. "It looks like New Dover way back when."

I studied it carefully, but I couldn't make it out. "Why are these sections colored in?" I pointed to four distinct sections of the map.

Tom snapped his fingers and turned the map ninety degrees so it aligned with true north. "Now does it look familiar?"

"No. Should it?"

"These shaded areas are cemeteries, Koz: North Street, Darrowville, Oak Ridge and New Dover cemeteries." Tom pointed to each as he spoke. "Is Rod Serling in here?"

"That is pretty creepy, Koz," said Jed. "Did your dad have some morbid fascination with cemeteries?"

"Not that I knew of." I thumbed the map, then realized there was another page beneath it. I slid it out and placed it next to the map. It was a charcoal drawing of what appeared to be a Native American man's face. The face was just an outline with a distinctive jaw line and a flat nose. He appeared to be wearing a fancy necklace. Below it was a single word, also sketched in charcoal: "KOMAKET."

"So, who is this Komaket dude?" Jed asked. "He's kind of spooky-looking."

We all looked at Gene, who put his hands up. "I told you already; I'm just the messenger. This is the first time I've laid eyes upon these papers and this, well, rather interesting-looking fellow."

"Submitted for your approval," Tom said in a decent Serling voice. He certainly had the eyebrows for it.

Tom made me smile but just for a moment. "That's really not

helping," I pointed out.

Gene shifted in his seat. "Dennis, there is one other issue I need to discuss with you. As I mentioned before, it's a personal matter that concerns your father but only indirectly. I don't think it's a good idea to involve your friends; but I'll leave it up to you to decide that because, hey, this is your night." He slid out of the booth and stood. "I'm going to hit the men's room. You decide how you're going to play this." He turned on what looked to be very expensive heels and was gone, at least temporarily.

"Koz, what the hell is this guy talking about?" Jed asked.

"I'm not sure. He told me he had business that concerned only me." I looked at the drawing of Komaket. "I assumed this was it. I didn't know there was a sequel."

"We're going to need another round for this." Tom attempted to get Stacy's attention.

"Or we could sneak out now while he's taking a piss." Jed turned his cap around, something he did when he was nervous. "You don't need this kind of drama on your birthday, Koz."

Part of me was halfway out the door, but I figured Gene had made this much effort to contact me on this one night, so I should see it through. Maybe he had more crazy drawings in his bag.

Stacy stopped by and we ordered another round. Drinks arrived just as Gene returned. Tom moved a Guinness directly in front of him.

"I took the liberty of ordering a beer for you, Gene the lawyer," Tom said. "I figure you're off the clock now."

"Good assumption." Gene took a strong pull from the bottle. I was fully prepared for him to take something from his bag, but he sat silently for several seconds; then he leaned in my direction. "Okay, Dennis, I'm not going to sugarcoat this. I also promised your father I would take care of your college finances. To that end, he set up a fund that could only be used for educational purposes." He took another long drink from his bottle. I could tell this was not going to be a short conversation.

"I know all that, Gene. My mom has sent checks to the university every year for several years."

"Actually, that was my doing. Once your parents got divorced, I took on the fiduciary responsibility. She sent me the bill and your father's fund took care of it."

7

I couldn't believe he came all this way to tell me something so obvious. "Okay, do you want a medal or something? Sounds like you were doing your job. I mean, for Christ's sake, writing out checks is so hard."

Gene twirled a napkin several times. "It's more than that and you know it. Let me first say that I knew Norm Kozma better than anyone on this planet—I dare say even better than your mother—and I really doubt he'd be happy with the way things have turned out."

"What the hell are you talking about?"

Tom leaned as far across the table as he could. "You've got a lot of balls coming here tonight, mister big shot lawyer. You make it sound like Koz is some sort of deadbeat dad or welfare mom. Well, as someone who knows him better than anyone on the planet—dare I say even better than his mother—I should point out that he's gainfully employed, never been in jail and is taking graduate-level courses. Things have turned out pretty well, for the record."

I really didn't need any help defending myself, but it was always good to have someone like Tom on my side. He'd been there for me many times before. I finished off the last of my beer and slammed it on the table. "And that's why I'm where I am today." I put out a fist and both my friends bumped it.

Gene also placed his bottle down a little harder than he needed to. "And just where is that, Dennis? I have full access to your academic records. I see you dropped out twice and changed majors at least five times before deciding on European History. History? Really? There's another name for majoring in history, by the way. It's called majoring in unemployment."

"Hey, he got his degree," Jed said. "That's a pretty good accomplishment."

"Actually, he didn't." He pointed his bottle in my general direction. "According to your official transcripts, you never completed the foreign language requirements necessary to graduate. All these so-called graduate courses you've been taking for over two years are just various piddly-ass electives and senior-level classes. In my day, we had a name for someone like you: professional student. Plus, I doubt your job at a pool supply store pays you much more than minimum wage." He nearly polished off his beer. "Hey, it beats getting a real job, right, *Koz*?"

Tom looked my way. "Is that true, Koz? I thought you had a degree in psychology."

"I could've sworn it was archeology," Jed said.

I waved my hands in front of them. "This is all bullshit. Why do you care what classes I take or where I work? Your cushy job is to sit on your ass and spend my dad's money. That reminds me, Gene, I sign up for classes this week and I'll need another check." This got me a fist bump from Tom.

He finished the contents of the bottle and placed it down. "Therein lies the real point of this discussion. The money is gone, Dennis—all of it. You're on your own from now on. The good news is that it's not too late to apply for a student loan, or maybe you can borrow from your mother. I'm sure that will go over well."

I nearly choked on my beer. I had been going to college for eight years. It was the only life I knew. I had every intention of taking that stupid foreign language class, then getting my Masters. I loved the university life and I loved to learn. What was so bad about that? Dad would have understood. I was no professional student because I had a plan—at least I thought I did.

Gene's phone went off and he dug it out of his bag. He quickly glanced at the screen, turned it off and stuffed it back in. "Gentlemen, I have to go." He slid out from the booth and stood at the end of the table. "I'll find my way out, thanks, anyway."

"Door's over there." Tom pointed while holding his bottle.

"Understood, but just one more thing…" He looked down and gently tapped the portrait of Komaket. "I'm not sure what all of this means, but there must be a reason he waited until you were twenty-five. He never shared that part with me, but that's what your father wanted."

"How the hell do you know what he wanted?" I asked. "Fifteen years is a long time."

"I think you'll find that it isn't. Let me remind you that your dad was always the smartest person in the room wherever he went." He shook his head and smiled, like he was recalling a Norm moment. "He was very ill when he came to me with this package. It's likely he had little time to gather the information." He got up in my face. "Finish this for him, Dennis. For once in your life, finish something."

I watched him as he made his way past the server's station. He pulled out a few bills and handed them to Stacy, who smiled and pushed a strand of hair behind her ear.

"Screw him." Tom playfully jabbed my arm.

"Yeah," Jed said. "Let's have another round, birthday boy."

They tried to get me back into the festivities, but I couldn't. All I could think about was the package Gene delivered and how I was going to pay for my next round of classes. I was never a real inquisitive guy by nature. To me, it was a bunch of papers and a drawing of an old Indian—another lousy gift, another ant farm, a total buzzkill. *Thanks a lot, Dad.*

Chapter 2

I didn't feel like staying much longer, even though it was my birthday. The package I had gotten from my dad sort of freaked me out and the lecture from Gene didn't help, so I left about an hour later. It's pretty pathetic when you're sober enough to drive home on your own birthday.

I shared an apartment with two other guys from school, both undergrads. They went back to live with their parents during the summer, so I had the place all to myself. The landlord gave me a good summer rate because it would otherwise be empty. We were not on the coast, so no one wanted to live around here in the summer—except me, because the alternative was to live at home again. *Not as long as Stan is there. No way.*

The papers and drawings my dad had left me were on the dining room table, so I opened the folder to have another look. It was hard not to stare at the drawing of Komaket. Although the drawing appeared to be unfinished, his eyes were dark, piercing, even mysterious.

I opened my laptop and did a Google search of the name Komaket. The only readable hits were in some weird language… Persian, one of the sites said. *Yeah, that would have been too easy.* After scanning each document, I backed everything onto a disk and set it aside.

I called my mom, Maureen, the next day. My parents were divorced when I was five, but they stayed fairly close until my dad died. I had to find out about the college fund and if she knew anything about these papers.

"Hi, Mom. I have something interesting to show you and ask you if you're going to be around."

"I'm not going anywhere, Dennis."

"So this would be a good time for a private conversation, then?"

"If you're asking if Stanley is home, the answer is 'no.' He's been gone all afternoon and I never know when he'll return."

That made me smile. "I'll be right over."

11

Jed called right after that and wanted to hang with me. It was Saturday, so he didn't have much else to do, evidently. He always liked my mom so he came along. Unfortunately, Stan's car was in the driveway when we arrived. We went in through the door on the side of the garage. There was something I had to show Jed.

"Check this out," I said.

The hood of Stan's car was open, and a large fan sitting on the workbench was blowing full blast towards the engine. The car was not running.

"He likes to cool off the engine after he drives," I said.

Jed looked at the scene and shook his head. "That's completely unnecessary. Why does he do that?"

"I don't know. He's just a nutbag."

Jed's eyes got real big when he scanned the wall behind us. "Whoa! Check out this tool bench."

The bench was spotless, and each tool was outlined on the pegboard with the name of each tool printed neatly beneath it.

"Is this guy anal or what?" Jed said.

"That's nothing. He alphabetized the spice rack. He wasn't too happy when I put parsley, sage, rosemary and thyme together."

"Seems like a fitting tribute to Simon and Garfunkel."

"He failed to see the humor in it."

We made our way into the kitchen where my mom had just finished cutting up some brownies, which happened to be a personal favorite of mine. The kitchen was immaculate, of course. Stan would have it no other way.

"Hi, sweetheart." She gave me a big hug, just like always, before she tugged on a few locks of hair sticking out behind my left ear. "You need a haircut, Dennis." I needed money for classes, but first things first.

Jed worked his way into the kitchen, and she hugged him too but said nothing about his hair.

"Hey, Mrs. Koz, it's good to see you."

"You're always welcome here, Jed." She peeked around the corner behind us. "No Tommy today? I made enough brownies for the three of you."

"He had to work." He hated being called Tommy, but I didn't tell her that. I looked at the large plate of brownies. "Somehow we'll get by."

Mom put four on a smaller plate, each spaced the same distance apart. Stan just had to have them that way. "I'll just take these into Stanley and be right back."

Stan was in the living room watching TV. I could see his bald head sticking out above the back of his recliner. He made no effort to acknowledge us, which was fine with me. That would require getting his fat ass out of his recliner. I wasn't worth it. Mom placed the brownies on an end table. Stan reached over and put his hand on her arm.

"Doesn't that boy know you've been Mrs. Woolery for the past ten years?"

"Oh, stop it, Stanley." She took a step back and his hand slid off her. "He's been calling me Mrs. Koz since he was four years old." She took one of the squares from his plate and walked away. "I think it's kind of sweet."

"Hey, hey, hey," he grunted. Mom smiled as she chewed the brownie. I loved to see her smile.

She wiped her mouth with the apron. "Now, what was it you wanted to ask me?"

"I saw Gene Clausen, Dad's lawyer, last night. He told me the college fund was empty. Is that true?"

She looked at Stan, then went into the garage. Jed and I followed.

"Yes," she said. "That's no surprise, though. You didn't honestly think it was a bottomless well, did you?"

"Of course not. It's just that I have to know how I'm paying for this semester, that's all. I guess I can get a student loan."

She motioned for me to keep my voice down. "I promised when you were eighteen that I'd take care of your education. Your father's fund was a good chunk of it, but some of it was mine too. I probably have just enough left for one more semester. Then you're on your own. I expect a Master's degree by Christmas. Deal?" She stood with her arms crossed, so there was no need to shake on it.

"Deal."

Weaver was an expensive private school, so it would have been a killer to take out a loan for even just one semester. I'd have to double my usual workload, but I could handle that.

"You said there was something you wanted to show me?"

13

We moved back into the kitchen and I scattered the papers on the table. The steely gaze of Komaket caught her eye immediately. She put on her glasses to look more closely.

"This is what I wanted to show you, Mom. Gene Clausen also gave me this stuff last night. He said Dad wanted me to have it on my twenty-fifth birthday. Any idea why?"

Mom examined the drawing and the map. She sneaked a peek over at me, then went back to the papers. I could tell they meant something to her.

"Well, I..."—she cleared her throat as she took off her glasses—"I can honestly say I've never seen this rugged-looking individual before." She tapped the picture of Komaket with the stem of her glasses.

"What about these legal documents?" I slid one closer to her.

She scanned it from top to bottom, shaking her head ever so slightly. Then she checked out the other page. It also meant something; I could tell.

"Mom, what is it?"

She turned and looked into the living room. "Outside," she whispered, pointing toward the back door. "And bring these other pages with you."

Jed helped me gather up the papers and place them in the folder. I gave him an I-don't-know look as we followed her outside. We stood near my car. "What is it, Mom?"

"I'd say they are P and Z documents."

"P and Z?"

"Planning and zoning. After we got divorced, your father ran for the planning and zoning board and was elected. Eventually, he became a tax assessor."

"I remember that. His picture was in the paper."

"A few years later he got into some trouble with the town, and he was forced to resign. None of it was true, Dennis." Tears welled in her eyes so she wiped them with her knuckle. "Unfortunately, that's how everyone remembers him. He passed away before he had a chance to set the record straight."

"Why would he want me to have these papers?"

She made a not-so-subtle glance back at the house. "I'll stop by your place later, Dennis, about 7 p.m. or so." She gave me a quick hug.

14

"Mom, are you all right?"

"I'm fine, honey. I... I have to make dinner for Stanley. He has a meeting tonight." With that, she slipped back into the house.

We were mostly quiet for the trip back, but I could see Jed staring at me occasionally while I drove. He turned the music down a few notches. "Koz, I just gotta know something." He fumbled with his fingers, then folded his arms. "Why the hell did your mom ever marry that guy?"

It was a question I had asked myself a thousand times. It sounded strange coming from one of my friends. "I'm not sure. I guess he's good company or at least he used to be. For what it's worth, he hasn't always been this bad. He was tolerable when I lived at home; but when they moved into this place a few years back, he turned into a total dickhead. I can't explain it."

Jed seemed satisfied with that answer and didn't bring up the subject again. Just as we pulled into my parking place, his cell phone rang. He talked while we walked up to my apartment; then he put his phone away.

"Gotta go, Dennis, but, hey, call when you hear the news. Sounds like your mom is on to something."

He always knew when to stay and when to go. I could tell he sensed that my mom wanted to talk just to me, and I appreciated his decision.

She showed up just after 7 p.m. with a small folder tucked under her right arm. I made some tea since neither of us were coffee drinkers. She sat on my couch and came right to the point.

"Just before he died, your father said you'd be coming around when you turned twenty-five, but I didn't know what he meant. Now I do. He told me to give you this, Dennis."

She handed me the folder and I opened it. On top were two documents similar to those Gene had given me. Beneath these were newspaper clippings.

"I almost threw this stuff away several times, but I know he wanted you to have it." She took a nervous sip of tea and held on to her cup. "We can't change what happened, Dennis, and I certainly don't want your father's name dragged around anymore. It was awful what they put that man through."

I spread out the newspaper articles on the coffee table to read the headlines.

15

R.M. Clark

Kozma Resigns as Tax Assessor

Town Lawyers to Decide Kozma's Fate

"Mom, I know about most of this already." I shifted a little closer to her on the couch. "I'm okay with it." It seemed as if she didn't hear me.

"He started acting different even before the legal trouble and well before he was diagnosed as... you know... terminal. He told me something big was going to happen, too big to explain."

I looked at the papers, then at my mom. Large wrinkles formed on her forehead as she peeked at her watch.

"There is one other paper," she said. "It got separated from the others, and I had no idea what it was. I don't know why I kept it."

She pulled out a piece of paper from her large pocketbook. It was a detailed drawing of a necklace. It appeared to be the same one Komaket was wearing in my drawing. I compared the two. They were a perfect match.

"Can you tell if Dad drew these?"

She looked at Komaket's picture, then shook her head. "I don't remember him ever having this kind of artistic ability. It takes a good eye to draw this well."

My eyes shifted to another document on the table. On it were four handwritten names and "2 of 3" written in the corner. I brought out a similar document from my Gene stack, which had five handwritten names and "1 of 3" in the corner.

"It looks like we have two thirds of the entire package." I turned in time to catch her peeking at her watch... again.

"Your father was a stickler for details. He dated, initialed and filed everything. I'd say he gave these to the people he trusted the most: Gene Clausen and me."

"So, Gene was '1 of 3" and you were '2 of 3'. Who was '3 of 3'?"

Mom took her pocketbook and put it on her lap. That was her way of saying she was ready to go. "Well, he mentioned someone but I didn't believe him. It was a very confusing time with all he was going through."

"Who else would he trust with something this important?"

She reached in for her keys. "Dennis, I don't want to be

16

involved. Just take all this stuff and do what you want with it." She tucked her pocketbook under her arm. "I have to go. Stanley will be home soon."

"Mom, please tell me. Who has the third set of papers?"

I did something I had never tried before. I blocked her path. She did not attempt to go around. Instead, she took her left hand, put it on my right shoulder and gave me a stern look.

"The only other person he really trusted was his brother, your Uncle Russell."

It was a name I hadn't heard in a long time. While I contemplated it, she slipped past me.

"Where is he, Mom? How do I find him?"

She opened the door, then paused for a moment. "Trust me, you won't have to. Russell Kozma will definitely find you."

Chapter 3

It was back to work for me the next day, so I put Komaket's picture on the refrigerator and made the short trip to Leo's Pool and Supply. I helped install swimming pools and hot tubs and occasionally got to deliver chemicals to our clientele. It wasn't my dream job, but it certainly wasn't the nowhere job Gene made it out to be. I had been working there for the better part of five years. It was a great job to have in the summer because Leo let me work as many hours as I wanted.

The day zoomed by, and I pulled into my apartment complex just after six, only to find a car with Vermont plates in my assigned parking place. My two roommates weren't due back until the following week, but I figured John must have returned early with a different car—he was from Vermont—or it could have been a new tenant getting an early start on the semester. It happened every year.

My apartment door was open, so it must have been that one of my roomies had returned. The bathroom door was closed, and I waited for either John or Mike to come out. I heard a loud belch. That would be John. No one could rip it like that.

The door swung open and there stood Uncle Russell.

"Dennis! Hey, buddy, it's great to see you again." He walked up and gave me a tremendous bear hug.

"How, how did you get in here?" My voice wavered as he patted me hard on the back.

"Front door was open. You really should lock it, you know. Lots of crazies out there."

I was positive I had locked the door, but it wasn't worth arguing over. The last time I saw Russell was when my mom had married Stan. Before that, it was at my father's funeral. He stood in the very back for the entire service. I didn't recall him even attending the family get-together later that day. He had a lot less hair now, and his wiry mustache was beginning to turn gray. He was a few years older than my father was when he died. Except for the hair and an expanding girth, there was an amazing resemblance.

"It's great to see you again," I said. "Can I, um, get you something?"

"Already taken care of, kid. I know you just had a birthday, so I brought you a little something." He opened the refrigerator. The shelves were stocked, top to bottom, with Guinness Draft bottles. I lost count after two cases. Another case was on the counter. "Nectar of the gods, Dennis."

Wow. "Thanks." Guinness Draft! My knees were practically shaking.

"You don't look too surprised to see me, which is good, so I'll grab us some brews and we'll kick this out."

He took out two bottles and opened them with a bottle opener attached to his massive keychain. I was still a little spooked at him being here, so it took me a while to get to the couch. Russell grabbed his backpack, took out a small folder and placed it on the table.

"Norm told me he left something for you to open on your twenty-fifth birthday, Dennis. When he was on his deathbed, I gave him my word that I would bring you this."

From the folder he pulled out a drawing of what appeared to be an ornate staff. It was similar in style to the other drawings and very detailed for a small drawing. Russell also took out a list of names with "3 of 3" written in the corner. "I'm not sure what these mean, but I'll bet you have more to go with it." He gulped down nearly the entire bottle.

I removed the picture of Komaket from the refrigerator door and showed it to him. Then I took the drawing and other documents my mom had given me and spread them out on the table. "This is the entire package he left."

Russell silently scanned each item, then picked up Komaket. "Dude is butt ugly, if you ask me."

I nearly snorted Guinness out my nose, but I managed to choke it back.

He started counting. "Eleven names in all. That's a good number."

"What's so special about eleven?"

Russell finished his bottle and placed it on the table. "I'll tell you what. Get your Uncle Russell another beer and I'll explain it to you."

I took his empty to the kitchen. He didn't wait for me to return.

"Matching double digits such as eleven, twenty-two and so on are called master numbers, Dennis. Many believe they inherently symbolize a stronger link to the unseen dimensions."

"I've heard of that. Numerology, right?"

"That's right. We're surrounded by numbers. It's impossible to deny their effect on daily life."

I had always thought numerology was a load of crap, but I didn't feel right challenging him on it. I decided to throw him a softball instead. "I just turned twenty-five. What's the significance of that?"

He ran his fingers through his receding hair and let out a massive belch. "Ha. Not a damn thing. All it means is that your car insurance will go down. But seeing that you have an addictive nature, like every male in this family tree has had since we were stomping our own grapes in Poland centuries ago, we'll just chalk up number twenty-five as a complete waste of brain cells." He used his opener to pop the tops on our bottles. "Your first master number as an adult has already passed. It means every decision you make will be huge. You'll probably never look better or feel better, so take advantage of that. When you hit twenty-five, you better have a good idea of what you want to do with your life."

He paused and looked at me, knowing full well that I didn't.

"In the meantime, go for it." He held out his bottle and I clinked it with mine. I was getting to like this guy.

We ordered some pizza and he insisted on paying, which was fine with me. While we waited for it to arrive, he told me about his cabin in Vermont and his booming on-line business. It took some time, but he finally got back on topic.

"So my brother sends his only son three drawings and a list of names. What do you make of this, Dennis?"

"I honestly don't know. Gene Clausen didn't know either, and they were best pals apparently." I polished off my final slice of pizza, washing it down with another Guinness.

"What did your mom say when you asked her?"

"She was pretty vague. Dad told her something big was going to happen, but she didn't elaborate. Apparently, he didn't trust too

20

many people, just you, Mom and Gene. You probably know more than I do, Uncle Russell. I hadn't even reached my first master number when he died."

He gave a squinty-eyed look, took another drink and placed his bottle down slowly. "Well, your dad and I were born pretty far apart, twelve years, to be exact. Our parents' marriage started to go south well before I was born, from what I was told. Then after what was likely a night of drunken, sloppy sex, Bingo! Along came yours truly. I tell you, if they could put birth control in vodka, the world would be a shitload better; but that's neither here nor there."

He stopped for another slice of pizza. The pause made that last statement linger in my brain a little longer.

"Anyway, your dad got the hell out of the house and went off to college. You think your parents were screwed up? You should have been around Gram and Gramps during my wonder years. Man, they took all the fun out of being dysfunctional." He reached down and slid off his sneakers without untying them, then brought his feet up on the couch and faced me. "As a matter of course, they got unmarried and I went to live with Pop in Wisconsin. I was six years old, Dennis. God, that sucked." He slammed the top of the couch with his bare palm. "Here's a free word of advice. Stay far, far away from Wisconsin. Don't live there, don't drive through it... hell, don't even fly over it if you can possibly help it. They entered the union as state number thirty, a number with some major problems. Trust your Uncle Russell on this one, Dennis. Wisconsin is evil." He poked me in the shoulder three times as he spoke those words.

He piled up a few pillows on the arm of the couch and stretched out. I moved to another chair.

"You have a girlfriend, Dennis?"

The question threw me off for a second. I shifted in my chair. "No, not at the moment. We broke up a few months ago. Why?"

"I just hope the Kozma curse does not befall you, that's all. We haven't exactly been role models in the father-figure department. To your credit, you're a good-looking kid with a good head on your shoulders. Hell, if you're like the rest of the Kozma men, you're probably hung like a rhino. That helps."

Wow. I truly wanted to ask if there were any chance he was adopted, but I thought better of it. A few moments of uncomfortable silence came next.

"Dennis, I should have asked sooner, but is it cool if I crash here tonight?"

"Of course, Uncle Russell. Stay as long as you want."

"Thanks, man." He pointed a finger at me. "You're a lot like your old man. Dude had a heart of gold." He sat up for a moment to drink the last of his beer, then plopped back down. "Norm never told me why he wanted you to have this stuff, and I never got a chance to ask, unfortunately. Life sure blows sometimes."

I didn't know much about my parents, pre-divorce, so I took the opportunity to find out. "Hey, Uncle Russell, I was wondering if you know why, uh, my parents... you know, how come they broke up."

"That's not a simple question, Dennis, but I'll give you my take. First off, I was surprised they ever got married. Every time I saw the two of 'em, they were bickering about something. Your dad was kind of a free spirit and Maureen, well, she was certainly more grounded. It helped when you came along because I think it gave them a focal point or something. Your dad was putting in a lot of time with his job and the town, and your mom wanted more of a Donna Reed life, if that makes any sense. Eventually, they just couldn't take each other anymore. It was never you, Dennis. Please know that. You were the one good thing that came out of the union."

We talked for a few more hours about anything and everything. I made a quick trip to the kitchen to put stuff away, and he was snoring soundly when I returned. I got a blanket from another room and placed it on him before heading to bed. It had been a long day.

Russell was gone when I got up the next morning. He had tidied up the couch and folded the blanket. There was one empty beer bottle on the coffee table with something sticking out of it. I pulled out a one-hundred-dollar bill. Attached to it were two small post-it notes. On the first he wrote his cell phone number and email address. On the second he wrote:

Finish this for your dad
RK

PS Keep me in the loop.

He had provided me the last of the documents my father had wanted me to have, all of which were spread out on the table. I left everything there as I fired up my laptop and made a cup of tea to wake up. My head was pretty clear after a quick shower and another cup of tea. A major sunbeam poured in from the side window directly onto the picture of Komaket. His face looked different, his eyes more menacing in the morning light. I clicked on the scanned image I had created earlier and brought it up on the screen. I took the paper and held it next to the laptop screen.

There was no doubt about it. Komaket's picture was changing.

Chapter 4

I double- and triple-checked the two images; the drawing had definitely changed. *How did that happen?*

My first thought was that Russell had somehow made enhancements to the drawing before he left, but it was still inside its clear plastic sleeve. I polished off a ham sandwich and sat down to think.

I scanned everything else and placed the items in a desktop folder, then checked my watch and realized that I had only ten minutes to get to work. The freak show would have to wait.

Over the course of the day, as I installed two hot tubs and helped with a pool filter, I thought about how to proceed. I knew I had to do some investigating, but I hated libraries so I really wanted to avoid heading to the local branch. There was a professor at Weaver who taught New England history, and he lived pretty close by. I had him during my sophomore year—well, one of my sophomore years—and he had a way of making local history somewhat interesting as he paced nervously in front of the class. He would bring in authentic weapons and costumes from various historical periods to use in his lectures. He once gave us a crossbow demonstration in the field next to his classroom. I could only hope he remembered me.

When I got home, I tossed my keys on the table and grabbed a beer from the refrigerator. My laptop was notoriously slow warming up and making a network connection, so I took the opportunity to put away a few dishes and clean the counter.

I found the email address for Dr. Jacob Overmann in the school directory and asked him if he knew about a Native American named Komaket. I told him I had a drawing if he wanted to see it. That seemed like enough information.

Surprisingly, he responded in less than an hour and asked for the drawings. I attached all three and sent the message. After a quick shower, I checked my inbox and saw his response:

DENNIS,
PLEASE BRING ALL THIS TO ME, IMMEDIATELY!!
J.O.

It was important enough to warrant an all-caps response, so I gathered up everything and headed straight there.

Dr. Overmann lived in Chepstow, the next town over. His house was a modest ranch-style in a nice part of town. I parked in the empty driveway and knocked on the breezeway door next to the garage. It seemed more inviting than the front door.

He greeted me wearing a dark blue sweat suit and jogging shoes. I remembered him saying that he was a former marathon runner who had done well in several Boston Marathons in his younger years.

"Dennis Kozma, please come in." He led me through the breezeway to his office. "I'm glad to see that, thanks to my inspirational teaching, you are now a full-fledged history hound."

"Thanks. I guess some just have history thrust upon us."

He laughed. "Could I get you a beverage, Dennis? I have coffee, water and soda."

"No thanks."

We both settled into comfortable chairs.

"So tell me about this picture of Komaket. How did you come to be in possession of it?"

"My dad—he died fifteen years ago and he arranged to have it delivered to me on my twenty-fifth birthday. He also arranged to have my mother and uncle bring the other ones." I decided not to tell him that the picture was changing... at least, not yet. "So who is Komaket?"

He took a drink of bottled water and unzipped his warm-up jacket. "Let me start by saying that it is a name I have not heard in a very long time... perhaps twenty years." He picked up the drawing and stared at it, seemingly entranced by it. "Every generation or so the legend grows"—with a flick, he let the drawing float back to the table—"and then dies."

This was how he was when I took his class: raise the anticipation level, then spend the next hour delivering the goods. I hoped this one wouldn't take an hour.

"Let me throw another name at you, Dennis. Surely you've heard of Komagansett, yes?"

"Sure, I've heard of him. He's the Native American who died protecting the sachem, who happened to be the first female leader

25

the tribe ever had. There's a statue of Komagansett around here."

"Of course, we have a statue of the great Komagansett. There's a stretch of highway named after him and a park and even an elementary school a few towns over. We all love Komagansett."

"You don't sound too impressed."

He stood. I knew he would have to go into pace mode eventually. He walked to a large bookcase, reached for a thick volume and pulled it out. He flipped open a few pages and set the massive book on the table in front of me. "Actually, Komagansett was as great as advertised. He did take a bullet for the leader, and that single event became the turning point of the war." He turned the book so it faced me. "It says so right here, so it must be true."

Dr. Overmann was baiting me into something, based on his sarcastic tone. I quickly glanced at the article as he paced the room. "So what does Komagansett have to do with Komaket? Were they brothers or something?"

He clasped his hands together and placed them on top of his head. "No, but research shows that they did have the same father."

"Stepbrothers?"

"And the same mother!" He turned and pointed to me as if to say, "Your move."

I had nothing. "I don't get it."

He lifted the book and placed the drawing in it. "Komagansett and Komaket are one and the same. The once living"—he slammed the book shut—"and the legend."

"How is that possible?"

"It's not unusual in Native American lore for a living person to blur the line between reality and mythological status. Komagansett is just another example. From what I've researched, the locals preferred Komagansett to be remembered as a hero. It's more appealing to history books and lore."

"Why does it matter what's appealing? You taught us history was immune to that kind of emotion."

"Indeed I did but when a legend is involved, it changes everything. It allows us to get emotional."

"I take it you prefer the legend instead?"

He shook his head disapprovingly. "I like the whole package, Dennis. As a historian, it is not my place to pick and choose." He placed a drawing before me. "Take a close look at the drawing of the necklace Komaket is wearing. Komagansett is also shown wearing a similar item in several artists' renderings, including the one on this page." He opened the book and pointed to a drawing.

"Okay?"

"What's interesting is that this object is not Native American, but rather a *crimpu*, a Mayan recording device. Komagansett's tribe was all about symmetry, color and function." He smacked his palm with the back of his other hand as he rattled them off. "The *crimpu* has none of these qualities."

With a couple of keystrokes, he brought up several examples of *crimpu* on his laptop. Komaket appeared to be wearing one.

"Clearly," he said, "this is an anachronism for the seventeenth-century native culture."

I took the picture of the staff and brought it to the forefront. It had a twisted, spiral-shaped shaft and a rounded top. "What about this? How does it fit in?"

He was off again, this time pulling a smaller book from a low shelf. He paced before me as he looked for his answer. "There are several examples of items like this in Komagansett's tribe. Unfortunately, he was a warrior, a soldier with no need to trifle with a sachem's staff. Besides, the locals were much more detailed in their ornamentation. The staff in this picture is not even from this continent."

I guessed. "South America, right?"

He placed the small book on the table. Several photos on the page matched the staff in the picture. "Africa, Dennis. It is most likely Zulu."

"Another anachronism?"

"Clearly." He zipped up his top and began to tighten his shoelaces. He was waiting for me to come up with an *aha* moment and piece it all together. He did this a lot during his lectures.

I was likely going to disappoint him, but I gave it my best shot. "Okay, so Komagansett and Komaket are the same guy. Komagansett walked among us, perhaps even on this very spot, some 300 odd years ago while Komaket existed only in the imagination of the local storytellers. Komagansett was a warrior and absolutely 100% the real deal. Komaket, on the other hand, was worldly and resourceful and a collector of some rather odd items." It was painfully clear I had no idea what I was talking about.

"Very good, Mr. Kozma. You've captured the duality quite well. What's missing is why Komaket had such odd items with his trick bag. That is where we separate man from myth, living from legend. You see, Komaket was a traveler. His tribe was nearly depleted by smallpox, so he went to faraway places and brought back those items needed to replenish the tribe—two of the earth and two from beyond." He closed the books he was showing me and began to place them back on the shelves.

"Komaket returned with a *shongo*," he continued, "an African tribal staff said to represent fertility and health. He obtained the *crimpu* from the Mayans for census-taking and recording the legends of his tribe because it was important for him to measure the population. Perhaps a bit of ego involved, but I think he earned the props. Those were the earthly possessions."

"That leaves two other items from two other destinations. I'd say Europe and Asia, right?"

"Outstanding, Dennis. Our weary traveler brought home the Roman concept of *triation,* using more advantageous patterns and structures to protect the village from intruders. Lastly, while in India, he learned the ancient concept of *jorva.* This was the most important concept of all: life, reborn from the hereafter."

"Reincarnation?"

"Amazing, isn't it? He brought everything the village needed." He counted them off on his fingers. "Health, recorded history, protection and the chance to do it all again; that is the legend of Komaket."

"Wow. That's quite a legend. I can see why the locals wanted to separate him from Komagansett."

As we spoke, another voice interrupted from somewhere in the house. Dr. Overmann once again tightened his shoelaces.

"Sorry, Dennis, but Melody, my running partner is here. We're due for ten miles today. You're welcome to come along, if you like. We can talk some more."

I hated running, plus it killed my knees. "No thanks, Dr. Overmann. I have to be going."

A young woman, perhaps in her mid-twenties, poked in for a moment, then returned to the kitchen. I only got a glimpse of her, but I liked what I saw.

Dr. Overmann retrieved a book from a high shelf and handed it to me. "Thank you for sharing these documents, Dennis. I do enjoy it when my old friend Komaket comes out to play. It's far too infrequent. There's more in chapter twenty, if you want to check it out."

I gathered everything up and tucked the book and folder under my arm. I thanked him and shook his hand as he began to stretch for his run.

"Thanks for the book and the lesson, Doc. It was quite enlightening."

"Any time." He looked up from his stretch position. "It's just a legend, Dennis."

"I know."

I didn't believe him for a second.

Chapter 5

I got called into my boss's office a few days later. Normally, this would be the time of year when I would ramp it down and get ready to go back to school. The pool business generally drops off in the fall, so it was a natural transition. I made my way past the floor-demo hot tubs and above-ground pools to Leo McNeal's office. We'd had this talk before.

He was on the phone when I arrived, soothing an irate customer as only he could. He motioned to me to sit while he finished the call, hung up and took a sip from a large stainless steel mug on the corner of his desk.

"Dennis, I have a slight dilemma and I was wondering if you could help me out."

"How so?"

"We just lost two full-time workers, Jack and Roger, in case you hadn't heard; and it has left me in kind of a pickle. I know you start school soon, but I was wondering if there were any way you could stay on, part-time, of course. I like the way you handle yourself on the floor, and your driving seems to be good. We need some help mid-week and Saturdays mostly. There will be more money in it for you, naturally, and your official title will be floor manager."

His proposal caught me off-guard, but it gave me the chance to float my own plan out there.

"How about full-time?"

He was about to take another drink, but he put his mug down. "But you're going for your Masters, right? There aren't enough hours—"

"I'm not going back this semester. I've thought about it for quite a while and decided to take a semester off." I didn't care what my mom or anyone else thought. It was time for a change.

He paused for a moment while he flipped a couple of pages on his clipboard. "Thirty-five hours a week is the most I can do. From my side of the desk, it's a great idea." He dropped the clipboard onto a stack of papers. "I'd love to have you, Dennis, but are you sure about this? You've got a degree and all."

I didn't want to get into the specifics of my academic record. "I love it here, Leo. You know that. School can wait. I have every intention of going back and finishing up."

***

The college fund was dry, and I was not too keen on spending my mom's money for another semester of random courses, including the much-needed foreign language class. My talks with Russell and Leo convinced me the best course of action was to keep working and figure out this Komaket business. I owed it to my dad.

It was sure to be an unpopular decision, but I had to tell my mom what I was planning to do. I preferred to have this conversation when Stan wasn't around, so I dropped by for lunch when I knew he wouldn't be at home. Mom had lunch ready when I arrived.

"School starts in a few weeks," she said. "I'll need a course schedule so I can send a check."

I grabbed a bottle of water from the refrigerator. "That's what I wanted to talk to you about. I'm not going back this semester."

If she had anything in her hands, she would have dropped it. "We had a deal, Dennis: one more semester to finish up and graduate. Do you remember that conversation?"

"Of course, I remember and I'm going to finish up and graduate... eventually. My boss pumped me up to thirty-five hours a week, plus a promotion and a raise. I really like it there, Mom."

She began to cry, then caught herself. "What do you think your father would say if he were standing right here?" She pointed to a spot in the middle of the kitchen.

"I don't know." I tried to get the cap off the bottle, but I had tightened it too much.

"Well, I'm sure he'd ask the same question I would: why? For the love of God, why can't you just finish something, Dennis?" Those last words lingered as she wiped her hands on her apron, leaving a large wet area.

I took out my phone and showed her the picture of Komaket. "This is what I'm going to finish. Dad gave me this for a reason.

Uncle Russell stopped by and gave me the rest of the package. I have all the pieces, and now I just need to put them together."

She took a large, covered casserole dish out of the refrigerator and practically threw it on the counter. The foil covering kept the contents from flying all over the kitchen. Now she had a knife. It glinted in the sunlight as she turned towards me. "If you listen to Russell Kozma, you're doomed to end up like him. You don't want to be a drunk, lonely loser, Dennis. You can do better than that." She took an onion from the counter and began to chop it furiously. "I can't believe you'd rather work for a pool company than finish college. Ridiculous." She held the knife up again. "Nice decision-making."

I tried to eat my sandwich, but I wasn't really hungry anymore. "It'll be fine, Mom. I promise."

She was crying again, but it may have been the onions. "Please go. I have to get this ready for Stanley." She removed the foil and covered the casserole with onions. The smell was unbearable. I was glad I wasn't staying for dinner.

***

My roommates, John and Mike, returned a few days later, so it got a bit crowded around the apartment. They were both very quiet, making no effort to unpack. Finally, they surrounded me while I was lounging on the couch watching a baseball game.

"Hey, Koz," John said, "we just thought you should know that we found another place and we're moving out. You're a cool roommate and all, but the new pad is a lot closer to campus."

"And cheaper," said Mike.

The news made me sit up. "You can't do that. We have a lease."

"Actually we don't," said John, "at least not for much longer. The summer lease ends on August 31st. I called the landlord and he said he'd give you a few days to find some new roommates."

"I already posted a flyer at the student union building," said Mike.

It was starting to sink in. "So you're just going to leave me here in limbo? You guys gave me your word you'd stay another year."

Mike spoke up first, "Sorry, man. It's just that this other place was too good to pass up."

"Hey, but you can keep the couch," John said with a stupid grin. "We won't need it."

These two douchebags had me by the short hairs, and there was nothing I could do about it. Such was life in a college town. Roommates came, roommates went. I'd find more. I always did.

I grabbed my keys off the table and headed out. This was a good time to go to the gym. "Fine. Have your crap out of here by the time I come back."

They were both packed and out the door when I returned. It was a semi-furnished apartment, and Mike took his chair and John a table and wall unit. John's ugly couch took up most of the front room. At least I had my TV, now on the floor, and the stove and refrigerator that came with the place. The picture of Komaket still occupied the front of the refrigerator. I hadn't paid much attention to it lately, but closer inspection showed that his chin and cheeks were more defined than ever. The *crimpu* and *shongo* had also filled in some. I still had no idea what it all meant or what I was going to do next. I should have been freaking out over this, but I wasn't. Dad kept me focused.

***

I badly needed a roommate or two, but I had no takers. I had been living in apartments around here for six years without a hitch. It seemed like all the places were filled up. The landlord, Lennard Chang, stopped by to let me know that he had new tenants for the place starting the first week of September if I didn't pay the full rent. Unfortunately, they didn't want me, or anyone else, as a roommate. I was seriously screwed.

The local paper had a few apartments listed, but they all turned out to be too expensive. I asked Tom and Jed if either had any room, but neither did. They were both well into their post-college careers, working full-time and saving money. Tom, with his finance degree, was an actuary, and Jed's business degree landed him a management job at the corporate office of a major grocery store chain. I felt funny driving around with my car packed full of my clothes, TV, computer and a few other possessions, but I had

ɔice. Jed let me crash on his couch for a few days while I
nued to search. At least I still had a job and some money.

My mom called me as I drove home from work later that day.

"Anything new going on, Dennis?"

"Not really, Mom. Work's been good." This was followed by
a killer silence. I pulled over on a side street.

"I went by your apartment yesterday, or should I say your
former apartment. Dennis, why didn't you tell me you'd moved? A
mother needs to know these things."

I swore silently. "Sorry, Mom. It's been a rough few days."

"I see. So, where is your new apartment? I'd like to come over
and see it."

"That's, uh, that's not a real good idea right now, Mom."

More killer silence followed. "Dennis, are you homeless? Is
that what it has come down to?"

"No, it's nothing like that. I'm staying with Jed for a few days.
I have a couple of leads on a new place—"

"Why didn't you come to us for help, Dennis? We're family.
You come to your family first for these sorts of things. We still
have a spare room, you know."

The thought of living under Stan's roof left me momentarily
speechless. "Sorry, Mom, I should have told you. Like I said,
things happened fast. My roommates pretty much screwed me, but
I'll be fine. I promise."

I could hear her stirring something. "What I wanted to tell you
is that I found some more old papers that your father left. I'm not
sure if they relate to the other ones he left you, but I thought you
might like them. I'll leave them in the kitchen for you if you
decide you want to stop by. Have a nice day, Dennis." She hung
up.

Damn. I hated it when she did that. It was best to let her cool
off before I went over, but I definitely wanted to see what she had
found. I stopped by when I knew they'd be gone and added the
Planning and Zoning papers to my ever-growing stack.

The next day Tom felt sorry for me and let me have his couch
while my apartment hunt continued. His roommate was cool about
it, especially when I brought over the rest of the Guinness Draft
Russell had left me. It bought me a few days, at least.

Tom and I sat on the small deck on the side of his apartment.

34

We grilled some burgers and drank Guinness as the sun began to set.

"Hey, whatever happened to that stuff your dad left for you?" He flipped a burger and backed up to avoid the high flames. "Did you file it away with the ant farm?"

I had been so busy that I had forgotten about Komaket for nearly a week. "It's in with my stuff. Plus, I got more from my mom and Uncle Russell."

I went to the corner of the living room where my belongings were piled and grabbed the folder. I placed everything I could on the deck table. There was plenty of light from the wall fixture.

"Besides our friend Komaket, I now have a drawing of his necklace, called a *crimpu,* and his staff, called a *shongo.* Dr. Overmann explained it all to me."

Tom listened intently as I tried to relay the whole Komaket/Komagansett story to him; then he gave me a crazy look. I couldn't do the legend justice like Overmann. Tom plopped the burgers on a couple of buns and sat down next to me.

"What about these?" He pointed to the numbered lists of names.

"We now have the complete set. I have no idea who they are, though."

Tom picked up the one marked "2 of 3." He read it, looked up to think, then read it again. "I've seen these names before, Koz."

"Where?"

Tom took a huge bite and I waited for him to swallow. "Darrowville Cemetery, the one in the west side of town."

"How would you know that?"

"I've seen them on the gravestones. I worked for the public works department during the summer a few years ago. I had the fun task of mowing and trimming the lawns at the local cemeteries." He polished off the rest of his bottle. "Trust me, when you work at a cemetery, you tend to focus on what's above ground rather than what's below."

He took page "3 of 3" and examined it, then smacked it with the back of his hand. "These are from the North Street Cemetery. I'm sure of it."

I showed him the final document. "Do these ring any bells?"

He studied it hard, then placed it down. "I only cut the lawn at the Darrowville and North Street. You have three sets of names and four local cemeteries. Our odds are fifty-fifty that these folks are in either Oak Ridge or New Dover."

Tom took the three lists of names and gave them a final scan. "One of these cemeteries doesn't get to join in any reindeer games. Only three sets of names."

He started in with the "Twilight Zone" music again. Now more than ever it seemed fitting.

It was dark and we were too wasted to be checking out graveyards. Tom put two more burgers on the grill while I put the papers away. I had been wrong about my birthday present from Dad.

This was certainly no ant farm.

Chapter 6

I was up bright and early, thanks to another uncomfortable night at Tom's place. His hospitality was first-rate, but his couch began to swallow me up after about four hours.

It was his day off, so we were out the door by 10 a.m., armed with the list of names. Our first stop was Darrowville Cemetery on the west side of town. It was the oldest and creepiest of the four big ones, with its meandering paths and oversized stones. It didn't take long to remember why I didn't like cemeteries.

Tom knew right where to go. I parked near a tree-lined area on the far side. We walked a good thirty feet until we came to series of headstones. The first name on the list was on the largest stone. Tom cast a long shadow on it. "Mason Wembley. I used to mow here every Saturday. His name sounds like a duke or an earl or something regal—maybe a baron."

On the way to the next name on the list, Tom took us past what he called a family vault. It was grass-covered with sloping sides, sort of like a large barrel buried in the ground. The door on the front was secured with a tarnished padlock. The name "WILLINGHAM" was spelled out in large letters.

"The next one is Gavin Newlands," I said.

Tom pointed out the Newlands gravesite. His stone also had the name of his wife and kids. "Twelve children? Gavin, you old stud puppet, you."

I showed him the next name, and he pointed to a section to our right. I headed over while Tom climbed to the top of the Willingham vault. He leaned over the front of it with his hands out to the side. "I'm king of the world," he yelled, before quickly descending. I looked around and, fortunately, no one was close enough to hear him.

"I've always wanted to do that." We found ourselves in front of a tall, monolith-shaped stone with names on all four sides. "My old friend, Mr. John Arthur Kistler."

The final name took us once again past the vault.

"Next stop, the family plot of Graham Skelton," Tom

37

announced in a pseudo-tour guide voice.

As I read each headstone and jotted down the information, I found no major similarities between them. All four men had lived and died around the same time, but nothing else on the stones jumped out at me. We moved on to the next cemetery.

The North Street Cemetery was located in the northwest corner of New Dover, along the main highway. It was newer than the Darrowville site and set up in more of a grid, complete with street signs for easy navigation.

Tom took us to a crowded section of the cemetery, where once again a large family vault towered above the others. He had no trouble locating all four of the men on the list. I wrote down as many details as I could.

"Okay, Koz. We finished '2 of 3' and '3 of 3' so which cemetery is the lucky '1 of 3'—Oak Ridge or New Dover?"

I looked at the names, then at the map. I guessed. "Oak Ridge."

"Why?"

"It just sounds older."

"That's exactly what I was thinking, my man. New Dover Cemetery has probably been around less than a hundred years. My money's on Oak Ridge."

We arrived ten minutes later with nothing to go on except the names on the list. We stopped at the front of the property and looked at the thousands of headstones before us. This was the biggest cemetery in town.

"Okay, where to start?" I asked. "Is there a directory of some sort?"

Tom took his sunglasses off and scanned the cemetery. "There is one in the office, but it's not open on Saturdays." He put his glasses on and gave me a weird smile. "We don't need it."

"You know where they are?"

"I have a pretty good idea. Go right."

I headed down the bumpy road toward the back of the cemetery.

"Take this left."

I drove a little further and pulled off the road. Tom took the paper and looked over the four names, then dashed out and began checking headstones.

I ran to catch up. "How do you know it's here?"

"Easy. The others all more or less surrounded a vault. So should this group."

"There are at least four vaults in here. Why this one?"

"It looks the oldest."

Tom was right about that. This vault was grass-covered like the other two we found. He compared the names on the list to the names below us as he walked around. "I got bingo!" He threw his hands up in the air.

After finding the first name, the others were easy. I wrote down everything. Then we headed back. It had been a long morning and we were both starving.

Using the one-hundred-dollar bill Russell left me, I sprang for a couple of steaks at the local supermarket. I figured Tom had been a ton of help, so it was time to splurge. He didn't argue.

Tom grilled while I sifted through the information we had gathered that morning. Twelve names were on the page, four from each cemetery. I still had no idea who they were.

I had made a crude map of each cemetery section while we scouted for the headstones that morning. Thanks to a surveying class I had taken during one of my freshman years, the map was a fairly accurate representation of what we had seen.

Tom held up the map and admired my artwork. "Not bad."

He put a steak on a plate and put it front of me. I was hungry so I dug right in. "Not bad, yourself."

When we finished, Tom took another look at my drawings. "Okay if I draw on these?"

"Sure. Just don't lower the resale value, okay?"

He laughed and grabbed a pencil. "Promise."

"What did you have in mind?" He had that look again. It was the same one he had at the cemetery when he knew which vault to look near. I could always tell when his mental wheels were turning.

Tom took the first drawing and made a circle around the vault, passing through the location of each headstone. "We knew right away that the four names in each cemetery surrounded a vault, right?"

"Yup. So what's buggin' you?"

He pulled his hair back, then let it fall into his face. "There's something about this circular pattern. I'm just not sure what." He twirled one of the pages around on the table a few times.

Then it hit me. I used a pencil to connect each of the four marks with a straight line. "Four points do not a circle make." I connected the lines for the other two drawings. "Some of us paid attention in geometry."

"I thought you were an economics major?"

"I was for a semester or two. Actually, this all comes from a surveying class I managed to not sleep through."

The first two patterns were nearly identical. The third was slightly off. I pointed to the Oak Ridge drawing. "Looks like I was losing my touch on this one."

"It's fine. But we can do better. I have some software that may help. We get the best stuff for our company computers."

He brought over his laptop and found a satellite photo of the Darrowville Cemetery. "This site has digital aerial photos of the entire region. We can practically read the names off the headstones from here."

Working quickly, Tom zoomed in on the section that matched my drawing. We found each of the four headstones, and Tom marked them. He used the mouse to draw a line between each point. It was nearly a square, close to what I had drawn, I was proud to see.

He zoomed in on the North Street Cemetery and repeated the process. It had the same pattern. Ditto for the Oak Ridge Cemetery. Fortunately, he didn't bring up how far off my artist's rendering was for that one.

"And finally"—Tom connected the diagonal points on each polygon—"we see that a vault is exactly in the geometric midpoint of each of these." He zoomed in perilously close, and the lines crossed right on the Willingham vault.

The pattern was mesmerizing. I had the nagging feeling that I had seen it before. I kept staring, hoping it would come to me. Tom was talking, but I heard none of it. *The pattern, the pattern, the pattern...*

"Komaket!" I nearly scared Tom out of his seat.

"What about him?"

I found the folder with his picture and brought it over. "Remember the first time I showed this to you, Tom?"

"Sure. Why?"

"Well, let's just say he's changed a little."

I took out the drawing and handed it to him. Komaket's face had twice the detail it had when we first saw it. Tom picked it up for a closer look.

"Sweet cartwheeling Jesus, Koz. That is crazy messed up."

"I agree, but this is what I really wanted you to see." I took out the drawing of the necklace—the *crimpu*—and showed him. It was the exact same shape as those on the screen. The four corner beads were connected, and two thicker strands crossed in the middle. Tom held it up to his laptop screen.

"Incredible. I have a newfound respect for your old man. He was certainly onto something."

"Yeah, but what?"

"I don't know, but I like it." Tom stared at the *crimpu*, then back at the maps. I could see the wheels turning, but I saw it first.

"Look closely at the necklace. See how everything works toward the middle?"

"Sure."

Lighter strands connected the perimeter of the necklace to the small circle in the middle. "That's what my dad wanted us to see. The vaults. The small stones are just the corners. The good stuff lies in the center point."

Tom clicked from map to map on his computer screen. I could tell he was onto something.

"Now what?"

He scratched the back of his neck, then began to go through all of my drawings. "Where's the map you showed us at the bar that night?"

I rummaged through a folder and found it at the bottom. "Here you go."

Tom nodded slowly as he looked at it. "That's odd. Your dad's map had four cemeteries shaded in but only left three sets of names."

I pondered it for a moment. It did seem strange that the New Dover cemetery was left out. "The only thing I can figure is that he really only trusted three people."

"Gene the idiot lawyer said your dad probably had little time to do all this. Maybe he knew you'd find the pattern and go with

R.M. Clark

it."

"So there's a fourth vault and it's at the New Dover Cemetery. Unfortunately, we have no names to go by."

Tom smirked as he brought up a map on the screen. "We don't need any."

I was about to ask why, but the answer was right in front of me. The aerial shot clearly showed that there was but a single vault in the entire cemetery. Tom adjusted the map to the same scale as the others, cut the four-sided pattern and placed the center point on the vault. Each corner touched a large headstone.

"Can you print this?"

"You bet."

We zoomed off to New Dover Cemetery, arriving in about fifteen minutes. We found the vault and, using the printout as a template, identified the stones at each of the corner points.

"So, Tom, we have a list of twenty names. Sixteen are from small gravesites, and four are from family vaults at the center points. Willingham, Stanwood, Hartin, Carleton: who are these people?"

Tom drove silently for a moment, then bounced his hand on the steering wheel. "I don't know, Koz." Bounce. Bounce. Bounce. "But there is somebody who just might."

Chapter 7

The New Dover Museum was located in a two-hundred-year-old red brick building that once served as the town's general store. It was only open to the public two days a week. Fortunately for us, Saturday was one of them.

Tom maneuvered his car into one of the few parking spots behind the museum. There didn't appear to be any other visitors. We walked to the front, and Tom pulled open the heavy wooden door. Fittingly, its large black hinges creaked in a low tone as it closed behind us. It didn't take long for the curator, Mr. Perry Sellers, to find us.

"Well, well, it's Dennis Kozma and Tommy Richcreek. Coming for a little culture, I'll bet."

Mr. Sellers held out his hand. We each gave it a shake. He was a retired teacher who had taught for over forty years in the New Dover school system. I was pretty sure that every kid who went through the school system had had Mr. Sellers as a PE or a health teacher at one time. He walked with a noticeable limp due to a bum right knee, but it never really slowed him down. He took over the museum duties after retiring a few years earlier. He was also the New Dover town historian.

"Great to see you again, Mr. Sellers." Like me, Tom always referred to former teachers as Mr. or Mrs.; it was a hard habit to break.

"Hey, Mr. Sellers, lookin' pretty good." I glanced at his severely-bowed right leg. "Although it looks like you may have lost a step."

"No chance, Kozma. Let's go outside right now and race to the next corner." He started for the door, then turned and gave me a modest back slap. It was great to hear his thick New England accent again. My name always came out as "Kozmer."

"Can we have a tour?" Tom asked. "I haven't seen the place in years."

"Sure thing, boys. We'll start in here."

"How much is it?" I asked.

"We'll take care of it later." His eyes looked huge through a pair of oversized glasses. As he turned, I noticed his gray hair didn't quite cover the hearing aid in his right ear.

Mr. Sellers led us into the main lobby, which had several glass cases filled with fairly boring local artifacts. Along the back wall was the general store, or what was left of it. The long, wooden counter was protected by Plexiglas with dozens of old photographs tucked beneath it. Provisions from centuries ago lined the shelves. It was the same stuff we had seen on a tour in the fourth grade.

Mr. Sellers let us go ahead of him as we entered the wing on the right side of the museum. We milled around a bit as he leaned against the wall. In the far corner there was a long glass case with much of a human skeleton in it. A small sign above it read:

Native American Warrior
circa early 1700s

"Hey, check out this guy, Tom." I waved him over.

"I remember this skeleton. Always gave me the creeps when I was a kid."

"I see you've met Bones," Mr. Sellers said. "He's one of our most popular displays. He's been here as long as I can remember."

We checked out the rest of the room with Mr. Sellers as our guide. I felt like a kid again.

"I'm guessing you didn't come here just to see Bones." Mr. Sellers straightened out a picture near the doorway. "Am I right?"

He was right. It was time to get down to the business at hand.

"Okay, Mr. Sellers, I have a list of names." I pulled out the paper from the pocket of my shorts. "We were wondering if you could help us find out who they are."

"Well, let's have a look."

He took the paper, held it an arm's length away and slowly brought it into focus. He mumbled the names as he went through the list.

"Impressive."

"So you know who they are?" Tom asked.

He peered at Tom from above his glasses. "These are some of most famous names in New Dover history. Are you writing a story or something?"

"Not exactly," I said. "We—"

"Let's just say"—Tom interrupted—"that they're people of interest."

"I see." Mr. Sellers limped to a small book display on the other side of the room and pulled a book from the bottom shelf. "I wrote this several years ago, but unfortunately nobody bought the damn thing. You can have this one." He tossed me a copy of *New Dover: The Early Years.* I caught it right before it hit my face. *Good thing it was just a paperback.*

"Otto Willingham, Josiah Stanwood, Syvanus Hartin and Lyman Carleton are all in there," he continued. "They played a vital role in the relationship between the settlers and the natives. You're probably better off reading about it rather than me boring you."

"Thanks, Mr. Sellers," I said.

He moved away from the book rack toward the main lobby. "Anything else I can help you boys with?" He glanced up at the clock. "It's getting near closing time."

Tom and I took the cue and followed him. "Actually, we were hoping to see more stuff on the local natives," said Tom.

Mr. Sellers stared at us, his eyes magnified greatly through his glasses. "Well, we have some arrow heads and pottery and old bones over there, of course." He laughed, which told me he knew that wasn't what we wanted.

"I'd like to know more about the great Komagansett," I said. "What can you show me?"

He limped toward the front door without answering. I guess he'd had his limit with us.

"I think it's time." Instead of showing us out, he flipped the sign to CLOSED and locked the front door. "You boys come right this way. I don't give many personal tours, so indulge me."

He led us through a side door into the small addition on the side of the museum. The windows were covered, most likely to keep out damaging sunlight. He flicked on a light, revealing shelves of artifacts, pottery, weapons and more.

"We keep a lot of native pieces in here. We don't have room in the main display area so we rotate them in every few years. Much of this just returned from a loan out with Chepstow Museum. It's quite a common practice in these parts."

I spotted a map similar to the one my dad left me on one of the shelves. "What's this?"

Mr. Sellers picked up the framed map and held it out. "That's the earliest map of the area, circa 1670 or so, artist unknown." He set it down, then worked his way to a shelf in the corner. With a grunt he reached up to take down a canvas-covered item. He slipped off the canvas, revealing a framed drawing. "Komagansett, artist and year unknown."

The drawing was a recreation of Komagansett's fateful final moments. A soldier was pointing a rifle at several lavishly-dressed natives. One man stood between the shooter and the sachem.

"Komagansett saved the leader," Mr. Sellers said. "The tribe rallied behind their martyr and fended off the soldiers. The rest is history."

I looked closely at the image of Komagansett. He was only about four inches tall in the portrait, but fairly detailed. "Hey, Tom, check this out."

Tom looked over my shoulder as I pointed to Komagansett's neck. "He's wearing a *crimpu*. Very interesting." He pointed to the staff in Komagansett's right hand, held high above his head. "He has a *shongo* too."

"What are you boys talking about?"

I struggled with how much I should divulge about the information I received from Professor Overmann, realizing, of course, that Mr. Sellers had been nothing but helpful. "Do you have any information on Komaket?"

Mr. Sellers looked up from the drawing of Komagansett, then back down. His eyes jumped around the drawing.

"Who?" He adjusted his hearing aid slightly, although I think he heard me.

"Komaket," Tom said, raising his voice.

"Ah, Komaket." He put the drawing down and shuffled along to his right. "I have not heard that name in a while. Fortunately, we at the museum deal with the past as a matter of reality and leave the legends to the storytellers."

"So you know about his legend?" I asked.

He began a slow journey toward the door. "It's closing time, Mr. Kozma and Mr. Richcreek."

"Please, Mr. Sellers, I'd like to know about Komaket. It's hard to explain, but it's something my father wanted me to find out. I don't know why, but it's what he wanted."

My pleas were not working. Mr. Sellers continued out the door. "Turn the light off on your way out."

I had one more ace up my sleeve. "Dr. Overmann told me a little about the legend. He told me about the duality between Komagansett and Komaket."

Mr. Sellers turned, his face slightly red. "You disappoint me, Kozma. Your first mistake was talking to Overmann. He overdoes everything. Have you read any of his books?"

I remembered I still had one and needed to read chapter twenty. "No, I haven't, but I hear he's the local authority on the native—"

"I'm the local authority, Kozma. Don't you forget that." His finger was up, but not quite in my face. "Overmann works behind those ivy-covered walls, and I work right here." He put his arms out wide. "I live it every day."

The light was still on in the side room, and he started back in. Tom stood in the corner, apparently happy with the way I was handling this.

"As I said before, there's really no place for legends in a museum, but if I put my town historian hat on"—he placed an imaginary cap on his head—"it all becomes clearer." He took a deep breath, clearing his throat on the exhale. "The thing you need to remember about most native legends is that they evolve over the years. A story will start one way, then take on a life of its own. Next thing you know, every generation has added a new twist." He worked his way to a small chair and sat down. "It complicates things."

"Are Komagansett and Komaket one and the same?"

He looked up. The dull light reflected off his glasses. "I don't think so, Kozma. I know Overmann has been floating that theory around for years. I suppose it adds to the hero status of Komagansett, but that's about it."

"What is the legend of Komaket then? What's your take?"

Mr. Sellers removed his glasses and polished both lenses with his shirt. "You've heard of the 'great epidemic,' right?"

"That sounds familiar. Smallpox was rampant back in the day."

"That's right. According to legend, when smallpox was wiping out a good percentage of the native population in the late seventeenth century, Komaket left the region for several weeks on a magical steed. When he returned, he cured all the tribes."

"How did he cure them?"

"Well, here's where the ride gets a little bumpy. The first recordings of the legend say he isolated the infected members and called on ten special wolves to spread out in a pattern around the people. When Komaket raised his staff, the wolves breathed on them and they were cured. Now, some say it was a famine, and others say Komaket built a bonfire and burned the sickness away; but that's the gist of it."

I thought back to what I had learned many semesters ago in a history class. "But the smallpox did go away, didn't it? They were cured somehow."

He shook his head. "The reality is that the disease ran its course after taking its toll on the masses. It was just the nature of the disease. The isolation part may have been rooted in truth."

"Where did Komaket go when he left? Dr. Overmann said he brought back four items, including a necklace from the Mayans, a staff from the Zulus."

He gave me a funny look, but there was a smile in there somewhere. "Legends are fair game, Kozma. I've heard worse variations. Mayans and Zulus? Ha! By the way, you said Overmann mentioned four items. What are the other two?"

"The concept of *triation* from the Romans to protect the village and something called *jorva*, which is a form of reincarnation."

"I've heard those too." Mr. Sellers got up from his seat and began to nervously rearrange the items on the shelf. "You might as well hear the whole story. In that legend, Komaket cures the villagers who are also as sick as the natives in the same manner and gives them the knowledge of *triation*. In exchange, he tells them that one day he will return and claim what is rightly his." He used his hand to dust off a small figurine. "I don't like the open-ended aspect of that particular version. Too much like a prophecy. Besides, the local tribes didn't believe in reincarnation, although Overmann disagrees."

"So what is rightly his? What will Komaket come back for?"

48

"I'm not entirely sure, Dennis. It's part of the natural order among the local natives never to leave a man behind in battle, so maybe that's it. Not real clear on that one."

Tom finally spoke up, "*Triation.* That's an interesting concept. How does it work?"

"Well, that term is not indigenous, and I wouldn't be surprised if Overmann started that one himself. I wouldn't put it past an academic prick like him to stoke his own fires. Anyway, the natives have long believed in the concept of *shingala*, the place where all the energy from the surrounding structures converge. Much of their artwork is done in this kind of pattern, and it's even said to be the design of our town, although I don't see it."

"*Shingala*," Tom said. "I've never heard that one before."

Mr. Sellers turned on his bad leg and began another trek toward the door. "A more modern term would be 'focus.'"

"Or 'center point?'"

"Exactly."

I could see Tom's wheels spinning. It clicked for me too. That was the term brought up earlier in the day.

"You boys have to go now." He waited for us to vacate the room so he could shut off the light. "Do come back and visit me, any time."

He took a key and unlocked the front door for us. We slid through as he followed us out.

"Thanks for all of your help, Mr. Sellers, especially about Komaket." I moved his book to my left hand and gave him a firm shake.

"Yeah, thanks," said Tom.

"Well, you're welcome and I'm glad I could be of some assistance. Not many people want to put up with my boring stories."

Tom shook his hand next. "Not boring at all."

"Great stuff, Mr. Sellers."

"Just remember this about Komaket, Kozma: it's only a legend."

"I know." I'd heard that somewhere. I still didn't believe it.

Chapter 8

When we got back to Tom's place, I realized my cell phone had been there all day. I quickly checked it for messages. One was my mom asking if I needed any food or if I needed to come over to do laundry. *Typical Mom.* The other one was a callback about a room for rent. I had almost forgotten about it in the past few days. I quickly called the number. *Please be available.*

I talked to a guy named Roger who said the room was still open if I acted quickly. As I hung up, I saw Tom out on the deck talking to someone on his phone. When he finished, I told him the good news.

"I might be able to get into a house over on Woodland Drive. There's one open room." I took out a clean shirt and pulled it on. "Oh, and thanks for all of your help today, Tom. If there's anything I can do for you, let me know."

He pulled out two beers from the refrigerator and offered me one. I declined. He opened his and took a much-deserved drink. "Well, there is one thing."

"Name it." I slipped on a pair of clean shorts.

"I promised my girlfriend a few days ago that she could come over and watch a movie on Blu-Ray tonight."

He leaned uncomfortably against the kitchen counter. "I mean, you're welcome to stay, but..."

I could take a hint. I had already overstayed my welcome, and I surely didn't want to be a third wheel. "No problemo, Tom. I have to go to check on this house. Then I'm going to grab a bite. I'll see you later on."

The rental in question was a large Victorian house that appeared to be in decent shape but was definitely in need of a coat of paint. It had a large wooden porch; and, when I walked up to the house, Roger met me at the porch stairs. He gave me a quick tour and I was impressed. The place was huge, especially the bedrooms. I would even have my own off-street parking place. I preferred a place with fewer roommates, but it was too late in the game for that.

"The other roomies, Jason and Mitch—they're grad students too," Roger said. "They're hardly ever here."

We shook on it, and I told him I'd get him first and last month's rent the next day. I had found a place. *Finally.*

I called my mom to tell her the news but she wasn't home, so I tried her cell number.

"We're on our way to dinner. You're welcome to come join us."

Two third-wheel offers in one day. Wow! "No thanks, Mom. I just wanted to let you know that I found a new place today. I'm a little short of t-shirts, so I was going to raid my closet if you don't mind."

"Not at all. There's a meatloaf in the refrigerator if you're hungry. Finish it up."

It was perfect timing. She made the world's best meatloaf.

I used my garage door key to get in. As I warmed up the meatloaf, it struck me that I was alone at my mother's house on a Saturday in a college town. Man, that had loser written all over it, but I was in transition.

It was the perfect time to catch up on my reading. I had brought along Dr. Overmann's book, so I flipped to chapter twenty while I ate. I got about a paragraph into it when my brain went into freeze mode. The day's events kept swirling around, dogging my concentration. Komaket, Komagansett, the cemeteries, *shingala*—my head was spinning. What did it all mean?

I really wanted a beer or something, but neither of them drank. When I finished, I washed my plate and put it away, then grabbed the extra shirts. I had to get out of my mother's house before she and Stan got home. I called Jed and happened to catch him as he and some friends were pulling into O'Reardons. He practically begged me to join them. Hey, at least I was a loser with friends who drank.

I gave Roger a rent check the next day and moved my things into the empty room. As I hoisted my final box through the living room, I noticed that several people had come and gone over the course of the morning. Roger had a lot of friends too, it seemed.

***

After a few days, I had settled nicely into the new house. There always seemed to be a baseball game on TV in the living room, which was fine with me. I pretty much had the kitchen to myself whenever I wanted to cook, which was most days. Roger turned out to be a very friendly guy, but his visitors usually didn't stay very long. I finally met the other two housemates, Jason and Mitch, but they mostly showed up late at night just to crash. I guessed they were serious grad students.

Roger caught me as I was heading out the next day. "Hey, Dennis, we'd like to have a party here later tonight. Sorry I didn't mention it earlier; but, you know, but we kind of had it planned before you moved in. Anyway, it's nothing big, you know, just some friends, maybe a coed or two. You cool with that?"

"Sure. Sounds like fun." It really did. I was thinking a party might do me some good. "You can call me Koz."

"Cool. Feel free to bring a friend, or three, if you want."

"I'll see what I can do. Anything I can contribute? Food? Music? Cash?"

Roger thought for a short time, then shook his head. "No, we'll take care of it, but thanks for asking."

I headed down the stairs toward my car.

"It's good having you around, Kozmo."

It was good to be there.

***

It was quiet at the house later that afternoon, so I began to make some headway on the books Mr. Sellers and Dr. Overmann had given me. Much of it was dry reading, as historical books tended to be, but each had a few juicy selections.

Dr. Overmann's book, specifically chapter twenty, dealt with some of the most popular native tales and legends, including Komaket. In his version, Komaket was born before many of the settlers arrived. He cured the settlers some twenty-five years later and told them he would return.

The most interesting reading was in Mr. Sellers' book *New Dover: The Early Years*. It told the story of how the early town leaders, notably Otto Willingham, Josiah Stanwood, Syvanus Hartin and Lyman Carleton, cooperated with the natives after the smallpox outbreak. These were the names of the four men in the grass-covered vaults that Tom and I had recently found.

Strangely enough, there was no mention of Komaket, just an unwritten understanding between the natives and the settlers.

The next page contained a photo of Otto Willingham's gravesite. The photo showed a close-up of the vault door and the name "Willingham" carved above. Next to the name was something I didn't notice when I had seen it in person. It was a symbol of some kind, but it was fairly worn. I took a magnifying glass to the image, but I still couldn't make it out. My computer was set up in my room, so I scanned the image and brought it up on my desktop. I opened a photo-enhancing application to see if I could clean it up, then messed with the tone and contrast. The symbol burst out before me: it was a *shongo*, nearly identical to the one in the drawing my father had left me. There was also a word written beneath it: "HERMILLION."

I tried to call Tom but he didn't pick up. If the other vaults had this same symbol, I needed to know, so I grabbed my digital camera and headed out.

The North Street Cemetery was busier than I expected, but no one was near the Josiah Stanwood vault as I searched for the information. The nameplate above the door was smaller than Otto Willingham's, but the symbol was unmistakably a *shongo*, also with the word "HERMILLION" beneath it. I had no idea what Hermillion meant.

Syvanus Hartin's vault in Oak Ridge Cemetery had only a small nameplate next to the door, but there was no sign of a symbol. Perhaps the connection was broken? It took me a while to realize that this was a family plot with a common headstone several feet away from the entrance to the vault. The area next to Syvanus Hartin's name was severely weathered, but something was there. I took a sheet of paper, placed it over the area and lightly traced it with the side of my pencil lead like I did when I was a kid. The image of the *shongo*—looking more or less like a lower-case *p*—came through clearly, along with "HERMILLION" beneath it. *Three for three!*

I was positive I would find the same thing at Lyman Carleton's vault in New Dover Cemetery and I was right. Four of our town's founders were buried in grass-covered vaults in four different cemeteries in the middle of a group of others. It was the same pattern.

When I got back to the house, I looked for information about the meaning of Hermillion. As bad luck would have it, neither Dr. Overmann's nor Mr. Sellers' book mentioned it. That would have been too easy.

In the short time I had been at the new house, I realized I hadn't had a chance to check on the drawings my father had left for me. I found a stack of folders near the computer and pulled out Komaket. He was nearly filled in completely, his cheekbones well-defined as was the cut of his chin. The deep-seated eyes that had once stared blankly at me were now piercing, perhaps even menacing. The strangest change was that the drawing was switching to color as a bit of flesh tone appeared on his forehead. It was frustrating not knowing his story. Did he really exist or was it wishful thinking on my part?

The *crimpu* too had begun to fill in with color. The borders were a pastel brown, and the center point was a pale green. The *shongo* drawing now had a clearly-defined spiral shaft, and the rounded top had the same distinct four-point pattern as the *crimpu.*

The final drawing in that folder was the old map, the one with the four cemeteries shaded in. I stared at it for quite some time, wondering why my father had chosen to leave this particular map for me. I used a pushpin to stick it to the cork wall behind my computer. I took a good look at the map with four shaded areas.

Then it hit me: the four cemeteries formed the pattern of the *shingala.* Better yet, the vaults of Otto Willingham, Josiah Stanwood, Syvanus Hartin and Lyman Carleton were the four points, so what was the center point?

I brought up the aerial map of the town and zoomed out to include all four cemeteries. I specified each gravesite as a waypoint and drew a four-sided shape. Crossing the diagonal points showed a center at a large plot of ground near the middle of New Dover next to the park. There were no houses or roads near it, just a lot of green. I clicked on an option to display the GPS coordinates of the center point and wrote them down.

Tom had to know about this. I called his cell phone and he picked up after four rings. I told him what I had found, and he absolutely wanted to go with me. He even volunteered to drive.

I found my GPS receiver in the bottom drawer of my desk and put in the coordinates of the center point. Tom rolled up a few minutes later and we were off.

He turned right onto Adams Road, and we followed it for about a half-mile. The GPS unit took us past Komagansett Park and was pointing to a field framed by some woods. There was a paved road that went around the perimeter of the property, but we thought it would be better to walk rather than drive.

"I've heard about this," I told Tom. "It's the land for the new cemetery. Apparently, the others are nearly full."

We followed the paved road along the field, then through a section of thicket and pine trees. I held the GPS unit out in front. "Seventy-five more feet."

Tom trailed behind me, then pointed to the opening at the edge of the woods. "There. Another field."

We bushwhacked through the final few yards; then we both stopped abruptly. I checked the GPS unit. The black arrow on the top of the display was pointing to a spot twenty feet away.

It was a grass-covered vault, just like the others, only newer. There were no other gravestones, memorials or any other indication that this was a cemetery... only this vault.

We went around to the front and found that it had a brand-new nameplate with a *shongo* engraved next to it and the word "HERMILLION" below that, just like the others.

"Okay, Koz, I have one question for you." Tom looked over at me, then back at the nameplate. "Who the hell is Ralph Pelson?"

Chapter 9

We stayed a little longer to assess what was going on. Neither of us had heard of Ralph Pelson or had any idea why he was buried here.

Tom broke the silence. "So this is the infamous center point your dad wanted us to find, huh?" He stood near the vault and tried to peek inside. "Frankly, I expected more, Koz. I'm not sure why."

I felt the same way. It seemed like a letdown for some reason. "Each cemetery has a center point, and this is the ultimate center point—Ralph Freaking Pelson."

"We're missing something." Tom had that look again. The wheels were turning. He pointed to the *shongo*. "This bugs me, Koz, it really does. Your dad wanted you to find the sixteen names that led to the four, and each of them has this symbol and the word 'Hermillion' next to his name. Maybe Overmann is wrong, and this isn't some Zulu staff used to cure the masses."

"That's been bugging me too. I agree that Hermillion is the key. Maybe it's a title or something? I don't know. I'll research it when I get home."

As we started back, I remembered about the party at our house. "Hey, Tom, there's a shindig at the house tonight. Since I live there, I'm allowed to invite whoever I want. I'll settle for you, though."

He laughed without looking my way. "No thanks, Koz. Jessica snagged me first. I'm supposed to meet some of her friends at some get-together over in Cardiff." He looked at me. "Trust me, man, a party at your house sounds a lot more fun; but, well, you know how it is."

I did know. Tom really liked this lady and didn't want to screw it up, even if it meant missing a kegger. He had only known her a few months, and he was already terribly, hopelessly pussy-whipped. Lucky guy.

When I got back to the house, the party was in full swing. Roger had placed his sound system in the optimal spot, had kegs flowing at both ends of the house and managed to squeeze a lot of people into a small space. I had been to my share, so I knew he had definitely done this before.

I worked my way through the crowd toward the kitchen. Roger was talking with a small group of partygoers, but he cut it short when he saw me.

"Kozmo, great to see you!" He had a habit of calling me that lately, but I didn't mind. "I got some folks I want you to meet."

He introduced me to his friends. Whether they were real friends or just party friends, it was hard to tell. Maybe it didn't matter. I shook four hands within a few seconds.

I tried to mingle but it wasn't really my style. I usually just zeroed in on some girl I wanted to meet and went from there. When Roger turned away for a moment, I took the opportunity to slip out. I used the back staircase to go to my room, clean up a little and check my texts.

There was one from Tom:

Koz,
Who knew your dad was such a wildman?

A wildman. That was the ultimate compliment from Tom Richcreek, even if it were given posthumously to Norm Kozma. It looked like he was thinking what I was thinking: based on what we've seen so far, we had just begun to scratch the surface.

A part of me wanted to keep researching Komaket, the meaning of Hermillion and everything else; but it was Saturday night, and there was a party going on ten feet below me. The research could wait. I was in my element.

Recharged and ready, I found a large, plastic cup near the keg, which was surprisingly not being used at the time. I filled it to the rim and began to work my way around. The party had the usual mix of college kids: jocks and posers in one corner, the goth crowd near the dining room table, a few frat boys and sorority girls in their house sweatshirts milling here and there. The small table in the corner was the site of a drinking game. The music wasn't so loud that the local cops would be knocking on the front door.

Even though I lived there, I still felt a bit like an outsider. All these people were in my house, but it wasn't mine really, at least not yet. Plus, I was probably the oldest person there, but I didn't have a problem with that.

I worked around to the living room and saw a familiar face on the other side of the room. Her brown hair was pulled back, and she flashed a full-toothed smile as she conversed with some guy in a Red Sox shirt. She was the same girl I saw in Dr. Overmann's house that day—his running partner, Melody. *That's a hard name to forget.*

The Red Sox shirt guy left and she was alone. I had met tons of college girls at parties over the years, but there was something different, something mysterious about her. I made the move to talk with her.

As luck would have it, no one intercepted her as I approached. She was scanning the other side of the room; then she scanned me.

"Melody, right? Hi, I'm Dennis."

She gave me the once-over, and I could tell my face didn't click. I probably looked and sounded like any other baby-faced party guy.

"I saw you at Dr. Overmann's house a few weeks back, remember? You were going out for a run."

Her face brightened. "Yes, now I remember. Dennis Kozma. You certainly got him going."

"What do you mean?"

She took a sip of wine which I complemented with a sip of beer. "Normally he's pretty quiet when we run, but that day he was particularly chatty. Are you a student of his?"

I had to move a little closer to be heard over the music. "I'm not a student here anymore. I did have him for history a few years ago and loved his class. What about you?"

"I'm a Ph.D. candidate in history, focusing on New England."

This was too good to be true. As we spoke, a rap song pulsed louder from the front room. Melody winced as the sound reverberated. Someone quickly adjusted the volume but not enough.

"It's kind of loud here. Want to go out on the porch?" That was bold of me but would it work? She didn't answer right away, which was not a good sign.

"Let me get a refill." Melody walked to a nearby table and filled her cup. I was sure I knew what would happen next. This is when the cute girl disappears into the party vortex, and I'm left holding my beer.

She said something to another wine drinker, then walked back my way. "Let's go."

I led her out front to our large, wrap-around porch. "It's a little quieter around the corner," I told her, although I had never been there before. We took a left turn and found a wide, sturdy porch rail to sit on. I desperately searched for something interesting to say. Fortunately, she went first.

"So, you don't go to school here anymore, but you still go to the parties, right?"

She looked even better in the cool glow of the porch. She had a perfect face and a lean, runner's build. Her teeth practically glowed.

"Actually, the party came to me this time. I live here. That's my room." I pointed to the corner bedroom. "My previous place fell through, and I ended up here just a few days ago. It was either that or move back home with Mom, and that wasn't really an option."

We talked for a good while about her family, my family, college life—pretty vanilla stuff—but I managed to keep her engaged the entire conversation. The party was still going full swing, with more people entering every minute. Her eyes moved toward the window as party people scurried past. I hoped I wasn't losing her.

"How long have you been running with Dr. Overmann? I hear he's a marathon runner from way back."

"It's only been a few months. He lost his wife to cancer last winter—she was a real sweetheart—and he took up running again for what he called therapeutic reasons. Anyway, we typically run as a group, you know, just a bunch of history geeks. It just so happened I was the only one who could make it that day."

"Geek?" That was the last word I would use to describe her.

"Did I mention I love history? In fact, I'm close to a degree in Euro History."

She gave me a cross look. "Really? Or maybe you're just saying that to impress me. You wouldn't be the first."

"Ah, but it's true. Just the other day, my friend Tom and I were at the New Dover museum talking to the town historian."

"Perry Stevens, right?"

"Actually, it's Perry Sellers." I could tell she was trying to trip me up.

"And what did you and the town historian discuss?"

I took a drink to lubricate my throat. "You know, the usual stuff: early town history, the great smallpox epidemic, Komagansett."

That got her attention. Melody pulled her feet up completely on the rail and leaned against the support column. "I'm duly impressed, Dennis. Why the interest in the great Komagansett?"

What could I tell her that didn't sound crazy? Then I had an idea. "Can I show you something?" I remembered that I had taken a picture of my dad's drawings with my cell phone. I brought up the picture of the *shongo*. "This is what I was asking Dr. Overmann about that day. Do you know what this is? We saw a drawing at the museum with Komagansett holding this staff."

She took the phone and examined the image. It was clear enough to make out on the small screen of my crappy phone. "It's hard to tell, but the lack of feathers and other details on the shaft suggests that it's likely a sachem's staff. They tended to be more ornamental near the crest than others. Komagansett was a warrior, so it's more likely he would have a weapon in hand."

"Dr. Overmann said it was African, a *shongo* of Zulu origin, to be precise."

She looked up, confused. "Zulu? That doesn't make any sense, but who am I to argue with him?"

Next, I showed her the drawing of the necklace. "This design is also at the end of the staff. Any idea what it means?"

She studied the image. "*Shingala.* I'm hardly an expert on the local native culture, but I've seen this pattern many times. It has something to do with concentrating energy toward a single area. Many tribes followed the principle." She took a sip, letting it go down slowly. "I won't bore you with the details."

Her thumb touched the next key, and the image of Komaket appeared on the screen. His name was still readable along the bottom. "Komaket?"

"The one and only Komaket, I dare say, a man of mystery and intrigue. Surely you've heard of his legend?"

She was transfixed by the image of Komaket for several seconds. "I told you, native history is not my strongest suit." She paused for a drink as she examined Komaket's face. "I do remember coming across his name once or twice."

I studied her face carefully. She went from flush to pale, then back.

"Sorry, I don't remember his story other than it involved wolves." She handed me the phone.

I didn't want to ruin a good thing, so thankfully I didn't have any pictures of the gravesites to show her; that would have been too weird, but there was one more thing. "What about the word 'Hermillion.' Does it ring any historical bells?"

"Hermillion?"

I nodded. "Oddly enough, this word and the image of the staff appear on the gravesites of four of New Dover's founders. Pretty crazy, I know."

She looked off into the night, then back at me. "Nope, never heard of it, but may I ask why you've been looking at gravesites?"

"Just some research I'm doing. It's a recent hobby."

Her cell phone rang and she answered it. "Hi... Yes, I'm still here... Out on the porch... No, I'm not alone... Yes... Why, yes he is... Okay." She put it away in her small backpack. "That was my roommate, wondering where I was. She's somewhere in the house." Melody got off the rail and stretched her back. "I have to go, Dennis. My roomie and I both have to work early tomorrow. It's been great talking with you."

Any other time, I would have used the opportunity to make a move on her. Under the circumstances, it didn't really seem right. It was just a party. "Can I call you some time?"

"Of course."

"So, is this when you give me the phone number of the pizza joint you used to work in?"

That made her laugh. "Nope, you get the real deal. I'll prove it. What's your number?"

I told her and she punched it in her cell phone. Mine began to ring and she put her hand out. "Don't answer it. I'm going to leave a message. Promise you won't listen to it until after the party?"

What the hell was this about? "I promise."

She walked to the other side of the porch as my voice mail silently kicked in after five rings. I craned my head around the corner and saw her leaning against the far porch rail, talking up a storm. The music from the party made it impossible for me to hear.

A tall, heavyset blonde walked out the front door, and Melody followed her down the front walkway. She looked back at me, smiled and emphatically put her phone away. "Goodbye, Dennis."

I kept my promise and avoided the message. The party was still rolling, so I went back in for a refill and to grab some food. Roger saw me and tried to get me into a drinking game, but I politely refused. Like most parties, I ended up talking with someone I knew from classes. The party died down after eleven and most people left, so I went to my room with a good beer buzz and crashed out. Then I remembered the phone message. My phone had trouble holding a charge, and it was down to one bar of power.

I brought up my voice mail and listened.

"Hi Dennis, this is Melody Bancroft. I just wanted to let you know that I really enjoyed talking with you tonight. I would really like to see you again; but, I'll warn you, I don't have a lot of free time." She paused until the party noise died down. "For the record, I've never worked in a pizza joint, but I did intern at the Stebbins Museum one semester. The curator once told me that there is a fine line between a legend and a prophecy. He said it all depends on what's at stake. Do you know what's at stake, Dennis?" There was a short pause. "Well, I have to go. See you later."

I couldn't stop thinking about her that night. I had to rub one out just to get to sleep.

Chapter 10

I stayed in bed as long as I could but still woke up tired and slightly hung over. When I went downstairs, the place had already been cleaned up. It looked as if a party had never happened. A couple of people were there to see Roger, but that was typical.

After pouring a cup of tea, I went out on the front porch and replayed the message Melody had left the night before. What was she saying about the legend and the prophecy? Why did her face go all weird when she looked at Komaket's picture?

I definitely wanted to see her again but decided to give her a day or two before I called. There was some rule about that or so I had heard. I hated those rules.

My pressing need for the morning was clean work shirts and underwear. Roger had quickly shown me the laundry room in the basement when I first toured the house. I grabbed my dirty clothes and headed down the creaky stairs. I pulled the string to turn on the light. There was a hand-scribbled "out of order" sign on the washing machine. Perfect. I started back up, then noticed a door in the far corner of the basement. There appeared to be a small amount of light—probably sunlight—coming from under the door, but it was padlocked closed.

I saw Roger when I came back up with my laundry.

"Hey, Roger, what's with the washer? I'm in dire need of some clean underwear."

"I feel your pain, Kozmo." His smile seemed genuine. "The damn thing broke yesterday. We told the landlord and he said he'd have a look ASAP. There's a coin-op a few blocks away; or, hey, you can borrow some boxers from me if you don't mind kittens on them, a gift from an old girlfriend."

"No thanks." Besides, I liked my tighty whities. "My mom lives pretty close, so I'll head there. If I time it right, I can get a nice lunch out of her too."

"There you go. Sounds like a win-win."

"Oh, and Rog? What's in the small room next to the laundry room?"

He paused as he opened the refrigerator. "Oh, that. It's a storage room for the landlord. He's the only one with a key, as far as I know."

That seemed perfectly logical to me. I called my mom and told her I was coming, then loaded the laundry bag into my car before heading out.

I took my stuff directly to the laundry room in the garage. My mom came out just as I began the first load.

"So when am I going to see this new house of yours, Dennis? I'm assuming, of course, that you actually did move into a house."

"Yes, I really did. You can come over this afternoon, if you like. We had some guests over last night, but it should be presentable." I didn't want to tell her we had a party. She wouldn't have approved of people—god forbid—actually having fun.

We talked in the kitchen while the clothes washed. As I had hoped, she made lunch for me which I ate at the small table. She made a sandwich for Stan, who was in his chair in front of the TV, as usual.

When I was done, I gave her a hug and arranged for her to come over to see the house. Stan never said a word, which was fine with me.

Someone had parked in my spot when I arrived home, so I had to park on the street. As I walked up the front steps, two guys came out of the house and zoomed past me. The first one said "hello" in passing; then they got into the car parked in my spot and drove away.

Roger was watching the Red Sox-Yankees game in the living room, so I dropped my stuff in my room and joined him. I had completely forgotten about my mom. When the game was over, I warned Roger that she was coming, then called her with directions.

I made sure my room was neat and the kitchen clean. Those were the two most important rooms to her. I ran a sock over the dresser and other wooden surfaces to get rid of the dust. *Close enough!*

There was a loud knock on the front door. It was too early to be my mom, so I assumed it was a guest of Roger's. I watched from the top of the stairs as a man in a suit took out a document and handed it to Roger.

"I'm Detective Sullivan from the New Dover police

department. We have a warrant to search the residence."

Two uniformed policemen entered through the front door and began to search. One headed toward the kitchen; the other rifled through the living room, then moved on to the dining room.

This couldn't be happening.

A plain-clothes officer, one of the men I saw coming from the house earlier, led Roger near the front door, then handcuffed him. Roger was read his rights and charged with drug possession and distribution.

My mind raced. *How did I get involved in this?* I thought back to all the visitors who had been over since I moved in.

Customers! How could I have been so stupid?

I seriously thought about making a dash for it down the fire escape at the end of the hall, but they would think I was involved when I clearly wasn't. I decided the best thing to do was to cooperate and let them know I had nothing to do with any of this. I slowly made my way down the stairs, heart racing, with my hands in plain sight.

"Who are you?" one of the officers yelled. I had never had a gun pointed at me before.

"Dennis Kozma. I just moved in here. I… I swear I have nothing to do with any of this."

The officer frisked me and led me into the dining room. "Don't move. Is there anyone else in the house?"

"No. Two other guys live here, but they don't show up much except at night."

Detective Sullivan entered the dining room as the frisking officer went upstairs. The other one went into the basement.

I never had a run-in with the cops before, and my heart pounded faster than I could ever remember. Detective Sullivan glared at me, then took a chair and turned it around. "Have a seat, Dennis."

I was shaking so much I nearly missed the chair. I corrected myself and sat up straight.

He pulled up his own and leaned close to me over the back of the chair. "What if I told you we've been watching this house for quite some time, Dennis? Add to that an anonymous tip and here we are."

It seemed like more of a rhetorical statement, so I kept quiet. I tried to make eye contact, but the detective's round face and scowl made it difficult.

"You say you just moved in here, right?"

"Yes sir."

"Have you noticed any unusual behavior since you arrived?

"Unusual? In what way?"

"Oh, I don't know. People coming and going, not staying very long—that sort of thing."

I took a deep breath and blew it out with puffed cheeks. "I... I have noticed that, yes. A lot of people come by to see Roger. I never really thought anything of it."

"Of course you didn't." He turned and looked up the stairs. "So tell me, what are we going to find in your room, Dennis?"

"Nothing. I swear, I don't do any drugs or sell any drugs. I lost my old apartment and needed a place to live. I never saw Roger or the other guys until I moved in here. That's the God's honest truth."

The officer came up from the basement, panting slightly. "There's a room with a padlock on it down here."

Sullivan looked at me. He was not happy.

I badly needed a drink of water, but I didn't dare ask. "Roger told me it was the landlord's storage room. I've never been in it."

"Get the bolt cutters from my cruiser," Sullivan said.

The officer from upstairs returned a moment later holding several small bags. "I found these in the bedroom on the left: four ounces of weed and what looks to be ecstasy."

"Your room, Dennis?" Sullivan asked.

"No. That's Roger's room. I'm on the far right."

"The others check out okay," the officer said.

He stood next to Sullivan with the contraband still in hand. Sullivan took a bag of marijuana and held it in front of me. The other officer with the bolt cutters headed into the basement.

"So, let me get this straight. Roger has been selling this stuff under your roof, and you had no idea?" He took the other bags and fanned them out in front of me for effect.

"Well, it's like this. I'm not a student like the other guys. I work for a pool supply place, which means a lot of evenings and weekends. I've only been here a few days, and we really don't cross paths that often. I never smelled pot smoke or anything like that. You have to believe me." I maintained eye contact with Sullivan and remembered to breathe. "Look, I'll take a drug test if you want. I'll pee in a cup right now if that'll help."

Sullivan motioned to the officer and he took the bags outside. The detective rested his chin on the top of the chair back and stared me down. "So what you're telling me is that you're just an innocent victim in all this, right, Dennis?"

I tried to speak, but nothing came out, so I cleared my throat loudly. "Yes."

The officer came up from the basement and interrupted our conversation. "Detective Sullivan, there are approximately twenty marijuana plants growing in that room—hydroponics, grow lights. It's quite a set-up."

Sullivan looked at me and shook his head. "And you knew nothing about this, I suppose?"

"I didn't, I swear. Roger told me it was the landlord's storage room."

He quickly stood and slammed his chair against the table. "Take Mr. Kozma down to the station for further questioning."

The officer made a come-on motion and led me outside. I mustn't have been too much of a threat because he did not cuff me. As I walked down the front stairs, I looked out across the street and my heart sank. Mom was standing next to her car, watching me being led away. As the officer opened the back door of his cruiser, I wanted to say something to her but words escaped me. He didn't force my head inside the car like I saw them do on TV so many times; I just got in and sat. Mom didn't appear to blink as she watched me head up the road to the police station.

Roger was there when I was brought into the station. He was sitting on a wooden chair, still cuffed, talking to the chief of police. I recognized the chief from the local newspaper. Chief Ruben Moniz was having a heated discussion with Roger, who nodded several times.

They took me to a small room in the back and left me there alone for fifteen minutes. Maybe they were hoping to sweat me out; I didn't know. Detective Sullivan came in a few minutes later, closing the door behind him.

"Your story checks out, Dennis. Roger told us you had nothing to do with his little operation."

"That's great." I resisted the urge to say, "I told you so." I just wanted to get the hell out of there. "So I can go home now, right?"

"Not exactly, Dennis. The house is still a crime scene. We can let you pick up a few personal items, clothes and what not. Everything else has to stay."

"What about my other stuff? My computer and TV?"

"Afraid not. Until we can determine which items are drug-related, it all stays. You'll have to check back later when the investigation is complete."

"How long will that take?"

He came toward me quickly and leaned across the table. "If it were me, I'd be thankful I wasn't arrested as an accomplice, looking at, oh, I don't know, five to ten up in Walpole. If it were me, I'd go back to the house, grab my shit and forget that I ever moved there." He stood and straightened his tie. "If it were me."

An officer I hadn't seen before drove me back to the house a little while later. He watched as I filled a small gym bag with some clean clothes. I was so glad I had just done laundry. He didn't seem to care what I threw in there, so I took Komaket's portrait and all the other papers and carefully placed them in a folder. I grabbed my cell phone and GPS too and put them all in the bag. There was a shirt on top of my laptop, so I scooped up the whole heap while the officer turned away for a moment.

My car was not confiscated, thankfully, so I threw my bag in it and backed out of the parking lot while the officer watched, arms folded, from nearby. I made it about a block when my emotions finally got the better of me. I pulled into an empty church parking lot and stopped. I smacked my hands against the steering wheel several times, but it didn't seem to help.

Where would I go? I couldn't impose on Tom again. He made it pretty clear that it was a one-time deal. Jed didn't have any room at his place. I had no choice. I was out of options. I dug through my bag, found my cell phone and began to dial with sweaty hands.

"Hi, Mom. Listen, I can explain."

Chapter 11

"Dennis, sweetheart, are you in jail? What happened?"

"No, Mom, I'm not. I was just taken down to the station for questioning. I was never arrested."

For the next ten minutes, I explained to her the events of earlier in the day. For the most part, she just listened and let me get it all out. I reiterated several times that I was not involved in Roger's dealings. It was a matter of me being in the wrong place at the wrong time.

"I had to watch my son hauled away like a common criminal. Do you have any idea how that makes a mother feel?"

"I'm sorry you had to witness that, Mom." My voice was still wavering, so I covered the phone and tried to compose myself.

"What about your belongings, Dennis?"

"Well, that's the thing. The officer who drove me home explained to me that they have to determine which items in the house were possibly, you know, bought with drug money. I'm free to go but my TV is still under arrest, if you can believe that."

"But Roger said you had nothing to do with it, right?"

"Detective Sullivan believed him too. I'm hoping it's just a formality."

"When are they going to let you go back, Dennis?"

My long pause pretty much answered the question. "I can't go back. I have to disassociate myself with Roger and that house."

"So you have a place to stay?"

"Not exactly."

"I see." She paused for a few seconds. It seemed like minutes. "Well, are you going to ask me or do I have to invite you, Dennis?"

I stuck my head out the window to get a breath of fresh air. "Mom, I have nowhere else to go. Could I stay with you until I can make other arrangements?"

"Dennis, of course, you can. I'll run it by Stanley, but I don't think that will be a problem. I'll get the guest room ready for you. No one has been in it since Stanley's brother came to visit."

"Thanks, Mom."

"By the way, I don't exactly like the idea of being your last resort, but I understand your dilemma. I've told you before that we're your family, and we'll always be here for you."

"Sorry, it didn't come out like I wanted. Anyway, I'll be over in a little while."

"Okay."

By the time I said, "Thanks, Mom," she had already hung up.

I rolled into her driveway about thirty minutes later. I took my bag and went in through the side door to the kitchen. Mom was there to greet me with an enveloping hug.

"Welcome home, Dennis." She pushed a few tears aside and led me to the small dinette table. She acted like I had just come back from a war. "Have something to eat. You've had a long day."

My stomach agreed with that last statement. She got me a steaming bowl of beef stew. It was one of her specialties. As much as I liked living on my own, nothing was better than her home cooking.

I had gotten two spoonfuls in when Stan came in from the garage. I fully expected him to walk right past me, but he came into the kitchen. He appeared to be smiling as he put out his right hand.

"Dennis, it's good to have you home."

I stood to shake his hand. He seemed sincere. "Thanks, Stan. I really appreciate the hospitality."

"I heard about your predicament. Talk about wrong place, wrong time. Anyway, our house is your house, Dennis." He went to the refrigerator and took out a diet soda. "Would you like something to drink?"

"Sure." I seriously wanted a cold beer or a shot of tequila but not in this house. "Soda is fine." He handed me a can and stood next to my mom as I sat down.

"You can check out the new toy when you're done." Stan flicked his thumb over his shoulder. "I moved up to a fifty-five-inch LCD hi-def TV. NFL Network too."

"Sounds great."

My mom rolled her eyes, then went to the sink to clean up. I looked over at Stan, then attacked the rest of my stew. He was being nicer to me than I could ever recall. Maybe this was a "new

Stan."

A few minutes later, Mom showed me the guest room. I had moved out on my own before they bought this house so I felt like a stranger. My old bed and dresser were in it, and she even managed to find some old posters of mine to put up. She opened up the middle drawer of the dresser.

"Lucky for you, some of your clothes are still here—nothing much, just some jeans, shorts and t-shirts."

Fortunately for me, that's all I ever wore. I unpacked my meager belongings and placed my laptop on the small desk in the corner. I was so glad I managed to sneak that out while the officer wasn't looking. The house was equipped with wi-fi, so at least I had that going for me. My crappy cell phone was nearly dead, so I set up the charger and plugged it in. I kept the stuff my dad gave me in the bag.

"I see you're traveling light," she said. "So if you need anything, just let me know."

"I will. Thanks for everything."

Mom couldn't help herself. She had to give me one more hug. I could hear her gently sobbing, so I patted her on the shoulder. I knew it was better not to say anything; just enjoy the moment.

It had been a long day, so I took Stan up on his offer to watch some TV. The Red Sox were on in high-definition. It was heavenly. Stan sat in his favorite chair and I took the couch. He took the time to show me how to use the elaborate remote control for the TV and other electronic equipment. I already knew, but I let him have his time.

I was dog-tired, so I went to my room a few innings later. My cell phone was done charging. I checked my voice mail and found two messages. They were from Tom and Jed wondering what had happened earlier in the day. I called each one back and gave them the short story. We agreed to meet at O'Reardon's sports bar the next night to get the long story.

After I hung up, I realized there was a text message from Melody waiting for me. I brought it up on the screen.

I found a painting you might find interesting
call me tonight

I found her number and called back immediately. She picked up on the third ring.

"Hi, Melody. This is Dennis. I got your text message."

"Dennis, I'm so glad you called me. I came across some curious information, and I'd like to show you what I found. How about tomorrow? I have a little bit of time in the evening."

A little bit of time? It sort of made sense coming from a Ph.D. student. "Well, I have to work until 6 p.m.; then I'm meeting some friends at O'Reardon's at 7. You're welcome to join us if you want. Tom and Jed know all about Komaket and the other stuff my dad left."

The line went painfully silent. *I just invited a girl I'm getting to know to a sports bar with two other guys. What the hell was I thinking?*

"That sounds great, Dennis. I'm looking forward to it."

"Can you give me a hint?"

The silence was killing me. *Are you always this theatric?* I thought.

"Words can't do it justice. I'll see you tomorrow at O'Reardon's."

"Would you like a ride?"

Another long pause followed. "No thanks, Dennis."

I was going to say, "Call me Koz," but Dennis just sounded right coming from her. Everything sounded right coming from her.

***

The only bad thing about work the next day was that I had left my work shirts at the "busted" house. Employees were supposed to wear matching dark-blue collared shirts with "Leo's Pool and Supply" written above the breast pocket. I explained what had happened to Leo, and he gave me a spare to use for a few days. It was a little small, but I had no choice.

I ate quickly when I got home, then explained to Mom and Stan that I was going out for the evening. Neither seemed terribly excited about it.

Jed picked me up just before 7 p.m. As we headed to O'Reardon's, I told him about Melody. "She's a grad student, going for a Ph.D. in history. I met her at a party and showed her some of my dad's drawings and, well, I think she took a liking to Komaket. She's going to meet us there. I hope you don't mind."

"A grad student, huh?" He sneaked a peek at me as he drove. "Koz, you animal, don't be so modest. It sounds like she wants more than just your drawings." He snickered louder than necessary. "Of course, I don't mind."

We found a booth in the back corner. I sat facing the entrance so I could see when Melody arrived. Tom showed up next, sliding into the booth next to Jed. He ordered the first round of beers.

"So tell me about this Melody chick, Koz. I haven't seen you this anxious in… well, ever."

I slid my hand down to stop my right knee from bouncing. Before I could reply, the waitress arrived with our drinks. I bought the first round. "Well, Tom, it's like this..." Then she walked in.

"Yowza!" Tom said but not too loudly. Fortunately, she couldn't hear him.

I leaned in the direction of my two friends. "Try not to be your usual douchebag selves tonight, guys." That made them laugh a little.

Melody had on a tank top and sweat pants with her hair pulled back in a ponytail and a backpack slung over her well-toned shoulder. I introduced her to Tom and Jed as she sat next to me with the backpack between us. Tom tipped his bottle in my direction, then took a swig.

"Can I get you a drink?" I asked her.

"No thanks. Maybe just some water; I have some more research to do tonight."

I brought everyone up-to-date on the drug bust at my former house and my subsequent release. A few eyebrows went up, but no one went out of their way to make me feel any more stupid.

"What's going to happen to Roger?" Melody asked.

"I'm not sure. He was charged with both possession and distribution."

Tom chimed in. "If it were just the pot, he might be all right. You mentioned ecstasy, Koz. That stuff is seriously bad news. I hope he has a good lawyer, or he'll be doing some time for that."

Better him than me. I fished through the drawings I brought and spread them out on the table, mostly in front of Melody who had never seen them before. The face of Komaket was more vivid than ever. She picked it up for a better look.

"Is this the same one you showed me before?"

"Yes. The drawing appears to be filling itself in, if you can believe it. Same with the necklace and staff. I can't explain why."

Jed, who hadn't seen the drawings since Gene had given them to me, was amazed. "Koz, this is wild. Is it some sort of magic?"

"I don't know what it is. My dad must have gotten hold of some special paper or something."

Melody slid the staff drawing a little closer. "I looked up some of these items, and this is definitely a sachem's staff. Each tribe had a unique shape, style and pattern. This square pattern, symbol of the *shingala,* appears to be favored by this particular tribe."

"These now have a clearly-defined focus or center point." Tom pointed to a spot on all three drawings. "That's where the good stuff is."

This drew confused looks from both Jed and Melody.

"I'll tell you what," I said. "Let's order another round, and I'll get everyone up to speed. You'll like this part."

Tom held up his empty, which caught the eye of our waitress. Melody looked closer at the drawings, then back at me. She pushed her water away.

"I think I need something a little stronger."

We ordered three Guinness Drafts, a glass of Chardonnay and settled in. I brought out the old town map and the lists of names, then laid them out. Tom and I took turns explaining how each set of names corresponded to a pattern of graves around a grass-covered vault of a town founder, and each of those formed the same pattern around the vault of Ralph Pelson, the center point in the new cemetery.

"Plus," I said, "each vault has the same symbol and the word 'Hermillion' on it. All the symbols match the one our friend Komaket is wearing. It's also on a portrait of Komagansett that's in the library."

Melody mulled over the drawings, slowly sifting through the stack. The drinks arrived and Tom took care of the round. Melody picked up her glass and downed a third of it. She stared at the drawing of the necklace for a long time. "Very interesting. May I see the original lists of names?"

The documents had worked their way to the far end of the

table. Tom gathered them up and handed them to her. She pulled out a pair of glasses from her bag, put them on and mouthed the names of many of the men on the list.

"Shadow Regiment." Her voice was barely loud enough to hear. "Just as I suspected."

"What?" I said.

She opened her backpack and brought out a printout of a painting. It appeared to be a battle scene from the Revolutionary War.

"We need a little background here, so bear with me. You've all heard of the Shadow Regiment, right? The local soldiers who defeated the British right here in our own backyard during the Revolutionary War."

"Yeah," said Tom. "There's a plaque in the park that explains the whole battle."

"I was at the Stebbins Museum yesterday, and I came across a painting by Phinneus Marley, a local artist who specialized in war scenes. Now, this painting has been on the lobby wall for years, and I've probably walked past it 1,000 times without noticing."

"Noticing what?" I leaned in to get a better look.

She moved the picture to the center of the table. "I took these with a digital camera. See the two flags the soldiers are carrying? One of them is clearly what was called a New England flag. It was not unusual for these ragtag groups to use their own variations of more prominent flags. The symbol on the other flag is what I'm curious about." She slid another picture out and pointed to a squarish pattern on the flag's white background. "I blew up the image a bit."

Tom saw it first. "The sign of the *shingala*. Why would it be on a Revolutionary War flag?"

"Great question. Any theories?"

I tried my best to work through all the information we had gathered in the past few weeks. Somehow it all came back to Komaket, but his legend was supposed to have existed over a hundred years before the Revolutionary War. Then an interesting thought popped into my head. "Komaket was keeping his promise."

Tom picked up on it. "He said he'd show them how to protect the town. What did Mr. Sellers call it? *Triation*?"

"Yes. Dr. Overmann mentioned *triation* too, something about using an advantageous pattern against an intruder."

Jed got in on the action. "The British attacked Fort New Dover; but a handful of local militia, the Shadow Regiment, came out of nowhere, surrounded the intruders, kicked their asses good and eventually forced them to retreat."

Tom hoisted his glass. "God, I just love a feel-good war story." Jed and I joined in and clinked ours with his.

Melody did not lift hers. She seemed content to let us have our fun. "Interesting theory, guys. Unfortunately, there's no record of a known military stratagem being used in this battle. The pattern we so desperately wish to see did not exist, at least in any annals I'm aware of."

"How did the Shadow Regiment surprise the Brits?" Jed asked.

"The details are sketchy, unfortunately, like many of the smaller skirmishes. The consensus is that the local militia drew the British soldiers toward Fort New Dover, then came out of the shadows to surround and eventually turn back the intruders. What's odd is that according to British historical documents—and trust me, they were quite thorough—the advance scouts reported that the entire colonial regiment was spotted at the fort just hours before the attack. When the Brits arrived, only a skeleton crew was on hand and the rest took part in the surprise attack. It was a real turning point in the war."

I looked down at the list of names on the table. "How are these names related?"

"I recognized a few of them: Nathaniel Talcott, Archelaus Perkins and Noah Feagin to name three. They were all members of the Shadow Regiment." Melody took the opportunity to polish off another third of her wine. She had definitely earned it.

"Why just these sixteen names?" Tom asked. "The so-called Shadow Regiment consisted of hundreds of soldiers."

Melody stared blankly down, then shook her head.

"What's really unusual," I added, "is that these men died over a century after the four town founders but still managed to get buried in a perfect pattern around the four vaults."

Tom looked away for a moment in deep thought. "So what's the connection?" he asked. "Where does Hermillion fit into all this?"

We looked at Melody, but she calmly took her papers and placed them back in her bag. "I have to be going. It was nice meeting you guys."

"I'll walk you out."

She moved quickly past the bar and out the front door. I had to practically run to keep up. I guess she was late for her research. She unlocked her car and got in, pausing a moment to lower the window.

I leaned my forearms on the door. "Hey, can I call you again?"

She looked up and smiled. It seemed sincere. "Sure thing."

There was something I had meant to ask, and it finally came to me. "You told me after the party that there's a fine line between a legend and a prophecy. Which do you think this is?"

"Legends are just stories, Dennis."

"Ah, so you think Komaket is going to return, right?"

She leaned over, grabbed the back of my head and kissed me hard. "Maybe he already has." Her words and her actions stunned me and I stumbled back.

"Bye, Dennis." She put up the window and drove away.

Chapter 12

When I returned to our booth, Tom and Jed abruptly stopped their conversation and quietly drank the last of their beers. I slid in just as they finished their drafts.

"You douchebags got real quiet all of a sudden. Don't tell me you're not impressed with her."

Tom slid a little closer. "Look, Koz, she seems nice and all, and she does seem to know her stuff. It's just...."

"It's just what?"

He looked quickly over at Jed, who leaned across the table to make his point. "I don't want to come off as some kind of asshole or anything, Koz, but she's holding back from you... big time."

"Yeah," Tom said. "Did you see her body language when I asked about the sixteen names?"

I saw her body all right, but not necessarily the language. I was pretty sure I had a solid read on this one. "Wait a minute, guys. She came to us, remember? She told us about the painting and the symbol on the flag and everything she knew about the Shadow Regiment. That doesn't sound like holding back to me." I hadn't realized how loud my voice had gotten or that I was standing up.

Tom noticed. He looked around, apparently checking to see if anyone else had noticed.

"All right, Koz. I'm sorry. I didn't mean to set you off." He raised his glass to mine. "Let's have another drink and just chill."

Jed sat back and watched, twitching in his seat. "Can I just say something here?"

"What is it?" I said.

"Why is everybody so, I don't know, cool with all this stuff?"

"Like what?"

He pointed to the Komaket drawing peeking out of the folder. "Well, for one thing, Koz, in case you've forgotten, the portraits are filling in by themselves."

"I'm aware of that."

"Yeah, but doesn't that freak you out? I mean, that kind of

thing doesn't happen every day." Jed turned his Yankees cap around.

"I don't pretend to understand it. I just accept it because I trust my father. I also accept the fact that things in this town were set up in this crazy pattern over the course of hundreds of years for reasons unknown and that soldiers came seemingly out of nowhere to win a battle over two centuries years ago."

Jed nodded but not too convincingly. He turned his cap back around and finished his beer. "One more thing: there is a question that I have not heard anyone ask tonight."

"Fire away."

"Koz, what does any of this stuff you just mentioned have to do with your father? You haven't forgotten about him, have you?"

He had a good point. It had been a while since I thought about how Norm Kozma fit into the big picture.

"The honest answer is that, frankly I don't know, Jed. We're just taking the information as it comes to us. On one end, he wanted me to know about the cemeteries and the grass vaults and Ralph Pelson. On the other, a crazy native legend resurfaced, and it may have something to do with a Revolutionary war battle… or not. Who knows?"

"There's a link still missing," Tom said. "I don't know what it is. Sorry to say this, Koz; but I'll bet Melody does or, at the very least, she knows how to find out."

I didn't agree with him about Melody, but it wasn't worth rehashing. "We need to find out more about this Shadow Regiment."

Tom pounded his empty bottle on the table. "I'm an idiot. The names are right there on the monument. It's still light out. Anyone want to take a quick trip across town and check it out?"

***

I went with Jed as we followed Tom to the Revolutionary War monument near the center of town. We parked diagonally next to the park, then made the short walk to the monument. There was a large stone in the center with all the names of the local men who died in the war. There were benches on the south and east. To the right was a three-foot square display with a map of the region detailing the attack on Fort New Dover by the British and how the Shadow Regiment surprised them from three directions. A column on the left side of the display listed the men in the regiment.

I took out my papers and began to scan for names. I handed one each to Tom and Jed. They began to look.

"All mine are here," Tom said.

Jed checked his page carefully. "Mine too."

I mentally checked off mine. "So all sixteen names on the list are present and accounted for."

"Why just these sixteen, though?" Tom asked.

The sun was beginning to set over the trees on the west side of the park. It cast a perfect light on the cenotaph. "Guys, check it out."

Tom brushed against me. "What is it?"

"The stone. Look at it from this angle. The sun hits it just right."

Jed and Tom both stood behind me and peered at the stone. It was a marble monolith with a top that sloped about forty-five degrees toward the west.

Tom cocked his head. "What are we looking at?"

"The shape, Tom. It's unmistakable. That's no ordinary four-sided object."

He moved his head from side to side, then saw what I saw. *"Shingala."*

"I see it too," Jed said. "That's not the only one." He pointed to the information sign. It too was a slightly irregular square.

The sun was dropping quickly, and the site soon turned into shadows. We began to walk to our cars. I gave the monument and surrounding area one last glance and saw an even bigger picture in the gloaming. "Tom, you're not going to believe this."

He came back and put his hand on my shoulder to see what I was looking at. It was the entire monument: two displays to the north and west, two marble benches to the other sides and the names in the center point.

More *shingala*. It made me smile. "Do we have any idea who built this thing?"

"There's a dedication plaque in the back," Jed said.

We rushed over and read the plaque:

Center Point

Dedicated to the courageous men of New Dover
Who fought in the Revolutionary War.
August 1940
Hermillion Club

"Hermillion Club!" We all said it at the same time.

"That's the name on the four grass vaults," I said. "How crazy is that?"

By then, the sun had gone down so there was nothing more to see. Tom took off to see his girlfriend, and Jed dropped me off at home.

***

The house was mostly dark when I returned. I had forgotten how early Mom and Stan turned in most nights. I checked the refrigerator for something to eat and found some leftover casserole. I warmed it up and made my way into the living room to watch a little TV.

Stan had the remotes lined up on his table from smallest to largest. I found the remote for the TV, but it required a password to unlock the keypad.

A password... that was typical Stan. I wasn't sure if he always used the feature or was just teaching me a lesson. I shut everything down and went to my room instead.

I opened my laptop to see if I could find out anything about the Hermillion Club. Fortunately, the wireless internet still worked. Unfortunately, I couldn't find a single hit. It seemed like nothing in this town was archived electronically.

It was one of the quietest nights I could remember. I closed my laptop and sat back in the comfortable office chair. The silence was wonderful. My mind drifted from Komaket to the grass vaults to Melody.

Melody—she wasn't like any college girl I'd ever met. Was she holding something back? Why would she? It was hard to tell.

The word that pounded hardest on my brain was *shingala*. It was everywhere. I liked the air of mystery surrounding it. My father had told people that "something big" was going to happen, but when and why? If his premonition were correct, then it had to

81

tie in with everything else. All the information I had was so old that it seemed unlikely to have any effect on today or fifteen years ago. Those links in the chain were too far apart.

I took out the papers one more time and looked them over. Komaket glared at me, his eyes glassy and cold.

Attached to one of the pages was the note Russell had left me.

Finish this for your dad
RK
PS Keep me in the loop

I had not thought about Uncle Russell for a long time. This seemed like a good time to bring him back in the loop. I opened my laptop and began to piece together what I knew. It was one of the longest messages I had ever written; but after reading it back, I sensed that I had nailed it. An hour after I started, I hit send.

Chapter 13

I played it cool for a couple days, both with Melody and at home. I called her just to say "hi" and got her voice mail, like always. It was tempting to do my usual thing and go out with my friends to drink beer and shoot pool, but I felt it would probably be better if I acted more like a family member than a boarder.

My mom made sure my work clothes were cleaned and pressed. She even made lunch for me every day. My living at home seemed to revitalize her, like she had a new purpose in life. Stan realized that the remote was password-protected and removed the feature. He apologized for it, although it was hardly sincere.

I was relatively happy in their house. That was a pleasant surprise. I didn't dare tell either of them that I was actively looking for another place, though. Losing my rent and deposit money from the last house was a financial setback, but I was quickly making up for it.

Melody was on my mind and I couldn't take it anymore. I had to see her again—just the two of us this time. I managed to get only her voice mail for three straight calls. I didn't want to seem like a stalker, so I cooled it and hoped she'd call back. Instead, she left another text message for me on a Thursday night.

How about a movie tomorrow?
My treat
Meet you @ the SUB caf @ 6:30

The SUB was Weaver College's Student Union Building. I texted back, *Okay!*

I arrived at the SUB just before 6:30. It was a spacious building with several study lounges that were pretty well-populated for a Friday night. I took the stairs to the second floor and entered the cafeteria. It was closing time, so most of the tables were empty. I scanned the room but saw no trace of Melody, so I sat at one of the tables, leaned back against it and waited.

A few minutes later, I felt something wet touch my arm. I

83

pulled it away and saw Melody cleaning the table with a washcloth. She smiled and continued wiping the tables in the vicinity. She had a dark brown zip-up shirt with "Food Services" on it. Her hair was pulled back in a bun with a hair net over it. She looked great.

"Hi," I said.

"I'll be done in two minutes. I have to punch out."

I watched her closely as she disappeared through the door behind the counter. She exited a moment later without the work shirt and the hair net. She looked even better.

"I work here a few days a week," she said as we made our way down the stairs. "It's mindless work, but it pays pretty well."

"So where are we heading?"

"The Micro. I think we can still make it."

The Micro Cinema was a movie theater located in a converted church a few blocks from the campus. The ground floor housed the box office, concession stand and restrooms. The theater was in the basement; seating was cramped and sparse, with room for probably no more than thirty patrons. They typically showed cult and "art house" films from as far back as the 1940s. I hadn't been to it in a few years, but it was an interesting place to take in a movie.

We walked quickly out of the SUB and away from the campus. There was a line forming at the Micro, and we moved to the back of the pack. The large poster in front displayed tonight's show: *Fitzcarraldo*.

I'd never heard of it. The poster showed a large boat being pulled up the side of a mountain.

We stood and chatted for several minutes, but the line didn't seem to move much. I peeked at my watch. It was 6:50.

One couple came out of the front entry, followed by another, then another.

"Sold out," I heard one of the guys say.

Melody slumped her shoulders, then began to walk away. "I really wanted to see that one, Dennis. I think you would have liked it. Sorry I couldn't get away from work earlier."

"It's okay. We can hit the Quad Cinemas downtown."

"Nah. I'm not a big fan of new movies." She slapped me playfully on the arm, then grabbed it and held on. "What do you expect from a history geek?"

I tried my best to come up with an alternate plan that wasn't lame, like mini-golf. Even though she invited me, I felt compelled to have a backup. Nothing came to mind, so we just kept walking. A block later she spun me toward her.

"I have an idea. How would you like to go someplace special?"

"Special?"

"It's a place very few people get to see."

A thousand things flashed in my mind. A few of them made me smile. "I'm game. Where are we headed?"

"Let me check something." She rifled through her pocketbook and pulled out a smartphone. She opened an app, saw what she wanted to see and nodded. "Let's go."

She took my hand and led me across the street, back toward campus. A couple of cars honked at us as we cut in front of them, but Melody kept up the pace. We took a side street near fraternity row, then up towards the administration building. We dashed across the large lawn and through the long shadows of the giant oak trees. Our pace slowed—actually, her pace slowed and I just went with the flow—until we came to a row of red brick buildings. I recognized the largest as the liberal arts building. I had taken a class in there as a freshman many years before.

"If this is a plot to get me back in class, it won't work." I clenched her hand a little tighter as we got near the building.

"You'll like this lesson, Dennis. Trust me."

I liked the sound of it.

We went to a side entrance of the building. Melody stopped and opened her pocketbook. "Lucky for us, I have a key. They let certain grad students have after-hours access. I just have to call it in so security knows it's me."

She took out her phone and punched in a number.

"Hi, Frank, it's Melody... I'm great, thanks. Hey, I have some files to pick up; could you clear for me? Thanks, ever so. Oh, I also have a guest." She put the phone away and took out her key. "The alarm will be off in a moment. Frank will check us out on that camera." She pointed to a security camera in the upper corner of the enclosure. "Then we can go in."

There was a faint click; then Melody put her key in the door and unlocked it. We entered the building and headed for the stairwell on the far right. The only illumination came from the low-wattage security lights. We climbed all the way up to the fourth floor and entered the main hallway. Halfway down, we stopped at a set of double doors. Melody took another key, unlocked the left door and pushed it open. She turned on one set of lights and the place came to life.

It was a museum.

"I'll bet you didn't know we had a museum, did you?"

"Actually, no. I thought I'd been everywhere, but I never hung around in this neck of the campus."

It was small by any standard and crammed full of artifacts. There were stuffed animals along one wall. One shelf was lined with pottery of all shapes and sizes, another with flints, arrowheads, beads and tribal jewelry.

"We mostly use it to show students how to set up displays," she said. "Lighting and background are crucial, you know."

I had to admit that this was the strangest date I had ever been on. During normal hours, this place was probably boring as hell, but the idea of being here after hours added a sense of intrigue. The crazy side of me thought maybe there was a couch in the back room, and maybe she had an ulterior motive.

She led me to a darkened area to the right. "When the subject of Fort New Dover came up the other night, it made me think of this place. I don't come in here too often, but I did in my undergrad days. It's mostly for museology students."

She flipped a light switch, and a set of track lights glowed from the ceiling onto a large, covered display. She pulled off the white cloth cover, revealing a scale model of the fort, complete with miniature soldiers.

"It's called 'Attack at Fort New Dover,' artist unknown."

The model was about two feet long on each side and four inches tall along the walls. The British soldiers in their red battle garb were fleeing past the fort toward the river to the south with the minutemen right behind them.

"Nice work," I said.

She said nothing as she nudged me to the left.

"Really," I said. "Great detail."

"So, do you see it?" She gave me an eye roll, grabbed my arm and moved me to the front of the display.

"I... I guess I don't."

She smoothed her hands over the display. "Look at the shape of the fort, Dennis."

It was a near square: *shingala.*

"Okay, I get it now." I walked around the entire display. "This pattern is everywhere in this crazy town. What does it mean?"

"I'm not entirely sure. Komaket showed the founding fathers this pattern, and they passed it on. How and why remain unknown at this time."

"It's just a square. There's nothing special about it."

"Empirical evidence says otherwise, Dennis. Just so you know, this is said to be the only model of the fort in existence."

We checked out the display for a few more minutes. I was fascinated by the detail put into it, especially in the soldiers. They were all different. I couldn't find two with exactly the same pose.

Melody stood nearby and said nothing as I checked out the display. I'm not sure how much time passed—fifteen, maybe twenty minutes—but it seemed as if this were the only reason she brought me here. I was glad she did.

I had seen enough and we moved to the front of the museum. I glanced back and a glint of light caught my eye. There was a plaque high on the back wall. I don't know how I missed it earlier. On it was written:

Exhibit made possible by
a generous donation from
The Hermillion Club

I turned toward Melody to ask her about it, but she was already in the hall holding the door open for me. There would be no naked rendezvous in the back room. It looked like this night was just about over.

Chapter 14

She hit the lights just as I was leaving; then she locked the door, shaking the handle to be sure. The fourth floor was back to its eerie, soft-glow look from the security lights. We made for the stairs at a brisk pace, but I wasn't sure why. Maybe there was a time limit on late-night visits.

"Thanks for the personal tour." I glided my hand down the stair rail as we went.

"I thought you'd like it." She took out her cell phone and punched in a number. "Hi, Frank, it's Melody.... Yeah, we're done here.... No, I didn't find the files but thanks for asking.... Okay."

We waited in front of the exit door until it clicked; then Melody gently pushed it open. "Wave to Frank." I decided to salute, instead, as we walked out.

It was dark out as we made our way back across the Weaver College campus. It was well- lit along the popular walkways but eerily dark near the large clumps of trees that surrounded the liberal arts and administration buildings. In the clearing just to our right, someone began to walk in a parallel path to us. I put my hand on Melody's shoulder to stop her, and the shadow person stopped too.

"There's someone in the woods," I whispered.

"I know. I saw him."

She took my hand and we continued up the lighted sidewalk. The stranger mirrored our movements. When we paused, so did he. The sidewalk split and we took the left route. It was a longer route back into town but took us past several well-lighted dorms. No one appeared to be tracking us, and perhaps no one really was. It was a big campus.

We made our way back into downtown New Dover and passed the Micro Cinema. There was a later showing of *Fitzcarraldo*, but she seemed uninterested. We continued silently. I put my arm around her and she did the same to me. I didn't know where we were going. I didn't care.

"How about a drink?" I asked.

"Sure. Someplace classy, though. No beer halls."

"The New Dover Hotel it is then." The New Dover Hotel was the tallest building in town. The bar was pricier and more upscale than most places, which scared away a lot of the college kids.

As we took a left turn, a car slowly turned the corner behind us. I'd noticed it in front of the Micro but hadn't given it much thought. The car looked familiar, but I couldn't see through the tinted windows. It followed us for another block, then turned right and out of sight.

From our corner booth, I ordered a Guinness for me and a glass of Chardonnay for Melody. She told me about her doctorate program and how much work it was. I didn't miss school at all after listening to her. She took small sips as she spoke, using her non-drinking hand to punctuate an occasional point.

"I know you tried to call me before, but it was way after midnight most of the time." She put her hand on mine. "Research is a bitch, Dennis."

I thought the time was right to ask her about something from earlier in the evening. "Did you happen to notice the plaque above the fort display in the museum?"

She glanced up, eyes wide as she took another sip. "What plaque?"

"It said something about a donation by the Hermillion Club. They also have a plaque at the Revolutionary War Memorial. I'm just wondering why that name keeps popping up."

She shook her head. "Like I said before, I've never heard of them. I can look into it if you like."

A waitress interrupted our conversation by placing another Guinness and Chardonnay on the table.

"We didn't order these," I said.

The waitress, Karen, picked up her tray. "These are yours, compliments of RK. At least that's what he told me to tell you."

Melody tapped my arm. "Who's RK?"

"I don't know." Then it hit me. "It can't be." Then I saw him walking directly toward us.

Russell Kozma was back in town.

"Hey, Dennis. Great to see ya again."

I stood to shake his hand, but he bear-hugged me instead. He squeezed so hard my eyes popped wide open.

"What brings you into town?"

"Just some unfinished business." He gave me that weird Kozma smirk I'd seen before.

"Oh, I'd like you to meet Melody Bancroft. Melody, this is my Uncle Russell. Russell Kozma."

He reached out and gently shook her hand. "A pleasure, Melody."

"Nice to meet you, Dennis' uncle."

He put his hands up above his shoulders. "Hey don't let me interrupt anything. I can see you two have made a night of it."

How did he know that? Unless...

"You weren't, you didn't..." I couldn't think of how to word it.

Melody finished it for me. "Were you following us earlier, Russell?"

"Well, yeah, sorry if it freaked you out a little bit. I went to your mom's house, but I didn't see your car. I don't have your phone number, but I got lucky when I saw you walking to the student union. When you two disappeared into that building, I thought I'd never find you."

Melody pulled her pocketbook closer. "I should be going."

"No, enjoy your time together. I'll just head up to my room, right above us in 221." He pointed straight up. "See you later, Dennis. A pleasure, Melody."

We finished the second round of drinks with little to say. Melody appeared to be irritated and made several peeks at her watch. Finally, she picked up her pocketbook and hooked it over her shoulder. "I have to go, Dennis. It looks like you have family business." She headed for the door while I followed behind.

"Wait. Come on, you can't leave now. I didn't know he was coming. He just shows up when he wants to."

We were out on the sidewalk, heading away from the hotel at a brisk pace.

"Thanks for the tour. I liked the museum."

"I'm glad you liked it." She stopped and faced me. "I had a nice time tonight, Dennis, but I have to get up early tomorrow." She pulled me in and kissed me. I could taste the wine in her mouth. Then she dashed across the street, causing a Hyundai driver to slam on his brakes.

At that point I realized that our night was truly over. Why was she always so damned mysterious? Anyway, she was gone and Russell was here, so I went back to the New Dover Hotel. I know he wanted to see me.

***

Room 221 was the last room at the end of a long hallway on the second floor. I knocked twice. Russell opened the door before the second knock had finished.

"Dennis, I'm so glad you could make it." He took the opportunity to give another bear- hug. I was getting used to them. He closed the door and led me in.

"So what brings you back into town, Uncle Russell?" I looked around the room and saw that the TV was off. His laptop computer provided the main lighting.

"Well, your long email message really got me thinking."

"About what?"

"About this crazy town. Hey, you want a beer? I stocked the fridge." He opened the small refrigerator to reveal a plethora of Guinness.

"Sure." I never turned down a good lager.

He took out two and opened them, then handed me one. I settled into a semi-comfortable hotel chair.

"Before we go on, Dennis. I just want to say that I didn't mean to interrupt your social life. I hope I didn't mess things up for you."

"No, not a problem, Uncle Russell."

"Good. Mind if I ask how old Melody is?" He took a long drink and cocked his head at me.

"Twenty-four. She's a Ph.D. candidate: history."

"Twenty-four, huh? Well, that's, uh, that's cool, Dennis." He made a strange sound as he exhaled.

It wasn't cool; I could tell. Somewhere in all his numerology nonsense, that number did not sit well. "Okay, I have to know. What's up with the number twenty-four?"

"Well, it's like this. I had to leave my last girlfriend when she was twenty-four."

"Why?"

"I found that twenty-four-year-olds are known for three things. One is a moronic affection for cheap Chardonnay. Two is a severely-convoluted sense of reality." He paused and took a long drink, then moved the computer mouse to bring the machine out of hibernation.

"Sooo, what's the third?"

"It's not important, Dennis." He clicked the mouse several times.

"Come on. You started it."

"Okay, number three is great tits."

I should have known better. I decided to try to keep him off these little tangents for my own sanity.

"It was just last year," he said, "so the memory is kind of fresh."

I found it creepy that we would date women the same age. It was just wrong. *Why... would... anyone... STOP IT!* I took a breath to compose myself. "Okay, let's get to the real reason you're back in town. I doubt it's to talk about your old flames or my current one."

"You got that right, Dennis. Sorry for the sideshow. C'mon over here. I have something to show you."

I moved my chair a little closer as he brought up a document on the laptop screen.

"I've done a little searching. It seems your sleepy little town has done a few peculiar things in the past few centuries."

"How peculiar?"

"Well, let's start with the information you sent me. There were sixteen names on the papers your dad left for you, right? And they all were part of this Shadow Regiment from the Revolutionary War."

"Right."

"And they're buried in this crazy pattern around four other guys. Otto Willingham, Josiah Stanwood, Syvanus Hartin and Lyman Carleton were all-around good citizens from what I can tell and helped put this town on the map way back when."

"Thanks, but I kind of knew all that."

"I know. Here's the good part. The cemeteries in question were once the properties of the aforementioned men. That's right; each of them owned farms somewhere else in town, then sold everything they had to buy one of these obscure plots of land. All four donated the land to the town with the provision that it had to be used for cemetery purposes only."

"Why would they do that?"

"I don't know, but I'll bet it pissed their families off. Anyway, since you discovered that everything happens in a pattern of five— four corners and a middle—this one is no exception. The land in the center of these four cemeteries is also a cemetery, thanks to a man named—"

"—Ralph Pelson." Wow, I had almost forgotten about him.

"Yes indeed. Ralph Pelson bought it and donated it to the town, just like the others. What's strange is that I checked the town records and found out the selectmen have turned down perfectly good opportunities to purchase land for a new cemetery even though the other four have been full or nearly full for years. It's as if they were biding their time... waiting."

"Waiting for this particular piece of land to be for sale, right?"

"That's what it looks like." He sat back in his chair and took a swig. I did the same.

"Why didn't those town founder guys just buy the land when they bought the other four? That would make sense."

"I don't know and yes, it would make sense. I traced the history of the Adams Road property, and it has been in the same family for as far back as the archives go. Ralph Pelson sells his farm and pays twice the market price to get the land at auction. The town agrees to buy it from him for a mere dollar as long as old Ralph gets a grass vault in a particular location. It's not even a family plot."

"How do you know all of this? I thought you were a small businessman?"

He gave me a wry smile. "I do own a small business. I'm also what you might call a corporate investigator."

"What? A private eye?"

"Not that glamorous, Dennis. More like an independent researcher. A lot of it has to do with local regulations and zoning laws and very uncool things like that. Google and LexisNexis are your friends, I've always said. The information is there if you know how to get it."

"And you do?"

"If the price is right, absolutely. I also do some pro bono work."

"Great. So what else is in your bag of tricks?"

"It all comes down to zoning, Dennis. Zoning laws are basically the same throughout New England, except for Maine, of course. It's too cold to even piss outside half the year, but that's neither here nor there. Anyway, nearly all the land around here is zoned for residential, commercial or industrial use and pretty much stays that way until the land is sold—basic Euclidean zoning codes. The Adams Road property that Pelson bought had been grandfathered as residential for many years even though all the businesses around it were zoned as commercial. It was worth more to the town if someone bought it, developed it and paid taxes on it for years to come. But the town knuckleheads simply let Pelson sit on for years, then let him essentially give it away."

"How could that happen? Don't we have advisory boards and such?"

"Of course. I'm pretty sure there was one person who tried to stop them."

"Who?"

"Norman Jackson Kozma."

I just about dropped my beer. I figured there was a connection between my dad and the cemeteries but not like this.

"What's scary, Dennis, is that your father was known for his use of understatement. If he said it might rain a little, I expected a downpour. He told your mom that something big was going to happen. That could only mean one thing."

"What's that?"

"Some serious hell is going to break loose."

Chapter 15

I gave Russell's face a good looking-over. There wasn't a trace of wry humor in his eyes or satire in his voice, no tangents.

I tried to recall what I knew. "I heard he was forced to resign in disgrace. I even read a few articles about it. If he had a smoking gun, why the hell didn't he bring it out when he had the chance?"

Russell closed his laptop, then swung around toward me. "I've been thinking about that too. Whatever information he had must have been bigger than him, bigger than you and me, certainly bigger than this squirrelly little town of yours. When he knew he was going to die, it would have done him no good to blare the trumpets. It was too soon."

"So whatever is going to happen..."

He nodded contently. "... is going to happen real soon, and he wanted you to be right in the middle of it."

"Lucky me." It was sort of a throwaway line, but I really meant it. The Kozma family name was at stake and I, for one, wanted the truth to be known.

We spent the next hour talking about my dad. Uncle Russell had story after story about the roller-coaster ride that was their childhood. Even though they were far apart in age, I was glad to hear they had an unusual bond that lasted right up until the end. Being an only child, it was a bond I'd never know, unfortunately.

It was well past midnight by the time I got out of there. I slowly unlocked the kitchen door and made my way into the darkened house. My growling stomach reminded me that I hadn't eaten in quite some time, so I got a bowl down from the cabinet for some cereal. The bowl slipped a little and made a loud noise on the counter. When I took the milk out of the refrigerator, a tube of biscuits rolled off the rack and smacked the floor. Damn. I was trying to be quiet. I finally had my cereal and washed the bowl out in the sink. When I turned around, my mom was standing at the edge of the kitchen in her bathrobe, arms folded. She scared the crap out of me.

"It's very late, Dennis."

"I know. I was out with Melody; then I went to see Uncle Russell."

"This is completely unacceptable." Her hands moved to her hips, and she gave a tired but focused stare. "We'll talk in the morning." She turned and disappeared down the hallway.

I wasn't very tired, but going to bed seemed like the right thing to do. I lay there for quite a while with a million things swirling through my mind, including how ticked off my mom was going to be in the morning. Finally, I managed to put it behind me and sleep arrived.

***

It was a late workday for me, so I took the opportunity to sleep in. I knew I had to have an unpleasant conversation with my mom and possibly Stan, so I slept as long as I could, then took a long, slow shower before heading to the kitchen.

"Good morning, Dennis," Mom said. "I hope your evening went well." She had her cutting board out and began cutting up stew meat to place in a crock pot.

I found my mug and a tea bag and began to pour a cup. "It was fine, Mom. Look, I'm sorry I was out so late. Uncle Russell's in town and he invited me to his hotel room."

"This is the third time this week you've been out late, Dennis. It would be nice to know where you are going and what time you'll be home. It's only common courtesy." She made short work of the potatoes.

"Mom, I'm young and I have a social life. Besides, I wing it most nights. Is that so hard to see?"

"No, not at all. It's just that you're out until god knows when, doing god knows what, with god knows whom. I admit we're old and boring, and we certainly don't approve of a party lifestyle." Next she chopped the carrots and slid them into the crock pot.

"I don't have a party lifestyle. I was out with Melody, the grad student I was telling you about. We went to the campus museum. Then Uncle Russell found me and had some important information about Dad to show me. It was too late to call. Really."

The crock pot was nearly full. She took a measuring cup full of water and poured it over the contents, then put on the top and turned it to high.

96

"Stanley and I have talked it over, and we think it's best if you curtail your late-night activities."

The thought of getting ol' Stan involved in the equation made me queasy. "What does that mean? A curfew?"

She moved her hands quickly under the faucet, then wiped them on her apron. "Call it what you want, Dennis. If you want to live in our house, the rule is that you must be home at a reasonable time. Let's say 11 p.m. on week days and midnight on weekends. Can you live with that?"

She had me, plain and simple. I was in no position to argue since my alternative was living in a cardboard box next to city hall. I sloshed the tea around in the bottom of my mug, then finished it off, including several loose grounds. The bitter taste didn't bother me.

"Is that a 'yes'?"

"Sure. I can live with that."

"Great. Now let me fix you something to eat."

I wasn't really hungry, but I let her fix me some eggs. It gave me a chance to find the classified section of the local paper and check the "Roommates Wanted" section. In truth, the new rule sucked, big time.

***

When I got home from work that evening, there was a message in my email inbox from Russell. He had to go back home to tend to his business, but he promised to return soon. He left me the link to his website that gave me access to additional information. "Don't worry, it's secure," he wrote.

I went to the website and saw there were links to several sets of documents. It looked like I'd have to do some digging. I brought up the first set of documents and read through them, but nothing on the pages was familiar. Unfortunately, it was the same for the second, third and fourth pages. It was tedious skimming through them all, but Uncle Russell assured me his search for something useful was narrowed down to this group. Finally, I hit pay dirt on the fifth set. There were four purchase orders for gravesites in the new cemetery. I noted the names. One of them, Kevin Van Houten, sounded familiar, so I searched and found that he was one of New Dover's three selectmen. The second person, James Flanary, was also a selectman. The other two men, John Partridge and Neil Hollinger, were members of the zoning board.

I checked the location of the four plots in the new cemetery and found that they were scattered pretty far apart. I was not at all surprised to find that they formed a near square around the vault of Ralph Pelson.

Russell's website also had a link to a series of town videos. Unlike the pages I skimmed through earlier, I had to listen to each town meeting to figure out if anything were useful. It took a little while to load each one, and the videos that came up were not of great quality. The sound was also less than stellar. I saw what I wanted on the third video and replayed it to be sure. If only I could make it bigger.

Then it came to me. *Use the big screen in the living room—* Stan's TV. I unplugged the laptop and found the right cables, plugged it into the back of the TV and used the remote to select the right mode. What a difference!

The video was from a meeting of the New Dover Planning and Zoning Board. The names of the board members, including John Partridge and Neil Hollinger, were visible on large prism-shaped nameplates in front of them. The third member was someone I had never heard of: Ken Cordeiro. The meeting was taped from a single, stationary camera in the corner of the room. I sat in a wooden rocker and watched the meeting unfold.

Ken Cordeiro sat on the far right of the long table at the front of the room. Like the other members, he had a small microphone in front of him. He arranged his notes and waited patiently for the proceedings to begin.

John Partridge, the director, called the meeting to order at precisely 7 p.m. After several short articles, he got down to important business. He took a swig from his bottled water and addressed the board.

"The next item concerns our old friend, Ralph Pelson. Mr. Pelson's attorney has sent a formal letter to the town stating that Ralph is willing to sell the Adams Road property to the town for the sum total of one dollar on the condition that it be used as cemetery land."

"What? A dollar?" Cordeiro said. "As I recall, he paid a lot of money for that piece of property five years ago."

Neil Hollinger continued, "Overpaid is more like it, to the tune of a quarter million. I know it's an unusual request, but that land would solve our cemetery problem for at least another generation, perhaps more."

"I don't know, gentlemen. It sounds too good to be true."

Hollinger made sure the few spectators could hear him. "Who's going to say they turned down a chance to save the town that kind of coin?" He looked directly into the camera. "Certainly not me." Two spectators nodded.

Cordeiro tapped his pencil on the table. "But why? What's in it for him?"

Partridge held up a piece of paper and read from it. "According to his attorney, he has one other stipulation. He wants a grass-covered vault, one of those barrel-shaped types. That's it."

"A vault?" Cordeiro appeared to be getting annoyed at the proceedings. "We haven't allowed vaults since, I don't know, the twenties maybe. Can we do that?"

"The monument restrictions vary by cemetery," Hollinger said. "We write it in so he can, then take it off later."

Partridge drummed his fingers on the hardwood table. "The way I see it, Mr. Pelson wants to do this and we should recommend approval. He's not some crackpot we've never heard of. The man has been an upstanding citizen for sixty years. If he wants to do his town a favor, who are we to judge?" Partridge took his glasses off and cleaned them. "Remember, folks, he sat in this chair for a long time back in the sixties and seventies. He was one of us." He turned in Cordeiro's direction. "What am I missing, here, Ken?"

Cordeiro shifted in his chair and leaned into the microphone. "What you're missing is rational thinking. Let's step through it, okay. Ralph Pelson sells his farm and his house to buy a piece of over-priced land at auction five years ago. The land is zoned commercial and he does nothing with it, even though he could grow something because he's been a tomato farmer for, oh, fifty years. Now he wants to donate the land to the town to ease our cemetery problem. Tell me this doesn't raise a red flag."

"I disagree," Hollinger said. "It's not unthinkable for a private citizen to make a major land donation to his hometown. A high percentage of the cemeteries and town parks in our part of New England were created in such a way."

"Not in this century or even most of the last century," Cordeiro shot back. "Three of our cemeteries go back to the 1700s, the other to 1699. Komagansett Park was turned over as a land grant in 1922. Since then, we have had to purchase every acre of land we've needed for schools, parks and town offices. Random acts of kindness—at least when it comes to land—are older than the Model T, gentlemen."

Partridge nervously straightened out his papers as the room grew silent. "Let's vote. A simple majority is sufficient to send a recommendation on to the Board of Selectmen."

Ken Cordeiro cast the only dissenting vote. He wrote a few lines in a small notebook and excused himself from the rest of the proceedings, shaking his head as he walked away.

The video was over and the screen went blank. I played it again to make sure I knew what was going on. Two members of the zoning board approved the cemetery deal, then bought plots in a pattern around the center point. Why?

I moved the laptop back to my room and checked the town website. Ken Cordeiro, who appeared to be the lone man out, was still listed as a selectman. It was time to pay him a visit.

Chapter 16

I sent an email to Ken Cordeiro to find out if or when he had office hours at the town hall. He got back to me later in the day and said he would be there on Monday between 3 and 4 p.m. Perfect—that was my early day, so I'd be done with work by then.

The New Dover town hall was a red brick building located in the heart of the historical district next to the public library. I pulled into a shady parking spot in the back and made the short walk to the side door with my laptop case in hand.

Ken Cordeiro's "office" was just a desk in a moderately-sized, wood-paneled room. The other two planning and zoning board members and a part-time secretary also had desks in the room. The secretary, a pleasant-looking young woman named Nancy Rinker, looked up from her computer screen as I entered.

"Can I help you?"

"Is Mr. Cordeiro in?"

She turned and looked. "He must've stepped out for a minute. He should be right back. You can wait there." She pointed to a pair of wooden chairs below a large bulletin board with "recent events" spelled across the top in cut-out letters. Some of the events were months old, but I decided not to mention it to Nancy.

I had sat for less than a minute when Ken returned to his desk from an adjoining room. I walked past Nancy and the two empty desks to Ken's area. He saw me coming and remained standing. He looked to be in his mid-forties with a stout build and thick, dark hair and eyebrows.

"Hi, Mr. Cordeiro. Dennis Kozma. I emailed you yesterday." He gave my hand a firm shake.

"Yes, Dennis, I'm glad you could make it. I love speaking with the young people of this town. What can I do for you?" He motioned for me to sit. I did. So did he. "Please call me Ken."

I had gone over what I was going to say several times but forgot most of it, so I winged it. "This might sound kind of strange, so bear with me. I was watching a video of a zoning board meeting from a while back, and was wondering if you could explain something to me."

"I'll try. Can you be a little more specific?"

I pulled out my laptop and sat it on the edge of his desk. "Sure. I have the meeting right here." I started the video and, although it was fairly low-grade, we could make out what was happening.

Ken focused hard on the screen. He nodded a few times; and when it was over, he sat back in his chair.

"I'm guessing you're some sort of reporter or blogger maybe, Dennis. First off, let me say that it was a mistake on my part to walk out of a town meeting in a huff. I apologized later for it and frankly had forgotten about it until now. It was not exactly a high point in my term."

"I'm not a reporter or a blogger, Mr. Cordeiro, and I'm not concerned about the walkout. My question is about the details of the meeting, more specifically the new cemetery. I'd like to know why the zoning board turned down perfectly good properties for years before the Ralph Pelson deal came along."

Ken's thick eyebrows pinched as he moved closer to his desk. "As you can see from the meeting, I was against the new cemetery idea; but with the town finances the way they have been in the previous few years, not spending on cemetery land seemed fiscally responsible." He blew out a breath. "I guess we got lucky. Does that seem reasonable?"

It did, but I had a nagging suspicion that he was holding something back. He moved the pen in his right hand in circles between his fingers.

As we spoke, a second board member came in and sat at the next desk. I recognized Neil Hollinger from the meeting video. He immediately picked up his phone and began dialing.

Ken sat back and seemed content with his standard, boilerplate answer. I tried another tactic. "You said in the meeting that the Pelson deal seemed too good to be true. Do you still feel that way?"

Ken glanced over at Hollinger, then gave me a serious look. "I admire your civic concerns, Dennis, but the fact is that the cemetery purchase was a low-priority item. The town saved a quarter million in that deal; then we moved on. It all worked out for the better."

I considered asking him about the tax revenue the land could have brought to the town, but he likely would have sidestepped that one too. It seemed uncomfortably crowded in the room, so I decided to wrap it up.

"Thanks, Ken. I appreciate your time." He remained sitting as I shook his hand. I put the laptop back in its case.

"Feel free to contact me anytime, Dennis."

"I will." With that, I grabbed my laptop case and headed past the secretary's desk, not at all satisfied with the lack of information I received. What the hell was he hiding?

***

I got called in to help with another home hot-tub installation that evening, and it took us well past 9 p.m. to finally get it delivered and set up. I really wanted to head to O'Reardon's for a cold one with Jed but thought better of it. That would be considered a "party lifestyle," wouldn't it? I went home and watched the Red Sox game on the big TV, just me and Stan and a six-pack of diet root beer.

I checked my email later on, and there was a message from Ken Cordeiro.

Dennis,

I apologize for the brevity of my responses to your questions earlier today. Believe me when I say that it was a bad time to talk about the subject matter (thin walls). If you would like to continue the conversation, please meet me tomorrow at 4 p.m. in the archives room located in the town hall basement (thick walls).

Ken

I smacked the desk hard with my palm. Now we were getting somewhere.

Fortunately, working late Monday made Tuesday a short work day, and I was done by early afternoon. I took the time to call Melody to see what she was doing; but, as usual, I only got voice mail. Moving on, I found the documents my dad had left, the ones that looked like official town papers, and took them with me. I parked in the same spot behind town hall.

The door to the archives room was located just off the main

hallway next a door with "Tax Assessor" written in curved text. Reading those words made me shiver. This was my dad's old office, and I remembered going in there when I was a boy. I opened the door to the basement and headed down.

I went past a small kitchen and several vending machines to a dark wooden door with a frosted-glass window. The sign on it read "Archives." The knob was so old, I could feel the springs extending as I turned it. I entered and looked around for Ken, who was waiting in the far corner.

"Close the door, please." He walked toward a table in the center of the room. "Again, I apologize for the tone of my answers yesterday. You brought up some interesting questions that deserve proper answers, but first I'd like to know why you have an interest in this. Cemeteries and zoning laws are not exactly exciting stuff."

I moved to the opposite side of the table and put my folder down. I thought about sitting but continued to stand. "It's for my father. He used to work in the assessor's office upstairs and on the planning and zoning board for a short time. I just came into possession of some documents he had gathered together before he died fifteen years ago. This information, along with some other stuff I've researched, seems to imply that something strange is going on with the new cemetery. That's about all I know."

"I see. What was your father's name?"

"Norm Kozma."

He nodded. "Of course. I remember that name. I wasn't involved in town politics back then, but I do recall him having some legal difficulties with the town."

"Yes, he was forced to resign. My mom claims he was innocent but never got a chance to prove it."

"Well, that would explain your interest. Now, back to your questions. Why did we turn down other potential cemetery sites in the years leading up to the purchase of the Adams Road land?" He used finger quotation marks for "purchase," but he didn't need to. "Of course, we had no way of knowing that Ralph Pelson would give his land away. He was a successful farmer and businessman for many years. Anyway, a few years before that, we considered a piece of land just past the mall. It was perfect for our needs and the price was reasonable. The finance and advisory board gave their recommendation and so did I. The two other members balked, saying that it bordered wetlands and we would need an environmental impact study before the DEM would approve the sale. Technically they were right, but those problems could be overcome fairly easily. Two other properties came up for recommendation, and they were similarly killed by the same members. Then along came Ralph Pelson's Adams Road property—which, incidentally, borders wetlands—and these guys jump all over it. Yes, I thought it was too good to be true. I just didn't know why. I still don't."

"Did you know that the other board members and two selectmen immediately bought plots in the cemetery? I think that's kind of strange." I thought it best to stick with town-related information and not to bring up the whole *shingala* phenomenon.

"No, I didn't, but there's certainly no law against that. I've considered doing the same thing, to be honest. Lord knows I'll need it someday."

I opened the folder and pulled out the first document my dad left for me. I slid it across the table to Ken. "Do you know what this is?"

He picked it up and reached for the glasses in his front pocket. It was a two-sided page. He flipped it over to read the other side.

"This is a zoning reclassification request. The property owner was requesting a zoning change from residential to commercial. We get these all the time, especially when the land abutting it has been changed. Much better chance of a sale."

"Can you tell where it is?"

He looked over the front page once again.

"Hmmm, the location is the Adams Road cemetery land. What's odd is that this reclassification was approved over fifteen years ago, but I know for a fact that it was still residential land when we bought it a few years back."

"Can you look it up?"

"Sure, we have all these documents stored on microfiche. The newer backups are all done on DVD, but the microfiche is still around for the older files until we can upgrade. The hard copies are kept in a storage facility on the other side of town."

He went to a file cabinet labeled "1993-1997" just below the handle. He opened it and ran his finger along the index tabs on top, found the file he wanted, pulled out several envelopes and spread them out on the table. They were standard-sized business envelopes, some thicker than others. Ken found the right year and pulled out a few microfiche cards. Holding one up to the light, he checked the date. Then he checked another and another. Finally, he found what he was looking for and placed the card in the reader. He motioned me over.

"Zoning reclassifications are filed by date. It should be somewhere in the middle of this card." The images flew by at a dizzying speed on the large display screen. "Right... about... here." He stopped and turned the knob back a notch. The document on the screen was not the one in his hand. "Very strange."

He checked every image on the card. There was no match.

"Maybe it's not official," I offered.

Ken pointed to the signatures at the bottom. "Signed, sealed and delivered. The owners of the land, Robert and Maria Riley, filed the paperwork and got approved; but something happened along the way."

"Can you tell who approved it?"

He checked the document again. "This is interesting. The signing authority for the zoning board was Norman J. Kozma."

I never thought of looking at the signature line. The legal mumbo-jumbo made me dizzy just reading it. We now knew that my dad had signed off on the document over fifteen years earlier.

"What happens to one of these reclassifications once it's approved?"

"It gets filed and the property is legally recognized under its new designation. It's all fairly standard stuff." He removed the card from the microfiche reader and placed it back in the proper envelope.

"So what happened to this one?" I spun it on the table several times using my fingertips.

Ken put the envelopes back in their folder, placed it in the drawer and locked it. "I don't know, Dennis. I can't explain it. It seems to have disappeared. The fact that your father kept a copy of it is, well, intriguing."

I started to put the papers back in the folder. I had assumed that they were multiple copies of the same document, but something caught my eye. The dates didn't match. I pulled it from the folder.

106

"Mr. Cordeiro, here's another one, only it's from 1995—two years earlier."

He quickly scanned it, then shook his head. "This land was reclassified twice and it never went through. I wish I knew what your father was trying to tell us."

That made two of us. I checked the folder again, but the only papers left were those with the names we found in the cemeteries.

"Dennis, it's getting late and we'd better wrap this up. I'm chairman of the Founder's Day celebration next month, and I have a ton of stuff to do to get ready. I'll see what I can find out about the Adams Road property and the zoning issues when I get a chance. Thanks for sharing this with me, and I assure you I'll keep in touch."

"No problem. I learn something new every day. When is Founder's Day this year, by the way?"

"It's the third weekend of October, just like it has been for a hundred years."

I shook his hand, gathered up my folder and left the archive room. As I made my way past the vending machines, I saw someone dash up the stairs and close the door behind him. I couldn't see who it was, but he was wearing dark pants. Perhaps someone had come down for a snack?

When I got back upstairs, no one was around. All the office doors were closed, all the lights turned off. I headed to the parking lot and only one other car was there, likely Ken Cordeiro's. I thought about how helpful he had been and why he had been reluctant to help me at first. It made me think of my dad. Dad gave me two ends to a puzzle, with Komaket at one end and the new cemetery at the other. All I needed was the middle. Middles, or so it seemed, were always the hardest.

Chapter 17

I planned as I drove back home. The best course, I decided, was to follow what I knew. The four town officials and Ralph Pelson were somehow connected to the Hermillion Club, which was then linked to our old friend Komaket.

There was a lot going on both in my life and in my head. It kept me awake far too long that night. I hadn't thought about Melody for most of the day, which was quite unusual. Tom and Jed had both left voice mails, but I was too busy to call them back. I needed all three of them right now to help me find the middle.

Unfortunately, it was a hectic couple of days. We were still selling and installing pools even though it was too cold to go in them. The prices were too good to pass up, apparently. I did two hot-tub installations and a maintenance check, all in one day. I called Melody again, to see if we could get together, but only got voice mail... again. Tom and Jed were working extra hours and had little free time. Things got better by week's end, and everyone was free to get together Friday night at O'Reardon's. I promised to buy the first round.

I arrived early and found a large booth. Surprisingly, Melody showed up next. She looked great, as usual, and slid in next to me. I was always told not to keep a lady waiting, so I ordered her a Chardonnay right away. Tom and Jed were not far behind; and, true to my word, the first round was on me.

Tom leaned in and started the ball rolling. "So, Koz, it's been a while. What do you have for us?"

"It all comes back to Ralph Pelson. From what I can tell, the land that he bought at auction, then sold to the town for a buck was pre-determined to go to him. My father had two zoning documents from the previous owners showing that they tried to change the zoning classification. The other zoning board members and two selectmen squashed it for reasons unknown. We know that Pelson is buried in a vault on the land and—get this—those same four officials have plots in the *shingala* pattern around Pelson. Pretty wild, huh?"

Tom took a strong pull from his beer and nodded. "Once again, the key is *shingala*."

"It's a classic example of historical pastiche." Melody sat back and started on her wine.

Jed gave a confused look. "Pastiche?"

"Yes. It's an imitation of style that often applies to music, but it works here as well. Komaket provided the original pattern." She made a square shape on the table with her finger. "Then members of this town faithfully imitated it for over 300 years. There is precedence for this, of course. The Mayans, you see, had a similar usage of pastiche dating back to the seventh century and continuing on until the post-classic collapse." She looked around the table at our cold stares, then smiled. "Okay, sorry. I've given too many history lectures lately." She picked up her Chardonnay and sat back.

I took out a small piece of paper from my pocket and unfolded it. "Somehow, selectmen Kevin Van Houten and James Flanary, along with zoning board members John Partridge and Neil Hollinger are all in this thing... plus, our old friend Ralph Pelson, of course."

"Hey, Koz," said Jed, "sorry I haven't been of much help. It's been a busy few weeks, and I've had to cover for some folks on vacation. Such is life on the bottom of the corporate totem pole."

"Me too," said Tom. "Busy, that is, but I want a shot at ol' Ralph Pelson. I know some good research sites, and I'll see what I can find out about him."

"Thanks, Tom." I found out earlier that he had broken up with his girlfriend, but I thought it better not to bring that up. "Ralph is all yours."

Jed moved in closer. "I'll look into those town guys. There has to be a connection somewhere. I can probably sweet-talk one of the research librarians into helping me."

"Great, Jed. Go crazy."

Tom tossed some popcorn in the air and caught it in his mouth. "So, Koz, what does that leave for you?" He tossed another and Melody intercepted it.

"We are going to take a little visit," she said before popping it in her mouth.

"We are?" I had no popcorn to toss, so I settled for a quick drink of Guinness.

"Yes. We should have done it a long time ago. We are going to see Dr. Overmann to see if he can shed a little light on all of this. I've already arranged it, Dennis. He's looking forward to seeing you."

"Okay." It struck me odd that she would arrange a meeting out of the blue. Then again, she was a little on the unpredictable side.

"In the meantime, I suggest we finish the first round and start on a second." Tom raised his bottle. "Here's to Komaket—one wild and crazy guy."

We completed the toast and drank up. His words reminded me that I had not seen Komaket in a while. I pulled out his folder.

"Let's see what the old guy is up to." I took out his portrait.

If I had had anything in my mouth, I would have spat it out. Komaket's face was glaring up at us in full color. His lips were pursed, and his eyes were like dark pools. His jet-black hair was tight against his head and contrasted with the deep creases on his forehead.

The drawing of his necklace—the *crimpu* with the *shingala* shape—was completely filled in with vivid detail; the same with the *shongo*, his staff.

"Holy Christ, Koz," said Tom. "That is one scary-looking dude."

Komaket's eyes appeared to follow me as I reached across for some popcorn. I didn't want to freak everyone out, so I closed the folder and put everything away. We spent the next hour or so talking and watching the Red Sox on the big screen. Apparently we all needed a night out.

Melody was the first to leave, as usual. I walked her out to the parking lot but didn't see her car.

"I walked," she said as we approached the sidewalk. The streetlight lit her face perfectly.

"So when do we see Dr. Overmann? He seems like a busy guy."

"He is. We're meeting at his place at 4 p.m. tomorrow. Bring comfortable shoes."

"For what?"

"Running. We're his jogging partners this week. Bye, Dennis.

See you tomorrow."

I hated jogging, but she was gone before I could tell her.

Chapter 18

I was home before curfew that night just to play it safe. It felt like I was thirteen again, but they weren't going to change the rules very easily. Saturday was my early day at work so I crashed out immediately. I would need my energy for the meeting with Dr. Overmann.

I was wardrobe-challenged when I looked for the appropriate jogging attire after work. Most of my workout gear was still under arrest in Roger's house. I had just enough time and money to head to a local sporting goods store to get a shirt and a pair of shorts that didn't look lame. My sneakers were fine.

Melody's car was already parked in front of Dr. Overmann's house when I arrived a little before 4 p.m. I could hear Melody's voice through the front screen door as I approached. I never made it in. They continued their conversation as they came outside. He closed the door behind him in mid-laugh.

"Dennis, so glad to see you again." His dark blue running outfit put mine to shame. "We'll stretch, then get started."

We moved to the empty driveway to stretch. It had been so long that I had to watch them to remember how. I leaned forward and cradled the back of each leg, feeling the burn of inactivity while trying my hardest not to wince. I put my feet apart and tried to touch my toes, but my lower back refused to cooperate. Melody looked at me as she quietly grabbed her ankles and formed a perfect jackknife position. It took a full five minutes to complete the stretch.

"And we're off!" Overmann led the way as we started down the driveway.

They were quickly ahead of me and I sprinted to catch up, which used up a good deal of my energy. I was already in big trouble.

"How far are we going?" I asked between large gulps of air.

Overmann turned my way, grinning. "For you, Dennis, we'll take it easy and only do five."

"Miles?"

"Of course, silly boy. We'll be done before you know it."

We made it out of his neighborhood, then headed north toward farm country. There were very few cars, and that made it good for running. My body started to adjust and my breath came back to me. I must have been what they called *in the zone.*

Not much was said for the first half-mile or so. Then they slowed down and fell in on either side of me.

Overmann broke the silence. "Melody tells me you have some questions, Dennis. I'm all yours for another four-and-a-half miles."

I tried hard to arrange my thoughts. My knees were already starting to throb. I wasn't sure if I could put a coherent sentence together. I took a deep breath and blew it out. "I want to know more about Komaket. I know it's just a legend but it fascinates me." Talking was more tiring than I expected so I waited a moment. "What I really want to know is how and when he will come back... according to legend, of course."

"Don't be ashamed of your fascination, Dennis. Many before you have inquired about the enigmatic Komaket, although none recently if I recall correctly."

I wasn't ashamed of anything, and I found it strange that he interpreted my words that way. Perhaps he really was the intellectual snob Perry Sellers made him out to be.

"Anyway," he continued, "the smallpox epidemic began to spread throughout the region; and Komaket went on his mighty quest to cure the villagers and his own people. When he did as he promised, he left the town fathers the concept of *triation* and *jorva* and told them that he would return for what was rightfully his. Unfortunately, no version of the legend has ever clarified what, exactly, was rightfully his."

I took longer strides to keep up with the experienced runners who were barely breathing hard. My shirt was mostly soaked, but I used it to wipe sweat from my forehead. It didn't help much. "So according to the legend," I said between gasps, "we don't know when he's coming back or even why?"

We came to a large puddle in the road, some ten feet across, so we moved left to avoid it.

"We must remember that his people didn't think in terms of months and years. They were much more traditional in their

113

approach. They were told that a wolf would guard, and perhaps guide, each generation—roughly thirty years—for eternity. They called it *mahica* or the cycle of the wolf. The legend stated that there were ten wolves, and Komaket would return when all ten completed the *mahica*."

I quickly did the math in my head. "So 300 years?"

"More or less, Dennis. Unfortunately, Komaket's window has closed. By the best case interpretation of the timeline, he would have appeared, oh, back in the 1980s."

I had another question but I was fading fast. I tried my best to sound coherent. "I don't get... the whole concept of *jorva*, this reincarnation thing...." I sucked in a huge gulp of air. "Did Komaket's followers believe... that they would return with him?"

"That was the promise, Dennis; when one life is done, another takes its place." He paused to cough, which was the first hesitation he had given the entire conversation. "Of course, the semantics of how it would play out have been bandied about for years. No one really knows and, well, it appears to be a moot point now, doesn't it?"

I was having a really hard time breathing, so I lagged behind, then stopped and put my hands on my knees. My lungs had never hurt so much in my life. They both stopped and Melody came over to check on me.

"Are you all right, Dennis?"

I wiped some spit off of my chin with my sleeve. "I can't go on... You two go ahead and... I'll walk back. I'm too much... too out of shape." I thought I was going to puke but I held it back. "Thanks for the info... Doctor."

They both waited for a moment; then I motioned them along with my hand. "I'll be fine. Finish your run."

They looked at each other, then started back down the road.

"I'll call you later, Dennis," Melody said.

"It's just a legend," Overmann added.

Of course, it is, you pompous, arrogant prick.

I took the advice of an old high-school coach who told me to always walk around after running to avoid cramping. I put my hands behind my head, sucking in as much air as I could. The ache in my side was slowly drifting away as I trudged through the roadside gravel. I sneaked a peek at my former running partners.

They were already far down the road.

The walk back gave me time to think about the conversation we'd just had. Melody set this meeting up, and I couldn't help but wonder why she had me go through so much turmoil just to get a few answers. Why couldn't I have just emailed or called the guy or met him in a bar like real adults?

A half-mile later I was feeling much better. My head was definitely clearing up. I needed to get off that road so I began to jog again, and I felt surprisingly good. When I saw my car up ahead, I went into a full sprint. I felt fantastic.

I opened the driver's door and got behind the wheel with my feet still on the driveway. It gave me an opportunity to ponder what Dr. Overmann had told me about Komaket. His window had closed.

What started as a grin morphed into a chuckle, then became a full-blown laugh. Everything my dad wanted me to investigate had checked out. Why wouldn't this one? I started the car, backed out and began the short drive home.

Was I experiencing runners' high? I didn't know. It didn't matter what the professor said. This was a moment of clarity unlike any other I had ever experienced.

I didn't know how or where, but Komaket was returning. I was absolutely sure of it.

Chapter 19

One of the good things about living at my mom's house was that I was socking away lots of money. They charged me rent, but it wasn't nearly as much as I would pay to live somewhere else. Regardless, it didn't feel like home. I still wanted out.

I checked the newspaper ads again the next day and even went to the college to check the bulletin boards. My plan was to stay relatively close to campus because I planned on keeping my word and enrolling next semester. I was not the quitter Gene and my mom thought I was.

Some of the places sounded promising until I did a drive-by. I found a lot of reasons to reject them: dumpy building, bad neighborhood, too far from campus—all dead ends.

At just after 2 p.m., I was on the couch watching TV. I heard the phone ring and Stan had a short, choppy conversation. He came in from the kitchen with a large grin on his face.

"How would you like to get your stuff back from the house, Dennis?"

I sat up quickly. "From Roger's? That would be great, but how?"

"Well, the police chief, Ruben Moniz, is a friend of mine. As such, I asked him if he could speed up the process a bit and he agreed. He's going to call me back when an officer is ready at the house to supervise the operation. It shouldn't be long."

Wow, who knew Stan had friends in high places? Who knew Stan had friends? "That's great, Stan. I can't wait to get my clothes and my CDs back. Thanks for arranging it."

"Glad I could help."

Three minutes later the phone rang. Stan answered. "Okay, 3 p.m. it is."

I had about a half-hour to find a rig big enough to haul all my stuff. I knew Jed's father had a small pickup, so I called Jed on my cell phone. He called his dad, who agreed to let me use the pickup. *Perfect.*

I was the farthest away, so it was quicker for me to pick up Jed

116

and head to his parents' house. I grabbed a few boxes from the garage and tossed them in the back seat. I hoped it was enough.

We got the Nissan pickup and arrived at the old Victorian in less than ten minutes. Officer Brian Tovey was there with clipboard in hand, and he walked with us up to my old room.

"I have the list of items you supplied us with a few weeks ago, Mr. Kozma." Officer Tovey pointed to the clipboard. "The department has verified that these items can be removed from the residence." He scanned the list again. "It looks like it includes everything from this room."

A week after the big bust, Detective Sullivan reminded me to file a personal-items list with the department. *I'm glad I didn't blow that one off.*

"Make it snappy, would ya?" I couldn't tell if Tovey was serious or playing me. I opened the closet and grabbed my work shirts and pants, then the rest of my shoes. I filled the other box with books, CDs and junk I had lying around. Jed helped me hoist the boxes, the dresser, my nightstands, my rocking chair and the twin-sized bed down the stairs and into the pickup.

According to the list, I still had a few items to get. There was a blow dryer, some towels and toiletry items in the bathroom. The only thing from the kitchen was an electric wok, my favorite cooking appliance.

I went back in for one last look.

"You're over your time limit," Tovey said with a stern look. A second later he winked and smiled. "There's probably something in the basement you may want."

I drew a blank. I was positive I had everything.

"Your bike?"

I gave myself a mock forehead slap. The bike was still down there thankfully. We placed it on top and tied the whole load down with rope. I thanked Officer Tovey and said good riddance to the house of doom and gloom.

As we drove away, Jed broke the silence, "So, Koz, where are you going to put all this stuff? I'm guessing space is a little tight at your current abode."

He was right. No way would Stan let me put this stuff in the garage. It wasn't worth asking. Then I had an idea.

"There's a storage place out on Route 38. I could rent a unit until I find a new place to live."

It was getting late and Jed took a quick look at his watch. "Let's hope it's still open."

He turned north and headed to the U Stor It. The front gate was still open so we pulled up to the office. We made it with an hour to spare, and it took us only half that time to unload the big items and lock the door.

"I owe you big time, Jed," I said as we drove back.

He smiled. "I know. I'm gonna milk this one for all it's worth too, Koz."

***

I wanted to make sure I was pulling my weight at home, so I decided to mow the lawn and clean up a little. Mom and Stan were gone in the afternoon—in separate cars, oddly enough—so the timing was right. I found the push mower in the garage, uncovered it—yes, he had a cover for the lawn mower—and wheeled it out. Stan had been nice to me since I moved in. It was time for payback.

The property was pretty small, so I made quick work of the lawn. I unplugged the grass trimmer and took care of the perimeter and around the trees, no problem.

The Red Sox had a day game, so I hit the couch and checked it out. A few innings later I heard the garage door open. Someone was back.

"Dennis!" Stan yelled. He probably wanted to thank me, or perhaps he needed help bringing something in. He was standing in the middle of the driveway, hands on hips, looking around the yard when I came out. "What did you do to my lawn?"

I figured it was a rhetorical question, but I answered anyway. "I mowed it for you. Nice job, huh?"

His face and bald head began to redden. "You should have asked me first. You really should have asked."

"Well, you weren't here and it needed mowing. What is your problem?"

He walked to the edge of the front lawn and looked at my handy work. "The pattern is all wrong. The first cut of the month is horizontal, the second is right-to-left diagonal, the third vertical, the fourth is left-to-right diagonal." He made the patterns with his hands as he described them, sort of like a mad conductor. "You went horizontal. You've completely ruined the pattern."

"You've got to be kidding me, Stan. I was trying to help around here. I've mowed other lawns hundreds of time, so I think I know what I'm doing."

Still fuming, he walked to the lawn mower in the corner of the garage. "You left the cover off."

He was right about that one. "Sorry about that. I'll put it back on."

"Don't touch it!" He moved between the lawn mower and me. "It's unclean. Can't you see that, Dennis? There's... there's grass on it."

"That's because I mowed the grass."

"Don't be a smart ass. The deck has to be cleaned on both sides after every use. I want my tools to last."

We were now standing toe-to-toe. I wasn't scared of this fat, middle-aged guy and I wasn't backing down. "Okay, Stan, I'll clean off the grass and have it as good as new in no time."

"No!" He acted like he was protecting a child and heck, maybe he was in his anal mind. He turned and took a cloth from a nearby drawer, rubbed the top of the handle, then down both sides. "Please leave, Dennis. You've done quite enough already."

"Are you forgetting something, Stanley?"

He wiped the deck and motor off with vigorous strokes. "I think not."

"How about, 'Thanks for mowing and trimming the lawn, Dennis.'"

He said nothing. The wiping continued.

"You're a real asshole sometimes, Stan."

He wrapped the towel around his right hand like he was getting ready to punch me, so I took a defensive position. If he made half a move toward me, I was ready to totally kick his ass. *Come on, Stan. Take a shot at me.*

Lucky for him, he backed away.

"You're a guest in my house. Don't you forget that!"

"Not for long."

I went in and watched from the window as he wheeled the mower out of the garage. It took him thirty minutes to clean it from top to bottom.

That was the Stan I remembered.

Chapter 20

I spent the next hour in my room, picking through the boxes of my stuff from Roger's house while trying not to scream. It was good to have my clothes back, especially my t-shirts. I had only a limited supply for a few weeks, but now my entire collection of Red Sox and Patriots shirts was safely back in my dresser.

I hung all my work shirts and dark blue pants—my uniforms—in the closet. I took out my CDs and lined them up along the back of the dresser, just like I always did. Death Cab practically begged to be played, so I put the CD in the player and let the music fill the room, not loud enough to disturb the bald douche nozzle in the other room but just right.

A knock interrupted my activities, and seconds later my mom was standing inside the room with a newspaper tucked under her arm. I turned the music down a bit.

"Stanley told me about the lawnmower, Dennis. He's quite upset right now."

"Mom, I was trying to do something nice. All I did was mow the damn lawn. He makes it sound like I wrecked his car or something." I pushed harder than I meant to, and the dresser drawer slammed shut. "I thanked him for getting my stuff back; that was huge, but when I tried to return the favor by doing a little extra around here—hell, doing anything around here—he goes all OCD on me." I slammed my fist down on the dresser. "I should just leave. That guy has too many issues."

"I know he does."

"What did—?"

She put her hand out to cut me off, then walked over to close the door. "I had a long talk with Stanley about the situation and what he did was wrong."

Wow. My mom standing up for me was not what I expected.

"But so were you," she continued. "There's never a need for that kind of language. Look, I don't expect you to understand how Stanley thinks. I know I certainly don't, but the number one rule is simple, Dennis: don't touch his things. If you can remember that one rule, life will be much easier and you won't have to move out.

Besides, we both know you have no place to go. Am I right?"

She already knew the answer to that one.

"He's very possessive, Dennis. You should know that by now. He's also very set in his ways."

"Yeah, I know, it's just that—"

"And let's not forget that he did you a huge favor by arranging to get your things back from that... that drug house."

She waited, probably to see if I had any last-minute smartass statements to make. Three or four swirled around my head, but I kept them in, nodding instead. "Sure thing."

"Very well then. I really came in here to show you this."

She held out a copy of *The Beacon*, our area's weekly paper. It was folded over to the wedding section. A familiar face was on the page.

"Your old girlfriend Darcy Millet got married last week, she and Chuck Barksdale—cute couple."

Darcy was my girlfriend through much of high school and a little bit beyond. My mom loved her like a daughter and couldn't understand why we broke up.

Maybe because she was a whiny, needy, little cling-on! "Good for her." It was all I could think of at the time. "Thanks for showing me this, Mom." *Thanks for kicking me when I'm down.*

"There's a nice write-up about them too. I'll just leave the paper on your bed." She placed it so Darcy's lovely picture smiled back at me. "Dinner will be ready in a few minutes."

After she left, I turned the music back up, sat on the edge of the bed and buried my face in my hands. *God, I hate living in this house.* I peeked through my fingers only to see the smiling face of Darcy the Wonderful, so I swept the paper off the bed with my right arm. The pages flew apart, and one page slowly worked its way back down to the pile. Another familiar face stared up from that page; it was Ken Cordeiro.

I picked up the paper, folded it back and read the headline above his picture.

Town Prepares for Founder's Day

The article by staff writer Lila Riddlemoser detailed the amount of work that went into organizing Founder's Day, the annual town celebration that commemorated the founding of the community back in the 1600s. The events included a cook-off, an art and crafts fair, an authentic eighteenth century village and even a Five-K run. The thought of running five kilometers made my legs hurt.

The quote from Ken in the final paragraph really caught my eye.

"We think it's important to remember those whose hard work put this town on the map. Otto Willingham, Josiah Stanwood, Syvanus Hartin and Lyman Carleton put the first town charter together and laid the framework for this community. We take one day a year to thank them and everyone else who has shaped our history. It's a great way to bring the people of New Dover together."

The four men he mentioned were the ones in the grass vaults in the four cemeteries, the ones who formed a pattern around Ralph Pelson's vault.

Founder's Day. Could it be? The timing seemed perfect. My dad said something big was going to happen, so maybe this was the day. I went to the calendar on my desk and circled the date with a red pen. The good news was that I finally had something to look forward to.

The bad news was that I had less than two weeks to figure this whole thing out.

***

I heeded my mom's advice and kept away from Stan and his stuff as much as I could for the next few days, especially after I found out he had changed the password on the TV. I was happy just going to work, going to the gym, hanging with my friends and heading to my room at night. My old tube TV would have to do.

I hadn't heard from Melody since we went running with Overmann. She did call me that night as she said she would. She left a message, but it was too late to call her back. As usual, she wasn't around the next day or the next. It was as if she lived 1,000 miles away.

Tom had some rare free time away from his job, and he wanted to get together with me and Jed. He said he had important information to share. We met at O'Reardon's, of course, and found a nice quiet booth in the sparsely-attended bar.

When the first round arrived, Tom took out an index card from his front pocket and waved it in front of us. "Ladies and gentlemen, I've got the goods on old Ralph Pelson. What a long, not-so-strange trip it's been."

"Bring it." I took a long sip. The Guinness tasted extra good that night. I even made a private toast to Stan and his asshattery.

"Ralph was born in 1920 in Fall River and moved to New Dover after high school in the late 30s. By all accounts he was a scrappy little guy, no more than five-nine and probably a buck forty in overalls. He served honorably in World War Two as a soldier and a boxer, then returned home to his farm... and that, people, is what he did for the next fifty years, give or take a few: he ran a successful produce farm. Ralph entered town politics in the 1960s and eventually became tax assessor, then went quietly into the sunset."

"Until..." I coaxed.

"I was getting to that." He took a strong pull from his bottle, then set it down. "Not really a peep from him until five years ago. Out of the blue, he bought the Adams Road land at auction for more than twice the going rate. He had to sell his farm to cover the cost. A few years later he sold the land to the town for the sum of one U.S. dollar for the sole purpose of using it as a cemetery. When the paperwork was done, he croaked and was strategically buried in a grass vault in the new cemetery. What a great guy, huh?"

"You sound disappointed," Jed said.

"I am. No smoking gun to report. The guy was a tomato farmer. I probably had more fun this summer than he did his entire life. Sorry, Koz, other than being a bit of a loon at the end, this guy appears to be squeaky clean."

"What was his wife's name?" I asked.

He checked a card. "The former Anne Clothier. As far as I know, she's still around. She was living with their daughter after Ralph sold the farm."

"How was his political life? Any scandals?"

"Hardly. I think the best word would be *unspectacular*."

I made a note of the information in a small notepad.

Jed moved his fingers around the side of his glass, then turned his Yankees cap around. He brought no written material with him. "I checked on the four town guys. They are about as boring as our friend Pelson. Kevin Van Houten and James Flanary, the two selectmen, went to New Dover High back in the 70s, a few years apart. Both went to local colleges, got married to local gals named Grace Tisdale and Jenna Lenhart respectively, and they've always lived here. They got elected within a few years of each other. Pretty generic stuff."

"Great. What about the zoning board guys?"

Jed took a sip from his glass. "John Partridge and Neil Hollinger took over their spots on the zoning board a little over fifteen years ago. Ironically, Hollinger came aboard when your dad resigned, probably because no one else wanted the vacant position. That's often the case in this town. Anyway, Partridge got elected the next spring on his own accord. They seem to butt heads a lot with the other member, Ken Cordeiro, but all in the name of town politics, I'm sure. Before you ask, I can tell you that Partridge also married a Tisdale, but, hey, it's a small town."

"You guys could have just emailed this info to me. I half-expected a major turn or something." It was good information but hardly groundbreaking. At least the beer was cold.

"There is one other thing, Koz." Tom put his cards down, pulled out a sheet of paper and unfolded it. "Remember that painting that Melody showed us, the one from the Stebbins Museum?"

"Yeah, the one with the two flags on it. Phinneus Marley painted it. One flag had the *shingala* symbol on it."

Tom looked at Jed, then back at me. "Or did it?"

"What do you mean? She showed us the painting."

Tom placed a photocopy of the painting before us. "She showed us a digital photo of the painting. Look here." He tapped on the white flag in the painting.

There was no symbol on it.

"I found a book of Marley's most famous works and came across this one. Clean as a whistle. I'd say your future Dr. Bancroft did a little photo-shopping before showing it to us."

"No, no, that can't be, Tom. She's been up-front with this stuff. She showed me the university museum and the model of Fort

New Dover and got me an audience with Dr. Overmann." I looked again at the flag. "Why would she change the photo, Tom? What's the motive?"

"I don't know, Koz." He paused and again looked at Jed. "Do you want me to be brutally honest here?"

"Sure, Tom." I did not like the sound of this.

"Okay. I'm saying this strictly as an observer." He blew out a big breath, then took another long pull. "I don't know why, Koz, but I think Melody's playing you. From what you've told me, she controls everything: when you meet, where you go. It's all on her terms. Then she mysteriously disappears for days at a time. She's a history geek, and you have this small piece of local history that she wants."

"Yeah, Koz," Jed added. "Do you even know where she lives? Has she ever invited you over?"

I couldn't believe what my so-called friends were telling me. Sure, Melody was a bit mysterious, but I never found her controlling—just busy. We would have great conversations and laugh with and at each other. "I'm smart enough to know when I'm being used."

They both sat back and drank their beers, neither making eye contact with me. I thought they were done, but they were just reloading.

Jed brought out some notes. "I did a little digging, Koz. I found out a few things about Ms. Bancroft."

"You checked up on my girlfriend?"

Tom practically jumped across the table. "Jesus God, Koz, she's not your girlfriend. You see, this is what we're talking about." He slapped the table. "A girlfriend is someone who wants to be seen with you and is there when you need her. A girlfriend is someone you take home to your mother and say, 'Look what I got.' Sure, she may rip your heart out, then stomp it into a million pieces and leave you for a pre-law frat boy with a Lexus; but that's a different story." He made short work of a napkin as he spoke, twisting it until it was pencil-thin.

"Anyway," Jed continued, "back to Melody. I hate to tell you this, Koz, but Bancroft is her married name."

"What? That can't be." *Married?* It felt like a kick to the gut. I knew she didn't wear a ring, but *married*?

"I know for a fact that she married some guy named Ellis Bancroft when she was twenty and apparently still is, according to the records I saw. I'm sorry, Koz; I really, really hate being the messenger."

I sat for the longest time, trying to take it all in. Maybe they were right and she was using me. An enhanced photo is one thing, but not telling me she was married was too much.

Tom refilled his glass, then mine. He always knew when to speak and when to wait. He stared at the football game on the TV, watching as a long pass went incomplete. He slapped the table, then turned back to me. "I'm thinking she was in one of those starter marriages, Koz—the kind that lasts a few years; then the couple realizes they made a mistake, quietly split and go their separate ways: no cash, no kids, no problem. Maybe they just haven't gotten around to making it legal."

"For what it's worth," Jed added, "her current roommate is male, and there is no sign of Ellis Bancroft in the immediate area; but there's more."

"Great. Next, you're going to tell me she was raised by gypsies."

"Even better. She's one of them, Koz."

"Them?"

"Her birth name is Melody Tisdale. It's the same family those town guys married into. I checked."

Now my head was really spinning. I tried to speak but could only muster a weak, fluttery sound. I closed my eyes and tossed back as much of my beer as I could handle, which turned out to be all of it.

"Remember your talk about finding the middle," Tom said. "You were looking everywhere for a connection." Tom polished off his beer and slammed his glass down once again. "I think you found one, Koz. She's not an outsider. She's way into this."

"It's almost certain she knows a lot more than she lets on," said Jed. "She has to. I'm not sure about her MO, but there's definitely something in it for her."

As much as I wanted to believe it wasn't true, I realized they were right. My somewhat casual pursuit of Melody made me blind to her actions. *How could I have been so stupid?* I gave myself a forehead slap.

"Don't be so hard on yourself, Koz," said Tom. "You need to get back on track… and pronto."

Tom was right, of course. I thought back to my father's words. Something big was going to happen. I composed myself and reminded them of the article I had read about Founder's Day.

"So you think that's the target date?" Jed asked.

"I do. Call it a gut feeling."

"Jeez, Koz, that's not much time," said Tom. "We still need more middle."

***

The trip home gave me time to think about Melody. What was her story? Part of me wanted to forget what my friends told me and see what path she took me down.

Apparently, I was pretty good at playing stupid. Another part of me wanted to forget I had ever met her.

When I got back to my room, I realized I had left my phone there, so I checked my voice mail. There was a message from Melody wondering when we could get together again. I checked my email and she sent the same message, plus a link to an animated greeting card. It was kind of funny.

The night was young, so she would probably still be around. I picked up the phone and punched in her number. Then the two parts battled in my head.

I pictured her face and her great smile. She had the best smile… and the best body.

She lied to me. She used me.

I put the phone away and deleted the email message. I was finished with Melody Bancroft.

Chapter 21

Of course, I couldn't sleep that night. Highly emotional moments always kept me tossing and turning. I got up about 1 a.m. for a drink of water and a change of scenery. It was no use; I was wide awake.

I turned on my computer and checked my email. There was another message from Melody. I hit delete without opening it.

When insomnia happened to me last time, I sent a long email to Russell to keep him in the loop. This seemed like the perfect time to do it again, so I took out my notes and began to type.

I gave him all the details about the zoning documents, Ken Cordeiro and everything else I could think of. I finally sent it about ninety minutes later, then crawled back into bed. I was looking forward to sleeping in.

There was another email message from Melody when I logged in the next morning. The subject was "*PLEASE READ.*" I sent it to the deleted folder instead. Her voice-mail message later that morning met the same fate.

I knew I would have to confront Melody eventually, but the time never seemed to be right. I worked late that day, thanks to a hot-tub install that took over four hours. I heard my cell phone ring several times that day, all of them from Melody saying, "Please call me, Dennis," or "I really want to talk to you, Dennis," plus one more I didn't listen to—delete, delete, delete.

My mom and Stan were gone when I got home, but the crock pot was still plugged in and Mom's stew was as good as ever. I had a can of soda and took the empty out to the garage to put in the recycle bin. Something new caught my eye as I scanned the garage. The lawn mower was now locked. A thin chain looped from the handle to a leg on the workbench, topped off with a padlock. *Typical anal behavior.* I was surprised he hadn't locked the refrigerator.

It was my night to hit the gym, so I got my gym bag ready and searched all over for my workout sneakers. I thought they were in the closet or under the bed. Then I remembered I had cleaned them, then left them in the laundry room.

I brought the shoes back in and stuffed them in the bag. As I did, a small chime went off indicating an incoming email. *Melody again?* I thought about ignoring it but checked my inbox just to be sure. Thankfully, the message was from Russell, so I clicked on it.

> *Dennis,*
> *Thanks for the info. Great stuff. You may want to check my website.*
> *Take care.*
> *RK*

I dropped the gym bag and sat down in front of my laptop. The workout could wait. I went to the secure website Russell had set up and entered the password. I had to laugh when I saw what he had on the front page. It was a large tab that flashed, "CLICK HERE FOR THE GOOD STUFF" near the middle. I did.

The first file was a document entitled "Cave-ins." I opened it and waited for it to load. It must have been big.

The first few pages were from a very old newspaper article about a series of unusual surface cave-ins that occurred back in the 1940s here in New Dover. One old photo showed a farmer standing next to a fence that seemingly disappeared underground, then appeared again after another twenty feet. The article stated that the depressions were officially classified as sinkholes. There were nine such sinkholes reported over a twenty-year span.

The next page was a document showing that the sinkholes were all filled in and repaired by a company called Tisdale Excavation. That was the same name as the town officials' wives... and Melody's maiden name.

The next document was a map of New Dover with the sinkhole locations marked. The nine areas were scattered around town in no discernible pattern, at least none that I could see.

I clicked on a link on Russell's new page. It took me to a website of a publisher called Four Seasons Press and brought up the page for a book called *New Dover Generations*. The short blurb described it as "a comprehensive look at a not-so-typical New England town." It sounded somewhat interesting, but why was this important? Then I noticed the author: Neil Hollinger, the zoning board member.

The link below this one brought up an article on *The Beacon*'s website. The article talked about the research Hollinger put into his book and that he wrote it because of his love for New Dover and its people, both past and present. The last line was very interesting: "Mr. Hollinger will be conducting a book reading at the New Dover Library this Friday at 7 p.m., followed by a book signing."

I made a note of it on my calendar.

Chapter 22

When I got home from work that night, there was a package waiting for me. It was a small cardboard box with Four Seasons Press in the return-address corner. I opened it and pulled out a shiny new edition of Hollinger's book, *New Dover Generations*. There was no note inside, but I knew it came from Russell. There must have been something in it he wanted me to read.

The book was not very thick and contained a lot of old photos, so I got through it pretty quickly. Hollinger's writing was excessively wordy, and I found myself having to reread some of the passages several times for clarity. It dragged to a crawl about halfway through. As a comparison, Mr. Sellers' book was much easier to read. It was the same for Dr. Overmann's. This new book was full of contradictions. Hollinger's look at town history was completely different from what Mr. Sellers wrote and told me. I couldn't believe something like that could get published.

As I slogged through, I made some notes and wrote down some questions. I figured since I went through all the trouble of reading the book, Neil Hollinger could sign it and answer a few of them.

I was curious what our town historian thought of the book and Hollinger's version of town history, so I emailed Mr. Sellers a few minutes later. It was late, so I closed my notebook and called it a night.

There was reply from him when I checked my mail in the morning.

Hi, Dennis,

Yes, I read his book. As town historian, I was given an advance copy but only after I refused to buy one. Can you believe he wanted me to pay for it? Anyway, there was no way I could give a positive blurb for the book jacket, which was all he wanted. I just couldn't do it. He was so far off, I had to check several times to make sure he was writing about New Dover and not some other town.

Hollinger is a piece of work. He's a decent town official, not much of an historian. He comes from a big family and knows lots of people. They'll all buy a copy. Hey, it's their money.
Regards,

Perry Sellers

I planned my Friday around the book signing. I would work until 4:30 p.m., then eat and head to the library. Neither Jed nor Tom wanted to go with me, so I told them to meet me after at O'Reardon's. It wasn't hard to convince them.

It was a slow workday, and only a few customers trickled in during the afternoon. At nearly 4:30 I was ringing up a sale of chlorine to an older man, looking forward to making this my last customer. After thanking him, I headed to the office to punch out.

"Hey, Dennis, glad I found ya."

Standing next to one of the floor-model hot tubs was none other than Uncle Russell. He came my way and gave me a giant bear hug, just like always.

"Hi, Uncle Russell." I had tensed up to prepare for the hug and managed not to lose my breath. "What brings you to town? Oh, and thanks for the book."

He walked with me toward the office. "We have some things to discuss, Dennis." He waited as I punched out and left the office. "Then we are going to a book signing."

***

"Dinner's on me tonight, Dennis." We made our way to the parking lot where he had conveniently parked right next to me. "You name the place."

"Sounds great, Uncle Russell, but I have to go home first to change out of my work clothes. I'm not big on wearing them in public. Hey, you should come over to the house. You can visit my mom while I get ready. She hasn't seen you in a long time, dude." I couldn't believe I called my uncle "dude."

He sat on the hood of his car, running his fingers through his thinning hair. "It's like this, Dennis: your mom and I never really got along, especially after your father died, and your stepfather—"

"Stan. I don't give him a title. It's just plain ol' Stan."

"Uh, yeah, okay. Stan, well, things didn't get better when he came along, to tell the truth. He's just, well, he's a real—"

"Asshat. It's the word I usually use."

"I like that, Dennis. I was thinking douche bucket, but, hey, asshat works too. Anyway, I'm sure they haven't missed me all these years."

Recent thinking had led me to believe that living back at home was a sort of penance. In a way, it had helped me focus on discovering what my father was trying to tell me. Now it was time to share the wealth.

"No deal, Russell. If you want to hang with me tonight, you have to come over. I don't mean just park in the driveway. You have to do a meet-and-greet dog-and-pony with my mom and Stan, the asshat douche bucket. You know where we live."

I got in and slammed the door shut. I was out of the parking lot in no time and managed to get a peek of him in my rearview mirror as I left. It was not a pleasant look.

I pulled into my usual parking spot at home and waited a moment. It felt strange just sitting there, so I went in and quickly got out of my uniform and into more appropriate attire: in this case a clean pair of shorts, t-shirt and sneakers.

My mom was in the kitchen wiping down the counters when I came by.

"Mom, I hope I didn't mess anything up, but I just got invited to dinner."

"No, we were just going to order out." She wrung out the cloth and hung it to dry. "Anyone I know?"

A car door closed in the driveway, and I caught a glimpse of Russell.

"Actually, yes. Consider it a blast from the past."

Russell came to the side door and waited. I casually opened the door and gestured for him to come.

"Hey Mom, look who's here."

He gave me a squinty look, then walked in.

Mom came around the corner, then stopped when she saw him. "Russell Kozma! Well, isn't this a pleasant surprise?" They gave each other a weak "in-law" hug. His appearance was definitely a surprise. The pleasant part remained to be seen.

134

"Hi, Maureen. You look great." This made her blush just a little.

"Come in. Come in." She led him into the living room. "Stanley, look who stopped by."

Stan turned off the TV, placed the remote in line with the others on the table and got out of his lounger. He didn't seem too surprised to see Russell. In fact, his expression went from neutral to confused.

"It's Russell. Russell Kozma… Norman's brother. He moved away right after Norman, um—"

"Oh, now I remember." Stan reached out and gave Russell a quick handshake. "Great to see you, Russell. It's been a few years."

"So what brings you back into New Dover?" Mom asked.

"Business mostly. I have a few ventures to check out. I told Dennis here that I'd take him out to eat next time I was around." That last statement was not true, but it sounded good. "You two are welcome to join us. My treat."

That statement was also false, and I could see the pain on Russell's face as he waited for a response. I already knew what she'd say.

"No thank you, Russell. That's a very kind offer. You two go off like you planned. I'm sure you have years to catch up on." Stan had already returned to his chair and TV. An impromptu dinner invitation was just not their style.

"Well, we should be going. It's was great to see you both again." Russell gave Mom a quick hug, then headed for the side door with me right behind him.

"Don't be such a stranger. Stop by anytime. We'll always be here."

"Will do."

I closed the door and ran a little to catch up with Russell. All I could think about was how phony the others acted. I'm not sure what I expected, but that wasn't it.

He drove to the restaurant with his eyes forward and the radio off. Normally he would be pointing out buildings and houses, yakking about people he knew from his time in New Dover with some oldies station playing. Now he was giving me the silent treatment. I had to do something.

135

"I'm sorry I asked you to come over, Uncle Russell. It really did seem like a good idea at the time."

He broke his straight-ahead gaze with a glance over at me. "You're the only honest one in the bunch, Dennis."

"I am?"

"Your mother, well, I know I'm not real high on her list of favorite people. I've been in town many times in the last fifteen years and never bothered to stop by or even call. She knows that. Sometimes you have to do things for the sake of family, and I messed it up big-time."

"Messed what up? You said before that you guys don't really like each other very much. Throw Stan in the mix and—"

"It's not about her and me, Dennis. It's you."

"Me? What do I have to do with this?"

By now we had turned into the parking lot of the restaurant. He parked the car and pulled up the emergency brake, then shifted his weight toward me.

"Do you realize you are the only blood relative I have left? My parents are both gone, and your father was my only sibling. I have no kids of my own and likely never will. We are the last of the Kozmas, you and me. I should have been here for you. That's what your mom's been trying to tell me all these years."

It was a side of Russell Kozma I had never heard before.

"You're here now, Uncle Russell. That says a lot. Besides, I'd like to think I turned out all right."

He put his thick paw on my shoulder. "Damn right you did. Now let's go eat."

I ordered veal parmesan, and he got some sort of seafood and pasta concoction. While we waited, he pulled out a small notepad and flipped over a page.

"Let's talk about Hollinger. He's a complete phony when it comes to town history. His book is revisionist history at its finest."

"But it got published. He had to be doing something right."

"Have you ever heard of Four Seasons Press?"

"No."

"It's not a typical publisher. It's a vanity press."

"You mean he paid to have it published?"

"That's right. He sent them a manuscript and a big check. It's extremely likely that he bought his own copies and now has to

136

pimp the hell out of them just to break even. He's an arrogant SOB who thinks he's a real author and historian."

Our food came and a young waitress named Colby placed the plates in front of us. I had to double-check the name tag because I had never heard of a girl named Colby before. Based on her accent, I figured maybe it was a common Southern name. She brought water with my order, and I downed much of it before she left.

I took a bite and swallowed quickly. "I asked Perry Sellers, the town historian, about the book. He refused to give a glowing review for Hollinger to use. No surprise, though. Sellers wrote a great book a few years ago, and no one read it."

Russell downed a forkful of pasta while I talked. He twirled his empty fork as he chewed and thought. "This guy claims to be an expert on the town, and you have a lot of unanswered questions, so let's just see how much he really knows."

Over the next fifteen minutes, he explained how we would handle Mr. Hollinger at the book signing.

It was the best meal I had had in a long time.

Chapter 23

We needed help with our plan, so I called Tom and Jed and convinced them to come to the library. I told them Uncle Russell would buy the drinks afterwards if they came and asked one question.

We arrived at the New Dover library fifteen minutes before the book signing. Tom and Jed were already there, lured in by the prospect of free beer for just a few minutes' work. I wanted to think they did it to help a friend, but who could compete with free beer? As we walked through the parking lot, Russell gave us some last-minute advice.

"Remember to set up your questions, men. Hollinger loves to hear himself speak, so make sure you kiss his ass and throw him a softball first—painful, yes, but necessary. Remember, these are questions he wouldn't answer if you saw him on the street, but I have a strong feeling he'll answer ours. He doesn't want to look stupid in front of his own people and so-called fans."

Russell told Tom and Jed their questions and where to position themselves in the room.

"No problem," said Jed, but his look indicated otherwise. I hoped he could pull it off.

"Sounds like fun." Tom's mental wheels were definitely turning.

There was a huge sign in front of the library announcing the event.

Author Neil Hollinger Book Signing
7 PM Tonight
Conference Room

We entered the library conference room and took our positions: Russell and me in the back corners, Tom and Jed along the sides. The room was still sparsely-populated, but there were quite a few people milling about the library waiting for the signing. A librarian began to quietly move the attendees into the conference room, asking them to take a seat around the large, rectangular conference table. We remained standing. Neil Hollinger entered the room, shaking hands like a politician as he made his way toward the wooden podium at the front of the table.

It was show time.

Hollinger spent the first ten minutes or so detailing how he went about researching the information for his book. As he spoke, I had to control the urge to laugh because his voice sounded like a higher-pitched Cliff Clavin from the old TV show "Cheers." Tom appeared to notice it too, as he held back the urge to snicker.

I scanned the room as Hollinger spoke. There were more than two dozen attendees by my count, mostly women in their thirties and forties, likely all his relatives and in-laws, including the Tisdales, if Mr. Sellers' theory were correct.

Tom and Jed were doing a great job from their vantage points, nodded along with each point Hollinger made as if they were genuinely interested. Russell stood in the shadows of his corner and showed no emotion.

"Next," said Hollinger, "I'd like to read a short passage that I have selected for tonight's gathering. I think you'll enjoy it."

He then gave a very tedious reading about how the people of New Dover welcomed home their Revolutionary War heroes and honored the fallen. The war heroes deserved better than what he had written. He paused for a moment, slowly closing the book for dramatic purposes. This was met with applause from those sitting at the table.

"Thank you." He waved politely. "You're very kind. I'd like to open the floor for questions now, after which I'll be signing copies. Don't worry, folks. I have plenty of books on hand."

A young girl in the front on my side went first. She held up a copy of the book. "Uncle Neil, how long did it take you to write all these words?"

There was some mild laughter in the room and Hollinger joined in; then he began to pace the room like a professor.

"After many months of exhaustive research, I began my manuscript a little over a year ago and submitted it to my publisher in late spring. We added some wonderful photographs, snipped here, clipped there and voilá, here we are."

Our plan was to intersperse our questions with the others

slowly over the course of the discussion. After a couple more cream-puff questions, Tom raised his hand.

"Yes?" Hollinger asked. "What would you like to know?"

"First of all, I'd like to say that this book is so good I'm going to buy a copy for Mother."

"Well, thank you."

"Your chapter on the history of the town parks, especially Komagansett Park, got me thinking about something; and I hope your expert knowledge can help me out."

Hollinger beamed. "I'll try."

"You mention in detail the exploits of the great Komagansett, which is cool because, hey, he's a hero and all. But I'm wondering why I found nothing in your book about Komaket, who some say is really the alter ego of Komagansett and provided his own bit of history to New Dover."

Hollinger rubbed one side of his face, then the other. He grabbed the sides of the podium and leaned in Tom's direction. "I admit you caught me off-guard with that question, sir. Hmmm..."

"I suppose I can call on the town historian, or maybe I can ask Dr. Overmann over at the university."

Hollinger nodded. "The answer is quite simple. Komagansett was real and, uh, the other... he was just a legend. All this talk about them somehow being connected is ridiculous and not worthy of discussion. You see, there are hundreds of native legends in this region, sir. I chose not to incorporate, uh, his or any other into my book for space and editorial reasons."

"Wow, hundreds. Sounds like a good topic for the sequel. I can't wait to read it. Thank you."

Good response, Tommy boy. That kept the room laughing.

More questions followed. A woman at the table asked Hollinger about his favorite chapter. Another wondered if he'd encountered any haunted houses during his research. He ate it all up.

Jed's hand shot up next. "Mr. Hollinger, I'm a big Revolutionary War buff, so naturally I was intrigued by your excellent chapters devoted to the war, especially New Dover's own Shadow Regiment."

"Yes, go on."

"I was wondering, sir, how they pulled it off. I read Dr.

Overmann's version and I wasn't thrilled by it. In your expert opinion, how did the Shadow Regiment surprise the British at Fort New Dover by having their men seemingly... I don't know... appear out of nowhere?"

Another moment of uncomfortable silence followed. Hollinger stared at Jed, who smiled back. Like Tom, Jed had nailed it.

All eyes in the room were on Hollinger. I could tell he was trying to find an alternate answer; but, as Russell had suspected, ad libbing was not his forte.

He cleared his throat and leaned against the podium. "It's not a widely-held belief, but I'm quite certain that the Shadow Regiment devised an alternate route to deploy troops behind the British as the Redcoats moved toward the fort."

"Like what? Did they fly?"

Several small children laughed, but Hollinger remained deadpanned. "Certainly not. There were, uh, many stone walls in the area... creeks too. It's quite likely they used these to, uh, hide as the enemy approached."

"I see. Wow, even in broad daylight. No wonder they were the Shadow Regiment. Thank you, you've been most helpful."

Hollinger was beginning to sweat along his brow. He took a handkerchief and dabbed away the moisture.

Next came another easy question, and Hollinger eased back into the discussion. A young boy declared himself to be Hollinger's biggest fan. As they conversed, Russell emerged from the shadows of his corner and got the author's attention. Hollinger pointed to him.

"Mr. Hollinger, I just love all the little nuggets of information you provide about New Dover. There's stuff in here I've not read about anywhere else."

"I'm glad you like it. Do you have a question?"

"Actually, I do. I've asked the town historian and he didn't know, so I figured you must. The word 'Hermillion' appears on the gravesites of town founders Otto Willingham, Josiah Stanwood, Syvanus Hartin and Lyman Carleton. There's a dedication plaque at the Revolutionary War monument from the Hermillion Club. What is the Hermillion Club and what role did they play in this town's history? I didn't see it in your book, but surely you know all about it."

Hollinger backed away from the podium as Russell headed back to his dark corner. The room was eerily silent. He waved a finger between Tom, Jed and Russell.

"Are... are you folks together?"

"Never seen them before in my life," Tom answered quickly. Jed shook his head.

Hollinger lifted a bottled water and unscrewed the cap. "That particular entity you asked about was abandoned over fifty years ago." He took a drink and screwed back the cap. "I fail to see why it's germane to this discussion."

"They also dedicated the Fort New Dover exhibit at Weaver College," countered Russell. "That sounds like an important society."

Hollinger squinted in Russell's direction as he grabbed the sides of the podium.

"Don't you know, Uncle Neil?" asked the girl in the front row.

A woman next to her quickly shushed the girl. "Of course he does," the woman softly said. "Uncle Neil wrote the book, didn't he? I want to hear this."

Hollinger smiled meekly at the girl and the woman. "Let me first say that my family has been in this town for many generations. Plus"—he raised his pointer finger for effect—"I had the good fortune of marrying into one of New Dover's most prestigious families." He winked at his wife who was standing near Jed. "They have given me insight into the town's history and I thank them for it. That said, I can tell you that my wife's grandmother was one of the last members, and she spoke to me about it one day many years ago. She said it was indeed a secret society, the key word being 'secret': no leaders, no membership list, no charter to speak of. As far as I know, they donated money to certain war-related endeavors, such as the monument and the display the gentleman in the back mentioned. I'll reiterate that there is a reason it was called a secret society. They wanted anonymity and they got it. That's really all I know."

Russell said nothing. He had a content look to him, so he must have liked what he heard.

Hollinger fielded two more questions from the table. The first was about the oldest building in town and the other concerned the old iron works on the north side.

"Are there any other questions?" He looked the whole room over. "Good. Let's move on to—"

"I have a question." I moved up a few steps.

"I guess we have time for one more."

I decided not to kiss his ass first. We'd heard enough of that. "Mr. Hollinger, near the end of the book, you claimed to have played a major role in cleaning up the town in the 1990s. What exactly did you mean by that?"

"Ah, yes, the final chapter. The town, in the opinion of many, was in financial shambles in the mid to late 1990s. There were funding issues and a major incident involving misappropriation of town money. I was on the oversight committee that investigated that particular incident. Once we removed the riff-raff, the town got turned around and is now stable and solvent. Again, I was just one of many who led the crusade."

His words were making my temples pulse. I breathed through it. "How exactly did you get rid of the riff-raff?"

He peeked down at his watch as he thought. Apparently, this had gone on far longer than he anticipated. It was fun to watch him squirm.

"It was in all the papers fifteen years ago," Hollinger said, "so there's really no need to rehash it."

The girl in front jumped in again. "Tell us how you got the bad guys, Uncle Neil."

A few others concurred, including Tom and Jed.

"Very well," Hollinger said, "but we really need to get to the book signing before they kick us out of here." He cleared his throat. "It has always been my personal feeling that if I get a chance to right a wrong, I will do so. Such was the case a few years ago when a town employee decided to funnel some town funds into his own account. We found out, of course, and gave the employee a chance to correct the oversight. He refused and was subsequently removed from office. Since then, we—"

"That's crap and you know it." I had heard enough of his lies.

"Excuse me?"

I made my way toward the front. "My father was innocent. You and your group framed him to get him out of office. He was on to you."

A librarian stepped in front of me. "I'm sorry, sir, but you'll have to leave."

Hollinger left the podium and took a step toward me. "You're Norm Kozma's kid? That explains a lot. I guess deviant behavior runs in the family."

From the corner of my eye, I saw Russell shoot out of the corner. Tom stepped in front of him. I tried to get to the podium, but several chairs and several Tisdales got in my way.

Jed grabbed my arm and turned me. "Time to go, Koz—I mean right now."

Tom had likewise turned Russell toward the back entrance. The room was loud with conversations and moving chairs.

"I don't know what you four are up to," Hollinger said, "but you've ruined the evening for everyone. Leave before I call the police."

It was clear passage to freedom as Jed and Tom steered us out the double doors, through the lobby and into the relative safety of the parking lot.

Jed let go and I stopped to collect my thoughts. I had lost my cool and put my friends in danger. "Sorry, guys. I just couldn't take any more of his crap."

"It's all right, Koz," Tom assured me. "The dude was crackin' on your old man. He was way out of line."

Jed kept a close eye on the back door as we moved away. "The important thing is no one got hurt. I just wish Hollinger would have told us something useful."

"Ah, but he did," said Russell, "and then some."

"Really?"

"Absolutely. I tell you what, let's head to O'Reardon's and we'll help Dennis find that middle he's been looking for. Beer's on me."

Chapter 24

True to his word, Russell bought the first round for us. Our waitress was Stacy, whom I remembered from my birthday visit. She put the tray of drinks on our table, then passed them out. She gave me a second look as she handed me a lager in a tall glass.

"Hey, it's the recent birthday boy. How is twenty-five treating you, sunshine?"

"It's been great, thanks." I found it amazing that she remembered me after a few months and hundreds of customers. Oddly enough, she never waited on me all the other times I had come here.

Russell pulled out a twenty and handed it to her. "Keep the change." After Stacy walked away, he leaned in to the center of the booth. "If you tip early and tip well, service will never be a problem, boys."

There was a short round of small talk; then he got back to the business at hand.

"So what did we learn from New Dover's newest author tonight, gentlemen?"

Tom jumped in first. "That a dickhead who marries well is still a dickhead?"

"True," said Russell, "but hardly earth-shattering news. Old Neil answered our four questions and gave away far more than he ever intended, at least from what I gathered."

"I asked about the Komaket/Komagansett relationship, and he shot it down."

"Did you notice what he didn't mention?"

Jed snapped his fingers. "He never mentioned Komaket, did he?"

"That's right. He did everything to avoid saying his name like it was his personal Voldemort. Plus, he wasn't at all comfortable talking about the Shadow Regiment and how they may have pulled off what they did. Did you see his body language? The way he stammered through it?"

I jumped in. "I believed the 'alternate route' part of his

answer. Everything else was crap. Same when I asked him about cleaning up the town."

"He took a lot of credit for that, didn't he?" Russell smacked the table with his palm. "I remember when your father was going through that whole ordeal. There was no investigative committee, at least nothing official. Norm resigned without incident. In fact, it wasn't clear why he resigned until after he died later that year."

"So Hollinger and others forced him to quit without a fight?" Tom tossed a balled-up napkin down in disgust. "That doesn't seem right."

Jed flipped his cap around. "Sounds like they had something on him."

"Komaket." It came out louder than I expected. "It all comes back to him."

"Norm Kozma must have figured out the connection. He found the middle, which brings us to your question." Tom turned in Russell's direction.

I interrupted. "I don't see what you could have gotten out of his answer. Yeah, it was a secret society and, yeah, his wife's grandma may have told him something about it. So what?"

We looked at Russell for his take on it. He seemed to be the best at observing basic human behavior. He took a long drink and slowly placed his glass on the table.

"I told you before that Hollinger's not that great at making stuff up on the fly. I've seen the videos from the town meetings and I'm sure of it. How about when I asked him about the Hermillion Club? He gave some song and dance about his family and his wife's family because he needed some filler while he thought of something to say. Does anyone know who his wife's grandma is?"

All three of us shook our heads.

"Kathleen Tisdale Merryweather. Ring a bell?"

Again, three heads shook at once.

"She was the town librarian for over fifty years. Her portrait is still hanging in the lobby."

I snapped my fingers. "She's the old lady in the painting?" There was a portrait in the library that had been there for as long as I could remember.

"That's the one."

"How exactly does that help us?"

"You'll have to ask her. She lives alone in a house over on Pierce Road."

"She's still alive? She's gotta be a hundred years old."

"Pretty close—ninety-two, according to town records. I suggest someone speak to her soon before word of our appearance gets around."

Tom and I looked at each other and raised our glasses.

"Tomorrow," we said in unison.

***

Mrs. Merryweather's place was an old ranch-style house not far from the library where she'd worked for so many years. Tom parked in the library parking lot, and from there we started the short walk. As we turned the corner, we decided the best approach was to tell the truth and ask her what she knew. Maybe our charm would win her over.

The window boxes along the front of her house were well-maintained, and there was a fresh layer of mulch surrounding the flowers and shrubs along the walkway. Someone made sure the place was kept up.

Tom went ahead of me and rang the doorbell. There was a moment of silence; then something crashed in the house, followed by swearing. A face appeared in the small window next to the front door and proceeded to look us over. The door opened slowly, and Kathleen Merryweather stood behind the Plexiglas in the screen door. Not surprisingly, her hair was white, but otherwise she still looked like the portrait in the library. She lowered a section of the Plexiglas, leaving only the screen.

"What do you boys want?"

"Hi, Mrs. Merryweather, I'm Tom and this is my friend Dennis. We'd like—"

"I know who you are." Her face was expressionless.

I started to freak out. *Is she already onto us? Hollinger or someone else must have told her. This is not good.*

"You're Denny Kozma." She looked me over. "Used to read *The Pokey Little Puppy* again and again, had to pry it from your sweaty little hands a few times. And you're Tommy Richcreek, loved those Dr. Seuss books with a passion. I used to save them for you before you came in every Tuesday."

Mrs. Merryweather was the children's librarian for many years before she retired. I had heard that she never forgot a face, but this was impressive, especially for someone over ninety.

"Now, what do you boys want?"

I moved to the front of her screen door. "We would like to talk to you about some town history, if you have the time."

She looked me up and down several times. "Normally I don't open my door under these conditions, but you boys seem harmless enough. Come on in."

She unlocked the screen, then pushed it open just enough for Tom to get his fingers in and open it the rest of the way. She led us into her living room, motioning us to an overstuffed sofa under the bay window. I noticed she moved rather well, without the use of a cane or walker. We both sat uncomfortably on the edge to avoid the line of pillows along the back.

"You boys don't have much time. I have a helper who comes by twice a day, and she's due here in about fifteen minutes to check up on me. Family says I shouldn't live alone, but I wouldn't have it any other way."

She sat in a wingback chair across from us. The coffee table between us was piled high with large-print books. One stack practically blocked our view of her, so she got up and moved the top few to another stack.

"I'm a little behind on my reading, but it beats watching TV. God, I hate TV—nothing but crap on these days." She sat back down with arms folded. "Nothing but crap for the last fifty years, if you ask me."

I decided to get down to business. "My father left me some information about the town, and there's something I can't figure out."

"I remember your father. He was a good man. Terrible what happened to him at such a young age."

I wanted to know if she had any stories about him but decided to press on. "Like I said, my father left me some information about a secret club that used to be around. Coincidentally, we went to a book signing for Neil Hollinger yesterday, and the subject of The Hermillion Club came up in a question. They put a lot of effort into sponsoring the war monument, and we were wondering what you could tell us about it."

"So you went to Neil's book signing, did you?"

"Yes, he mentioned that he's married to your granddaughter."

She pointed a bony finger at me. "Well, I told her a long time ago she made a big mistake with him. Would you believe he hasn't been to see me in over twenty years? I read about him in the paper quite a bit. Saw him on the town-access channel last week. He still sounds like that Cliff fellow from "Cheers," don't you think?"

Tom nodded. "Yeah, definitely."

"That particular club disbanded over fifty years ago, so there's not much to say."

"But what was its purpose?" I asked, not wanting to be too pushy.

Her eyes locked onto the table in front of us, and she was silent for several seconds. *I guess I went too far.*

"Excuse me, boys, but I've been rude by not offering refreshments. Tommy, would you be a dear and bring two cans of soda from the top shelf of the refrigerator? I still have my tea from earlier."

"Yes, ma'am." Tom was up and in the kitchen in no time. He returned with two cans of root beer and handed me one.

We both thanked her. I felt like a fourth-grader again, but maybe that was to my advantage.

"To answer your question, Denny, the club paid tribute to the men who took care of our town. Most of it was behind the scenes because we women chose not to call attention to ourselves. We've always made certain the cemetery plots were maintained. There were others, of course. The war monument is the most recent. That model of Fort New Dover is the only scale model of the fort in existence. It took the artist three years to get every detail just right. I haven't seen the art gallery over at the college, but I hear it's a beauty."

Art gallery? I've never heard that one before.

Tom jumped in. "What's the significance of the name 'Hermillion'? Who came up with it?"

She thought for a moment. "Syvanvus Hartin's granddaughter married a wealthy ship builder. When he died, he left her with quite a sizable fortune: 'her million.' Get it? Anyway, she financed the club for as long as anyone could remember."

"Thanks again for the information, Mrs. Merryweather," I said. "I was wondering, did anyone in your society ever mention Komaket?"

She rocked forward in her chair, then pretended to fix the cover on the armrest. "I think you boys had better be careful. The past has a way of catching up, you know." She stood and tottered toward the front door. "You best be going now. My assistant will be here very soon, and she doesn't like it when I have uninvited guests."

We stood and politely thanked her. As we made our way out the front door, a car pulled into the driveway and parked. We slipped around the corner, then back toward the library parking lot.

As I walked, I pondered what she had told us. The art gallery was intriguing. The middle was becoming clearer than ever.

Chapter 25

I had just enough time to get home, get dressed and head into work. I got the call to perform a pool maintenance check for a family on the other side of Cardiff. These types of calls were not unusual at this time of year as families buttoned up their pools for the season. Mike said they asked for me personally, so I took the small company pickup and headed out.

The drive gave me a chance to think about what Mrs. Merryweather had told us. I had never heard of an art gallery at Weaver, but I made plans to look for it when I got off work.

The other item swirling around my head was her declaration that my father was somehow set up and money got deposited. I remember from the newspaper clippings that he was accused of some sort of financial impropriety. I made a mental note to ask my mom about it.

I finished winterizing the pool just before 4 p.m., then headed back across town to return the truck. Traffic was pretty bad, but I made it okay even though it seemed like I was getting honked at, tailgated or cut off at every turn.

After dinner, I brought up the delicate subject of my dad's fateful final months. "Mom, did Dad leave any financial statements? You know, bank books and such?"

"May I ask why you need them?"

I took a large bite of apple pie and washed it down with some milk. "I'm pretty sure I know how he was framed. I can prove it if I had his records."

She gave me a less-than-supportive look. "Everything from his office was put into a box or destroyed. The box is on the top shelf of the closet in the spare... well, your bedroom."

"Thanks, Mom." I gave her a kiss on the cheek, which took her slightly by surprise. I loved to surprise her.

The box in question was heavier than I thought it would be. I struggled to pull it down from the closet shelf, and it made quite a thump when it landed. I took out a small knife and cut the tape that held on the lid.

Inside I found bundles of canceled checks going back three years before he died. There were several Manila folders filled with papers, bound with rubber bands and divided by subject: insurance forms, household receipts, automotive, travel. At the very bottom was one marked "Bank Records." I pulled it out and slid off the rubber band.

Most of the documents were checking account statements. Some had small checkmarks next to the line items from when he balanced his checkbook. I looked over the statements, not really knowing what I was looking for. From what Mrs. Merryweather had told me, someone placed a large amount of money in his account. I checked the entire stack and saw nothing unusual. I removed everything from the box and stacked it on the floor. At the very bottom of the box was a thin, blue book with a plastic sleeve—a savings passbook.

I thumbed through it and noticed it covered over five years of savings transactions. It was pretty standard stuff, with roughly the same amount added every two weeks. He must have had the same amount direct deposited every paycheck. That was just like him. There were only a few withdrawals: a couple hundred here and there, just enough to keep the running total between $7,000 and $8,000 for a few years in a row—not a bad nest egg.

I thumbed through it, hoping to find some unusual spike in the deposits, but it remained remarkably steady until the last page. There was no smoking gun here.

Then I double-checked the dates and realized it only went to early March. I knew for a fact that he had worked and continued to get paychecks until he became too sick in late April. Why would the deposits stop? The answer made me laugh a little. Passbooks only got updated when you took them to the bank and had the teller place it in a small printer. Most people had moved on to on-line banking, but this was still the way to go back in the 90s. All I had to do was take it to the bank to have it updated.

I had an account at that same bank, but where the hell was my passbook? I didn't take it with me when I moved out of the other house all those years ago. Nothing in this house was mine except the dresser. I checked every drawer and found the passbook in with some other personal items in the bottom right drawer. *Thank you, Mom, for not tossing everything!*

My plan was to get my passbook updated and see if I could get Dad's done too. Our branch of The Great Northern Bank was open late one day a week—Thursday—so I had exactly twenty-five minutes to get there and get that passbook filled in. I stuck them both in my back pocket and hurried out of the house. It couldn't wait until Friday.

It took me ten minutes to maneuver through traffic and make it to the bank parking lot. A few customers were still inside, so I knew I was still in luck. I swung open the glass door and got into the teller line between two velvet ropes. Three other customers were ahead of me with fifteen minutes to go. There were two tellers helping the walk-up customers and another handling the drive-through window. I recognized the closest teller immediately. It was Darcy Millet, now Darcy Barksdale, my ex-girlfriend, the one who was recently married. We had split up on pretty good terms, and I was sure she would help out an old flame if I just gave her a chance. She finished with a customer, and the person in front of me walked up to her bay. The other teller opened up at the same time.

"Can I help you?" the non-Darcy teller asked while leaning forward.

Fortunately, someone was behind me, so I motioned her along while I made like I was checking my pockets for something.

With five minutes to go before closing time, Darcy said, "Next, please." I stepped up and she recognized me immediately. "Dennis! How are you?"

"Fine, Darcy. Great to see you again. Hey, I heard you got married. Congratulations to you and the lucky guy." She still had a great face and a great smile. She was probably still a needy cling-on, though.

"Thanks, now what can I do for you?"

I slid my passbook over. "I'd like to withdraw fifty dollars, please."

"Sure thing." She filled out a short form and I signed it. Then she put my passbook in the printer and it clicked away, updating my book with what I was sure were pennies of interest after all those years. She counted out the bills and handed me back the entire package. "There you are. Anything else?"

"Thanks. I do have one other thing." I put my dad's passbook on the counter. "I'd like to update this one too."

"Sure thing." She took it and entered the number. She had a concerned look as she checked the front page again. "I'm afraid this account is frozen. That's what we do after ten or more years of inactivity."

"I know. It was my dad's account and he, unfortunately, died fifteen years ago. Can you still update the transactions? There's something I have to know. It's very important. Please?"

She reached across and gently touched my hand. "I remember you telling me about your dad and what a great guy he was. So sad what happened." She slid another withdrawal slip toward me and lowered her voice. "I'm not supposed to do this since your name's not on the account. In fact, I'm not even sure we have records that old in the system, but sign this because we're probably being watched."

I gave the slip a quick scribble signature and leaned in a bit as she began to update Dad's passbook. The printer was doing something, so that part was encouraging. Darcy took out the passbook and flipped the page, then reinserted it. It was done a few seconds later, and she handed it back.

"Anything else I can help you with?" Her voice was back to normal.

"No. That's it. Thank you so much for your help."

"You're very welcome, Dennis. By the way, we're closing."

I didn't dare look until I was outside. A female employee stood near the front door and gave a pleasant, "Good night," as I left.

Once out, I opened the passbook. The normal deposits were entered right up through the middle of April. I flipped the page and scanned the fresh ink. Bingo! There it was at the bottom: a deposit of nearly $10,000 on April 23rd. I thrust my fist in the air. "Yes!"

The transactions continued on the following page with a normal set of deposits and a final withdrawal for the entire amount about a month later... well, not quite the entire amount; he left exactly one dollar in the account. Soon after that, all deposits stopped, which coincided with the time he became too sick to work.

Ten thousand dollars! He must have known about it. Why didn't he say something? Do something? Plus, he must have left a dollar in the account so it would remain open—easy pickings for any investigator worth his salt.

These questions bugged me as I drove home. Nobody said anything to me when I got there, so I quietly went to my room and sat on the edge of my bed. I was convinced there were no more answers to be found.

I tossed the passbook down and it tumbled off the document stack, then onto the floor. I picked up the stack labeled "Travel" and began to place it back in the box. Unlike the other folders, it was not secured with a rubber band so the contents began to slide down. One item came out. His passport.

I picked it up and examined it. The first page had his picture in the lower left corner. He was in his thirties and still had a handsome, youthful look. I don't remember him traveling much, but he must have gone out of the country at least once.

The next page provided his one and only location: Bermuda. Then it came to me; he went to Bermuda with his girlfriend just before he got sick. Wow, whatever happened to her? I remembered that Mom had been really pissed at him for taking that trip with his girlfriend, even though they had been divorced for years.

He arrived in Bermuda on April 20th according to the passport. I got my first international postcard from him on that trip. In fact, I still had it somewhere. I got up and checked my top dresser drawer for an envelope in which I kept some old birthday cards and such from him. His presents may have sucked big time back then, but his cards were great. I found the envelope under a stack of wool socks. I fingered through them and pulled out the postcard. "Greetings From Bermuda" was printed across a photo of a beautiful, sandy beach. I checked the postmark, and it was stamped April 23rd. Something about that date didn't seem right. I took out the bankbook and looked at the date of the large deposit: April 23rd.

My dad was in Bermuda when the deposit was made to his account. He couldn't have put the money in on that day because he was well out of the country. Then who did? And why?

Based on the newspaper accounts I had read, the funds were found in his account about a month later; and soon after that, he resigned. He must have known it was a set-up, but still he resigned his post. That didn't seem right at all.

Next on my to-do list was the art gallery Mrs. Merryweather had mentioned. I did an online search of local galleries and found nothing. I checked the Weaver College site and found that they had an Art Department, but no gallery *per se*.

I emailed Russell to let him know about my findings. He was still in town on some other business and promised to get together with me when he was done. In the past he would have taken off back to Vermont without warning. It sure seemed like he was trying to change.

There was a voice-mail message on my cell phone from a guy with an apartment for rent across town. I had forgotten that I had called about a few places earlier in the week. I quickly called him back and he said if I wanted it, I had better come right away.

It took me about ten minutes to get there. A guy named Gary showed me around the place, which included my own bathroom. It seemed too good to be true. Gary said that his roommate had to drop out of school and return home for family reasons the week before.

It was a little more than I had planned on, but we shook on it. I agreed to pay him first and last month's rent plus security deposit the next day. I had been saving like mad for just this occasion.

No more living at Mom's house. No more Stan. This day was looking better and better.

***

I went to work the next day with a spring in my step and a smile on my face. I helped customers and did inventory for two hours until the boss, Leo, arrived and called me into his office. Everything seemed fine until he closed the door behind me. He had never done that before.

"Dennis, I'm not happy." He sat at his desk with his hands on cheeks, elbows on desk. "Not happy at all."

"What's wrong, Leo?"

He gave me a good, long look, then took a drink from his stainless-steel mug, keeping one hand on his cheek. "Your maintenance call yesterday, Dennis. Tell me about it."

"Well, it was pretty routine, if that's what you mean. I came. I saw. I buttoned it up, just like you and Mike showed me a bunch of times, Leo. Why?"

Leo stood, then began to walk behind his desk. He wasn't one to sit down for very long. "I got a call from the customer last night, Dennis, one Veronica Breezewood... wonderful lady. She's been a faithful customer for years. She was very, very angry."

"About what?"

"About you. She said she didn't like your attitude. Said you swore out loud several times while you were there, and—"

"What? I never did!"

"Don't interrupt. She also said"—he pulled out a notepad from his shirt pocket and flipped it open—"that you insulted and tried to kick her dog, played your music too loud after she told you nicely to turn it down, plus left several empty chemical bottles on the scene, which her grandchildren later found. If that weren't enough, you drove across her front yard on the way out."

He slammed the notepad on his desk. "This is completely unacceptable, Dennis."

I waited to see if he had any more. "Can I talk now?"

He glared at me as he paced behind his desk.

"Okay. Leo. I'm really confused, here. As I said before, I never swore... at least, I don't recall doing that. Secondly, my little dinky radio won't go that loud. Mrs. what's-her-name even told me she liked the song I was listening to. I promise I won't bring it with me anymore. As for her dog, the little mutt tried to bite me so I put my foot out for protection. It was self-defense." I had to think to recall the other "charges" against me. *Yes, the bottles.* "She told me to leave the empty winterizer bottle because she had room in her recycle bin and was getting ready to take it out. It was just one plastic bottle. Finally, I most certainly did not cut across her lawn. That's just... just wrong, Leo. Nothing happened the way she told you."

He didn't say a word as he paced. This whole scene was crazy. Who was this lady and why was she out to get me?

"I'd chalk it up to a bad day and give you the benefit of the doubt if it stopped there, Dennis."

"What? There's more?"

He opened his desk drawer and pulled out a small stack of paper. "You know that sticker on the back of the company truck, Dennis? The one that says 'How's my driving?' with a 1-800 number?"

"Sure. Lots of company vehicles have them."

"Any call to that number goes to a service that reports them to me. I've only gotten one report in four years and that was for good driving." He fanned out the reports on his desk. "There were four reports for bad driving filed yesterday. All of them gave the license number of the truck at the time you were driving it. Complaint one said you were driving like a maniac. Number two said you cut him off on Route seven, then flipped him the bird. Nice."

"But I didn't—"

"I'm not done. Number three says you tailgated so close he could practically, oh, how'd he say it?" He picked up one of the sheets. "He could practically see your nose hairs—another pleasant thought. These really make my day. Finally, 'Your crazy driver pulled a U-turn on a busy road and nearly forced me off. Thank God I saw the bumper sticker.' For Christ's sake, Dennis, what the hell got into you?"

This was almost too much for me to comprehend. Someone had it in for me. "Leo, you have to believe me. This is not the way it went down. I did my job and I came back. I'm shocked. I'm blown away by what you're telling me because none of it happened that way."

He stopped pacing long enough to take a long, steady drink from whatever was in his mug. "I've dealt with Veronica Breezewood and the other Tisdales for years. They are some of my best customers. Now—"

"Did you say 'Tisdale'?"

"Yes, and for god's sake, please stop interrupting. The entire Tisdale clan has threatened to take their business elsewhere. That's a lot of service contracts, Dennis."

"Tisdales! I should've known." There was so much I wanted to explain: Hollinger, Komaket, *shingala*; all of it tied in some way to the Tisdales. None of it would've made any sense if I tried to explain it. This was Melody's doing, I was sure of that. It was a perfect set-up.

"Dennis, I want to make this easy on you. You've been a great worker and I really like you, but I can't lose my customer base. Business gets slow this time of year, and I was going to make

158

some changes anyway. I don't want this to be a black mark on your career, so I'm going to pay you for the rest of the week and call it a layoff. You can keep the shirt and drop your keys off at the front desk. I've already informed Maria, and she has some paperwork for you to sign. I'm sorry it turned out this way."

He opened his door, inviting me to leave. I made the trek to the front desk as the door closed behind me. Maria said nothing as I dropped my set of keys on the counter. She handed me a clipboard, and I signed the document without reading it. What did it matter?

Maria gently touched my arm. "I'll mail you your final paycheck, Dennis. I've really enjoyed working with you."

I managed a barely audible, "Thanks."

As I left the building, it dawned on me that my chance to move out of the house ended that day too. There was no way I could afford the place on just savings. Sure, I could get another job but nothing as good as the one the Tisdales took away from me.

I had time to think as I drove home: no job, no classes, only a few days until Founder's Day. The only thing left to do was devote my attention to figuring this whole thing out.

Chapter 26

The first thing I did when I got home was call the guy back about the apartment. It killed me to tell him "no," but he understood when I explained I had just lost my job. I was resigned to living in the House of Stan until the next semester started in late January. There were sure to be some acceptable places then. *There had better be*, I thought as I hung up.

I called Russell to tell him how the Tisdales ganged up on me and got me fired. I also told him about my dad's bank account and how the money got put in while he was out of the country.

He paused for a moment after I told him. "That doesn't seem right. I seriously doubt he would have wired that much into his own account from a foreign bank. That's just asking for trouble. I talked to him right after he resigned, and all he said was, 'They got me.' I never believed him, and there was something unconvincing about his tone. Unfortunately, he was gone just a short time later, so I never found out."

"What do you know about his former girlfriend, the one he went to Bermuda with?"

"Her name was Kiwi or something; I can't quite recall." He snapped his finger. "Kiki! That was it. I only met her one time. She was a piece of work. As soon as she found out Norm was sick, she was out of his life—a total no-class, as far as I could tell."

Like much of this investigation, the thought of that made me pissed, but I kept it to myself. I needed to find her. "Do you know where she is now?"

"She used to live in the north part of town. Damn, I wish I could think of her name. I tell you what, let me poke around and see what I can find."

"Thanks, Uncle Russell."

"No problem, Dennis."

***

My plan was to break the news of my unemployment to Mom and Stan at dinner that night. I waited until everyone was sitting down because that seemed to cause the least amount of drama. I could fit it into the usual small talk.

"So, how's work been going, Dennis?" Mom asked, almost on cue. "Are you doing well as a floor manager?" I could hear the sarcasm in her voice.

"Funny you should ask. Leo called me into his office and told me they are cutting back for the fall and winter seasons. I hate to say it, but he let me go. I did get a full week of severance pay out of him, though."

"What? You got fired?" She appeared to be on that fine line between crying and screaming.

"Technically, I was laid off."

Stan said nothing as he cut his steak into exactly nine pieces, like always. Mom glared at me. I didn't think this would go over too well.

Finally she spoke up, "People don't get a raise and a promotion, then get fired—excuse me, *laid off*—after only a few weeks. What aren't you telling us, Dennis?"

"Well, it's like this." I told them what happened over the course of the day, trying hard not to leave out any details. Neither of them seemed too sympathetic to my story.

An uncomfortable minute passed; then Stan said, "You may have a lawsuit on your hands for improper termination, if you're willing to fight, of course."

My mom pounded her fists on the table as she glared at Stan. "He won't fight it. He's a Kozma. He'll just walk away, like his father always did... just like his uncle always does."

"It's not that simple. I was set up. Somebody wanted to get me fired."

Another minute passed with no chewing or drinking involved. *This conversation sure went downhill quickly*. Mom slammed another spoonful of potatoes on my plate. It was her idea of comfort food, but I hardly felt comforted.

"Let me see if I have this straight, Dennis. In the last few months, you've dropped out of college in your senior year, been taken to jail, lost an apartment and a house and now you've been fired from your job. What's next? Are you going to surprise us with a grandchild? Or better yet, you can start smoking crack. I hear that's all the rage."

She stared at me with the spoon still dripping potatoes. I took another bite and looked away. "Seriously, what are you going to do with this free time now?"

I was in mid-chew, so I quickly swallowed, washing it down with some milk. I wished it was a tall glass of Guinness. "Well, I'll look for another job until I head back to Weaver next semester. In the meantime, I'm still looking into some of those documents Dad left. I think I can prove that he was set up. Uncle Russell's helping out."

I waited for the *look* or the *sigh* but got neither. She flipped her hand at me. "Do what you have to do, Dennis."

"Thanks, Mom. Hey, I know this might be a touchy subject, but you wouldn't happen to know what happened to Kiki, the lady Dad went to Bermuda with that one time?" I braced myself for the response.

Mom calmly picked her plate up and headed to the sink. "Why do you need to know that?" She rinsed the plate, then placed it in the dishwasher.

"I want to know what happened on that trip. It looks like someone placed a bunch of money in his bank account while he was out of the country. I'm pretty sure it wasn't Dad, and I think she can verify that."

My plate was next, rinsed and in it went.

I continued, "I'm not even sure if she still lives around here or what her last name was."

Stan had finished his meal and his plate left the table. She put a couple glasses on the top rack; then she slammed it closed.

"I didn't really want to get involved in this. I told you that some time ago."

"I know, Mom, it's just that—"

"But it seems important to you, so I'll help." She wiped her hands on a dishtowel and replaced it on the rack. "Her name is Kiki Russell and, yes, she's still around. She runs the golf center and driving range up on Route seven."

"Thanks, Mom. Can I help you clean up?"

"No, please don't. Go do what you need to do." She shooed me away.

***

I had driven past the Oasis Golf Center many times but never stopped in. I pulled into the brightly-lit gravel lot and parked next to a massive SUV. I walked past the rows of driving bays—about half of them occupied—and into the main building.

The woman behind the desk had on a dark green shirt with "Oasis Golf Center" on the front. She politely handed a customer change and thanked him for coming. I edged my way up to the counter.

"May I help you?" She had well-chiseled features. Her dark hair was pulled back and under a visor. I could see how my dad would have been attracted to her.

"I'm looking for Kiki Russell."

"You found her, sport. I prefer to be called 'Kay' these days, but I answer to 'Kiki.' How can I help you?"

"I'd like to ask you some questions about my father, if you don't mind."

"Is he a customer here? A lot of people want to know how their parents' lessons are coming along." She looked right at me, and I really wanted to remember her; but it was too long ago, and I had been far too young.

"My father was Norm Kozma."

She looked away and used the mouse to click on something on her computer screen. "I see. So you must be..."

"Dennis."

"Yes, of course. Well, I can certainly see the resemblance."

A large man with a matching green shirt entered through a side door and immediately began straightening out a bin filled with putters used for the mini-golf course. He hummed away as he placed the long, medium and short clubs in the correct bins. In an instant, he was done and preceded through the front door.

Kiki leaned over the counter and pointed toward the driving range. "Outside. Pretend I'm giving you some lessons."

The man came back through the lobby, snapping his fingers to an imaginary tune.

"Jack, take the counter," Kiki said. "I have a customer."

"You got it, babe." He proceeded past us, then stood outside the door, watching the golfers practice.

She turned to me. "Buy a bucket of balls and meet me on bay

163

seventeen. It's all the way down on the right." She pointed out the window behind her.

"I didn't bring any clubs."

"Not a problem." She reached under the counter, pulled out a driver and a seven-iron, then handed them to me. "See you on bay seventeen."

"Thanks." I began to make my way out.

"Oh, that'll be four-fifty for the bucket of balls."

"Right." I pulled a twenty from my pocket and placed it on the counter. I didn't want change, just information. "Keep it."

I walked past Jack onto the sidewalk behind the driving bays. There was no sign of Kiki, so I put a ball on a rubber tee and grabbed the driver. I swung hard but pulled it far to the left. I teed up another and topped it badly. The third went dead-solid perfect. It felt so good, I hit another.

"Not bad, but your legs are too far apart and your backswing is too short."

"I didn't come here for a lesson."

"I know but if you want to talk, we have to do it out here. If you're out here, you have to golf. Those are the rules." She wasn't wearing her visor and she looked even better.

"All right, I'll just check out this seven-iron then. Mind if I hit off the grass?"

She motioned to the grass in front of the tee box and I directed a few balls there. I hit the first one and it went nearly straight up in the air. I prepared a second.

"Dennis, I've never told anyone about the short time your father and I spent together. I'm married now, and quite happily, so this will be the last time I'll talk about it. For what it's worth, he was a fine man and what happened to him was nothing short of tragic." She paused for a moment as she teared up. "So, what is it you wanted to know?"

I sliced a shot up against the screen that ran along the right side of the driving range. "You two took a trip to Bermuda in April of that year. At any time during your trip, did he go into a bank and wire money to the U.S.?"

She shook her head quickly. "I'm positive he never entered a bank. Of course, we were only there for a day, so it hardly qualified as a trip." She reached over and rotated my right hand

164

slightly on the club. "Move your thumb over too."

"One day? But he sent me a postcard from there three days after you arrived. I still have it. Look." I slid the postcard out of my back pocket and showed it to her. "April 23rd."

She looked it over, then handed it back. "I was with him when he sent this to you, Dennis. Take a real close look at the postmark."

I looked again and clearly saw "April 23" above the beautiful picture of Bermuda. The rest of the postmark, the writing in a circle around the date, was slightly smudged and the ink blended in with the background. I held it out to capture the lights from above. Then I saw it: "Charlotte Amalie." Below that was the name of their real destination.

"You went to the Virgin Islands?"

"Yes, we stayed a day in Bermuda, then took off to the Caribbean. Norman didn't want anyone to know where we were going. Of course, back then we didn't need our passports to get in. He bought the postcard in Bermuda and sent it the day after we arrived in Charlotte Amalie. He figured you wouldn't notice."

"But why did he want to go to the Virgin Islands?"

The caged tractor that picks up range balls rumbled by us, interrupting the conversation. I was tempted to take a shot at it with my seven-iron, but it was moving too fast.

"Dennis, this is getting into very touchy territory, here. I'm... I'm not sure how much you really want to know about this."

"Please, Kiki, tell me everything. I'm pretty sure... no, I'm positive that my dad would want me to know. My mom and my uncle both said he was very quiet after he got back. Then he got sick and, well, you know the rest."

She looked at the main building, then picked up the other club. "Let your left hand guide you, Dennis." She showed me a better way to grip.

I figured her answer would cost me a few shots, so I lined up another and gave it a whack. The new grip helped and the ball went straight and true.

"He went to the Virgin Islands for treatment, Dennis. He only had a few months to live and—"

"Hold on! Wait a minute now, Kiki. He told everyone that he was diagnosed in May. You're saying he knew sooner than that?"

"It's true, Dennis. He got the grim news just a few weeks before we left. His doctor gave him less than six months to live. He researched alternate treatments and found a doctor in the U.S. Virgin Islands who had had some success with his form of cancer. It was radical and experimental. I'm sorry, Dennis. I didn't know he hadn't told anyone else. Really."

I couldn't golf anymore after hearing her story. My hands trembled and I dropped the club. He knew he was dying. Why did he keep that information from his family for so long?

"This might seem like a strange question, but do you remember the doctor's name?"

"Why is that important?"

"I want to know. I need to know."

She picked the club up and placed it against a short rack between the bays. "It was a very unique name. Dr. Ulysses Avila. I remember his office was way out in the boonies. We drove by it the first day just to find where it was. On day two, I dropped him off and went back to the hotel room. I wanted to stay with him, but he refused."

"So how many treatments did he have?"

She was starting to well up again. "None. The doctor told him it was too advanced. We stayed for a few more days, then went home."

"You came home so you could dump him, right? Real classy."

She took my shoulder and turned me toward her. "Is that what you think? Is that what your family thinks, Dennis?"

"Well, my uncle said—"

"How dare you! God, Dennis, I'm no monster. I wanted to stay with him, but he didn't want to see me get hurt. I went to the funeral, you know. I watched from my car because I didn't want to be a disruption."

As I heard her words, my throat tightened up. I could hardly breathe. Everyone had been wrong about her. "I'm sorry, Kiki. I had no idea."

"You were just a kid. I know he had some rather unfortunate trouble with the town, but he wanted the best for you and your family. Oddly enough, the last thing he told me was that you would come to visit me in fifteen years. I'm glad you did. How do you like that?"

I liked it a lot. Dad did a lot of planning in his final weeks. The conversation had run its course, so I gathered up the last of the golf balls and put them in the basket.

"Thanks for talking with me, Kiki. I'm on a quest to prove that he was not a thief. Someone framed him."

"Good luck, Dennis. Norman would be very proud of you."

I walked away and headed back to my car. I turned just before the parking lot, and she was still in the same place.

"You would have been a cool stepmom," I told her... but not loud enough for Jack to hear.

She smiled and gave me a get-out-of-here wave.

I decided not to drive home right away. I took off down the highway, heading nowhere, just to think about what Kiki told me. Another day, another interesting morsel of my dad's life revealed.

I called Tom and Jed on the way back to see if they wanted to join me at O'Reardon's. They were both eager to get out. I pulled into the parking lot a short time later but didn't see either of them. Maybe they were already inside.

I pulled open the front door, and immediately Melody Bancroft thrust a finger in my face.

"We need to talk."

Chapter 27

My knees practically buckled when I heard her voice. She looked worse than I had ever seen her, with her hair only partly clipped up and her clothes disheveled. I knew why she wanted to talk; I just wished it wasn't right then.

"Tom and Jed are stopping by. Care to join us?"

"No. Dennis, this can't wait. Forget your idiot friends for one night. I've been looking all over for you today. You won't take my calls or answer my emails and the pool place told me you don't work there anymore. Now that I found you, I'm not going to let you go."

I took a small step to my right and she stepped in front of me.

"Okay, we'll go outside and talk." I opened the door and gestured her through. "My car or yours."

"I didn't bring a car. Let's sit on the patio."

I really didn't want to hang outside, but she looked pretty pissed off, so going with her flow seemed like the best thing to do. We headed toward the patio around the back that, fortunately, was unoccupied. The wind picked up, and I wished I hadn't left my jacket in the car. I sat. She stood.

"First of all, I don't appreciate being ignored. If you didn't want to see me anymore, you should have had the balls enough to tell me. Honestly, you act like you're thirteen years old sometimes."

"Maybe, but at least I never lied to you, Mrs. Bancroft?"

"Is that why you ran away? Because I didn't tell you that I'm legally separated and waiting to get a divorce? My ex and I haven't seen each other since he moved to California with his boyfriend over a year ago. It really seemed irrelevant, Dennis."

"Is the guy you live with irrelevant too?"

Her face tightened and she appeared to bite her lip. "Great, so you spied on me. For the record, I live with two other people to save on money. The guy, Albert, is gay and the woman... well, I'm not so sure about her. Full disclosure here: she and I are not an item."

168

I couldn't take her looking down at me anymore, so I stood on the other side of the table.

"Great, Melody, now that you've come clean, everything is just great. I feel like one of Phinneus Marley's paintings."

"What are you talking about?"

"You know, the one from the Revolutionary War that had a *shingala* on the flag. You couldn't wait to show it to us on your cell phone. I found a picture of the original. You lied about the painting and I'm not sure why. You used me. How could I trust you after that?"

She slowly sat down and buried her head in her hands. I expected the water works to start, but she looked up at me with clear eyes. "I can explain that."

"I'm listening."

"Look, I admit I knew more than I let on, okay? I've known about the Hermillion Club for years but not why it existed. I went to the party to meet you after Dr. Overmann told me about the email you sent him."

"Why did you want to meet me?"

She was starting to cry, wiping her eyes with her long sleeves. "Because I'm a historian, and the whole mystery about how the Shadow Regiment operated has intrigued me. For my thesis I want to be the first person to accurately report how they did it. Dr. O told me that Komaket was somehow the root of all this, but I didn't know how they were connected."

"So you used me."

"We used each other. I can distinctly remember providing you with information. It's true I messed with the photo of the painting to keep you interested, not just in your journey but also in me. I wanted to be a part of it."

A couple came out the back door and walked near us toward their car. She took the opportunity to fix her falling hair.

"Look, Melody, I just about have this thing figured out... without you, I might add."

She shook her head violently. Her eyes were now swollen and puffy. "You have no idea what you're getting into. Please, I'm begging you to stop what you're doing. It's too dangerous."

She had shot too many blanks in the last few months for me to believe her. My dad told me something big was going to happen, so she was telling me nothing new.

"They arranged to get me fired. No big deal, I can get another job."

"They will get what they want, Dennis."

"Don't you mean 'we,' Melody? I know you're a Tisdale. You're one of them. Wait, I guess you forgot to tell me that too. The points in your column are really starting to pile up."

"For the record, I disowned my family a long time ago, or maybe they disowned me. It's hard to tell. Why do you think I kept my married name? I moved out when I was seventeen, and I've supported myself ever since, including my education." She took a tissue from her pouch and blew her nose. "Some of them are evil. You and Dr. Overmann were the only people I could trust."

"Then it's simple, Melody. Go to the fabulous Dr. O for all your information. You two seemed to have hit it off pretty well. Write your thesis and wow the academic world."

"That's not possible."

"Why not? Did you rack up too many frequent liar miles with him too?"

She grabbed me by the front of my shirt and shook me hard. "Because they killed him, Dennis. My God, don't you read the papers or watch the news?"

"What happened?" A big lump of bile worked its way up my throat. I tried to swallow it but it just lingered. I wished I had a beer to wash it down.

"We... we told him not to run alone. He was struck by a car on a country road with no witnesses. The police called it a hit-and-run."

"God, that's awful. I'm sorry." I thought back to the night of the reading at the library. We brought up Dr. Overmann's name that night. I hoped to God that had nothing to do with it.

We had managed to drift closer over the course of the conversation. She gave me a look I couldn't resist. We simultaneously reached for each other and held on tight.

"Now do you believe me?"

I said nothing. She squeezed me so tight, I could hardly breathe. Finally, she let go.

"I'm not going to stop. Somebody set up my dad and I'm

going to find out who. Then I'm going to prepare for Komaket's return, if that's what all this means."

"You're making a big mistake doing this by yourself."

"I'm not by myself. I have Uncle Russell and Tom and Jed... people I can trust."

"They can't help you like I can."

"What do you mean?"

"They won't hurt me, Dennis. They won't go after one of their own. I know it. Blood runs very thick in the Tisdale family. Plus, you have my word—everything on the up and up."

The chilly wind finally got the best of me, and I began to shiver. Melody unzipped her sweatshirt and wrapped it over my shoulders. Her expression had changed. She no longer looked vulnerable. She even managed to smile. I loved that smile.

There were only three days left until Founder's Day, and I still didn't have all the answers, in spite of what I'd told her. I had a feeling she did.

"Okay, Melody, you're in. Now let's get back inside where it's warm. My idiot friends are waiting for me."

I took off the sweatshirt, gave it back and she hugged me again. Later, as I held the door open for her, I couldn't help but wonder what Tom and Jed were going to think.

We found them in a corner booth, each with a tall draft nearly polished off. Tom's look said volumes, and Jed's highlighted it. I was the biggest moron in town.

Chapter 28

Tom moved to the other side so Melody and I could sit together. I motioned her in, but she zipped up her sweatshirt and took a step back.

"I have to go. Dr. Overmann's wake is tonight. I should stop in."

"Do you want me to go with you?" I was hoping she would say "no."

"No, thanks. I'm meeting up with some of the others from the runners' group." She gave me a quick hug, then walked away. "Stay safe," I heard her say as she turned the corner.

I sat down, preparing myself mentally for the onslaught. I was sure Tom, with his many past loves, was going to take me to task. Jed, who had a girlfriend at another college—although I had never met her—was sure to chime in, but neither one said a word as they watched the college football game on TV.

A waitress came by so we ordered a round. Tom waited until we all had beer in hand, then held his up. "Koz, my man, welcome to the Pussy-whipped and Proud-of-It Club." He touched it to mine. "You're just a dumb son-of-a-bitch like the rest of us."

I knew exactly what he meant, so no one dwelled on the subject. Instead, I filled them in how I lost my job, my talk with Kiki Russell, Dr. Overmann's untimely demise and what we had to do before Founder's Day. Finally, I got around to telling them about Melody. "She warned me that the Tisdales were dangerous, but I was safe if she were around. Besides, I think she still knows more than she's saying. There's not much time and that could be useful."

"How can that possibly be useful, Koz?" Tom asked.

"Yeah, I'm pretty sure we tried to tell you that already," Jed said.

I took a drink to emphasize my point. "She's way into this whole Komaket story, and only I can get her what she really wants."

"And what's that?" Jed asked.

"A piece of the historical action. That's what motivates historians like Mr. Sellers and Dr. Overmann. Be the first. Be the best. Be the authority. I can make that happen for her."

"I don't know, Koz," Tom said. "I hate to say it, but I still think she's playing you."

"She was. I admit that, but now it's time for me to start playing her."

We had to drink to that.

***

On Thursday morning just two days before Founder's Day, I turned on my laptop and sent an email to Russell, reminding him what I found out about Dad's trip to the U.S. Virgin Islands with Kiki. The large folder with all the papers my dad gave me worked its way out from the pile of stuff on the corner of my desk. I opened it and scanned them. I needed some inspiration to get me going and point me in the right direction. I saw the cemetery maps with the graves forming a perfect pattern around a grass-covered vault in four different cemeteries. I unfolded the large map that showed the four vaults forming the same pattern around Ralph Pelson's vault in the new cemetery where Fort New Dover used to be. It still creeped me out to see those crazy patterns.

My eyes came back to the vault in the very center, Ralph Pelson's. I never did establish his connection to this whole puzzle. I thought back to something Tom had said after he gave me the report on Ralph: his wife was still around. The Pelson house was in the area, so I sent a text message to Melody letting her know about my findings. I was sure she would find this information intriguing.

As I got cleaned up and ready, I thought about how to approach Ralph's wife. Would she answer the phone? Would she answer the door? The drop-by visit won out, so I took the file of documents and maps with me, just in case.

With the window down, I put the car in reverse and backed partway down the driveway. I stopped when someone came into view. My feelings were correct.

"Going somewhere?" Melody stood on the sidewalk, arms folded.

"As a matter of fact, I'm going to visit Ralph Pelson's widow. Why?"

"I told you how dangerous it is going solo, Dennis. I'm going too."

I unlocked the passenger door and she slid in. What a difference a day made. She looked fresh and invigorated, and her hair was neatly pulled back. She buckled up and I backed out of the driveway.

"Shouldn't you be in class?"

She gave me a look. "I'm a Ph.D. candidate. I don't go to class, remember?"

"Of course." *Must be nice.*

"So, what do we know about Anne Pelson?"

"Not much. She lives over in Greenwood Estates with her daughter's family. I didn't call ahead or anything. I figured it would be best to wing it."

"What do you expect to find out?"

It was warmer than I thought so I put both front windows down a bit. "I want to know why her husband spent so much money on a piece of land, only to turn it over to the town. My father approved the zoning variances of other properties, but the town somehow wanted to shoehorn in Pelson's."

"Why would she want to talk with you?"

"I don't know." My voice was louder than I anticipated, so I turned it down a notch. "Because I'm such a charming guy, I suppose?"

She caught on to my sarcasm and smiled.

Ten minutes later, we were at the home of Julianna and Jeff Brightman, Anne Pelson's daughter and son-in-law. It was a modest ranch-style house in a middle-class neighborhood. There was a single car in the driveway, and I chose a spot next to it close to the road. I started to open my door but Melody stopped me.

"So you're just going to walk up to her and start asking questions? Just like that, out of the blue?"

"That's the plan. I take it you don't approve."

"I don't want to see you get the door slammed in your face, that's all."

"I told you before: the old Kozma charm will guide me through." That got me a well-deserved eye roll.

A rumbling sound interrupted the conversation. The garage

door rose up. A woman emerged from its midst and approached us. She appeared to be in her fifties, fairly hefty with a baggy sweatshirt pulled down over her sizable hips. She came over to my side and leaned over.

"May I help you folks?" Her tone was pleasant and friendly.

I wasn't prepared for anyone other than Mrs. Pelson, and this clearly was not her. "Hi, I'm Dennis Kozma and this is my friend Melody Bancroft. We'd like to talk with Anne Pelson. I was told she lives here."

The woman took a hard look at me and Melody. "What's this about?"

"My father had some dealings with the town over the land that Ralph Pelson donated to the town. I wanted to talk to her about it."

"That won't be possible, I'm sorry to say. She's in the hospital; she had a stroke just a few weeks ago."

"I see. Well, I'm sorry to hear about her condition." I looked at Melody but she said nothing. It looked like a dead end.

"Thank you. Oh, I'm Julianna Brightman, her daughter." She reached in and shook both our hands. "You're welcome to come in for a bit if you like. Maybe I can help. I'm not heading back to the hospital until later this morning."

"Sure," I said.

We got out and followed Julianna into the garage, then into the house through a side door. She took us to the living room where we sat on an overstuffed sofa. The place was immaculate.

"Beautiful house you have here," said Melody, beating me to it.

"Thank you," said Julianna. "Now, you mentioned something about the land my father bought."

I found myself slouching so I sat up. "Yes. My dad used to work for the town many years ago, you see. When he was on the zoning board, he approved several lots that would have made excellent cemetery sites; but for some reason, the other members really wanted the land your father eventually bought and gave away. I've never been able to figure out why."

"I remember your father. When you told me your name was Kozma, I knew who you were. I mean, how many Kozmas can there be? Ha! Now, back to your question." She cleared her throat and shifted to the other side of her chair. "I wasn't around at the time my dad went to the auction and bought the land on Adams Road. Jeff and I had moved to Portsmouth, Rhode Island, back in the early 90s when he took a job at the War College. We moved back after Dad died so we could take care of my mom. Sorry, but I don't know anything about the zoning board or other cemetery sites. All I know is my father was not the crackpot he was purported to be. From what I heard, he wanted to give something back to the town, so he bought the land on Adams Road and sold it back for a song. My parents had plenty of money and even left some in a trust for my kids. Does that sound deranged to you?"

"No," I said, "and I'm sorry if that's how I came off. I still can't figure out why he wanted that particular piece of land and why he wanted a grass vault at a specific spot in the cemetery."

"Well, I'm afraid I can't help you out there because I honestly don't know. Perhaps my mother would, but she lost her ability to speak after the stroke and may not get it back for a while, if at all. I can ask her when she's better."

"No thanks, that won't be necessary."

A bizarre ringtone interrupted us. Julianna examined her cell phone. "It's the hospital. I better take this. Excuse me."

As Julianna went to the kitchen, I sat back and took a quick look around the room. The furnishings were modern, right down to the quirky artwork on the walls and sculptures on the far table. The lady certainly had a sense of style. Melody's grip interrupted me. She shook my left arm and pointed to the painting directly in front of us.

"What?" I said. "Yeah, it's a cool painting."

"Don't you see it?"

"See what?"

"The pattern. Look really hard at the pattern."

I looked again. It was an abstract painting with lots of straight lines and varying color patterns. Like so many others, I couldn't tell what it meant or even if it were any good. Then I saw the basic shape in the center. It jumped off the canvas at me like one of those Magic Eye pictures.

Shingala! It couldn't be a coincidence.

Julianna returned a moment later. "Just routine hospital stuff, thankfully."

"I was admiring your artwork," Melody said. "I love these

paintings, especially that one." She pointed to the one in front of us. "Are you an artist?"

Julianna laughed. "God, no. That painting has been in my family for years. I asked for it when my parents sold the farm. It's beautiful in its own unusual way, don't you think?" A short "ding" sound came from the kitchen. "Would anyone like coffee? I started a pot before you got here and it's ready."

I raised my hand partway like I was in school. "I would."

Melody gave me a strange look as Julianna left for the kitchen. "Since when do you drink coffee?"

"I don't. I just want to get a shot of this painting." I took out my cell phone and moved a little closer.

"Dennis, what are you doing?" Melody asked through gritted teeth.

I lined it up the best I could and snapped off a picture. I was still standing in front of it when Julianna came back in.

"Cream and sugar, Dennis?"

"Yes on both." I was pretty sure she didn't see the phone. She left immediately. I took another picture, then put it back in my pocket.

Julianna held a serving tray with two cups on it when she returned. She placed them on the table as I continued to look at the painting.

"Well, I must say that no one has ever been so fascinated with that painting before. I'm glad you like it."

I moved in a little closer. "I'm looking for a signature, but it appears to be unsigned."

"Like I said, its origin is a mystery."

There was something in the corner that didn't appear to be part of the artwork. I moved in a little closer and tilted my head to get better light. I moved over, caught the painting just right and saw something astonishing.

I sat back down and tried a few sips of coffee just to be polite. Fortunately, Julianna loaded it with sugar to make the taste passable. We made small talk for the next few minutes and got the complete rundown on her husband, who was away on business, and her sons, both of whom were grown and living on their own. It was clear she was lonely. We provided a nice diversion before she had to head back to see her mother in the hospital.

177

Julianna walked us out to my car and we said our goodbyes. She managed a smile as we backed out and headed off. Melody immediately turned to me.

"You saw something else in the painting, didn't you?"

I pulled out my phone and brought an image up on the screen. The first was slightly off-center so I clicked to the next one. *Perfect.*

"You can barely tell from here: the spiral shaft, rounded with a four-sided pattern on top."

Melody squinted to see. "A *shongo?*"

"Yes, and not just that. At the right angle, I noticed something truly remarkable."

"What's that?"

"The painting was loaded with 'em."

Chapter 29

As we drove on, I could feel Melody's steely gaze. After we left the subdivision, she reached out and smacked my left shoulder.

"So are you going to tell me what the painting means?"

"I don't know exactly. I need to see the painting blown up a bit more to tell; but I do know that Ralph Pelson, the man in the center point, was certainly a key player in all this."

We went back to my house to get my laptop. I was relieved to see no car in the driveway.

"Want to come in?"

"No thanks." Melody flipped her hair back and rested against the headrest. "I'll wait."

I dashed in, unplugged my laptop and grabbed the download cable for my phone. While still in the driveway, I downloaded the good photo and displayed it on the laptop. The image was much clearer, making it easy to see the *shingala* pattern in the center.

My cell phone rang as we watched, so I unplugged it from the laptop.

It was Russell calling. "Dennis, I have something interesting to show you. Can I meet you some place for lunch?"

"Sure, how about—"

"Any place but O'Reardon's, okay?"

I laughed. "Sure. How about the Cabot Diner on Route seven? Melody is with me. Is that okay?"

After a short silence, he said, "Yeah, bring her along."

I put my phone away. "Lunch with Uncle Russell. Are you game?"

"Sure, why not?"

We were there in fifteen minutes. On the way, I filled Melody in on what I had found out about my father's trip to Bermuda and the U.S. Virgin Islands.

Russell was sitting at a large, round table in the corner. As soon as we sat, a waitress served us water and brought menus. The conversation then turned to my father.

"I did a little checking on that doctor Norm went to see, one

R.M. Clark

Ulysses Avila. Interesting fellow—he's a doctor, Dennis, but not a medical doctor. He has a Ph.D. in archaeology and teaches at the local university. He's an author, an artist and, strangely enough, a gourmet chef. It looks like he dabbles in a lot of stuff."

"But he went there for a radical cancer treatment. Kiki was with him." I thought about it for a moment, trying to remember what she told me. "Actually, she said she dropped him off at the office, then went back to the hotel. I guess he didn't want her to know."

"Know what?" Melody asked.

"That he went there for another reason," I said.

Russell handed me a slip of paper with the address on it. "I'm glad you brought your laptop. I want you to bring up this website." It was slow going, but soon the site was loaded.

"What are we looking for?"

"This is Dr. Ulysses Avila's website. The man has written a lot of books on various subjects, as you can see when you click on the far right tab."

I clicked it. Book covers popped up on the screen.

"If you scroll past the crazy cookbooks and archaeology books," Russell said, "we get to the really good stuff. Try page three."

I clicked on the small three at the bottom and another set of book covers appeared.

"Scroll down," Russell said. "There are a lot of books on this page."

I did and the screen filled with books on the occult, black magic and local island legends. All were written or co-written by Dr. Avila.

"The man is certainly prolific," Melody said. "Oddly enough, I've read dozens of local history books and I've never heard of Ulysses Avila."

"He considers himself the expert on North American legends, including many of the Native American ones," said Russell.

"I'll bet that's why Dad went to see him, right?"

"Looks like it. Now, check out the art work. There's a tab at the top."

I clicked on it and slowly the page began to load. The image was huge, but I knew what it was once it got past the eyes. *The*

180

same drawing my father had left me. "He drew Komaket? This is getting wild."

"Can you guess what's on the next page?"

I knew but I clicked on it to be sure. It was the necklace. On the page after that was the staff.

I was curious to compare them with the drawings my father left me. I opened the folder, pulled the pages on the bottom and spread them out.

"What the—?" I held the first one up to the light and only saw a trace outline.

The image of Komaket had vanished.

Chapter 30

"Dennis, did you lose them?" Melody had spread open the folder in search of Komaket and the other drawings.

"No. He used to be on this page. I can tell by the small tear in this corner. Besides, there's a slight outline if you hold it up to the light."

The other two were also barely visible on the page. Russell held them up and confirmed it.

"So what does it mean?" Melody asked.

I really didn't know, but I gave it my best guess. "It means his journey is complete. Komaket has returned."

Melody gave me an odd look. "You don't really believe that, do you?"

"It makes as much sense as anything else."

Russell shook his head quickly. "I'm not so sure. It could mean a lot of things. The drawings were clearly getting fuller as the weeks went on, and now they have, well, come full circle."

I glanced at the page again. "So we've reached the end."

"Or the beginning," said Melody.

I was about to make a point when my hand hit the mouse. This brought up another drawing on Ulysses Avila's website.

"Oh, my god," said Melody as the image loaded.

"What is it?" asked Russell. "I don't recognize that one."

I took out my phone and brought up a photo. "We just went to visit Julianna Brightman, Pelson's daughter. This is the same painting we saw in her house. She said it has been in the family for longer than she can remember. Look at the square pattern in the middle."

Russell tilted the view screen inward to compare the shots. "Interesting. It does verify that Komaket and Pelson are directly linked."

"And these little marks; they're the symbol of the *shongo*. They're all over—about twenty or so of them by my count." I took a good look at the painting from the website and the positioning of the *shongos* on the screen image. Where had I seen that before? I focused hard on the abstract art, but it didn't come to me.

We finished our lunch and offered to pay for our own, but Russell took care of it for us. Before leaving, we went over everything we knew just to keep everyone up to date. It was an amazing volume of information, but there was still much to learn and not much time to learn it.

As we walked out to my car, Melody stepped in front of me. "I have to go to a workshop this afternoon. I can't get out of it. Do you think you can handle staying out of trouble for a few hours?"

The slight smirk on her face made me smile. "I'll try my best. I'm going to go over all this stuff and see if anything jumps out at me. Call me when you're done, okay?"

"Sure. Maybe we can get together later."

"I'd like that."

She pressed herself against my chest and kissed me hard. Her hand brushed against my pants, probably not by accident.

"We have the place to ourselves," I managed to say between tongue lunges.

She pulled away and smiled. "I really have to go."

"Need a ride?"

"No, thanks. I prefer to walk."

I thought about what may have happened if Melody had taken me up on my offer and my mom caught us having sex in the house. I shook it off with a laugh. Walking up the sidewalk, I noticed the lawn needed mowing and, surprisingly, was several days overdue for a trim. Stan the Man was slipping.

The table in the living room was much larger than the one in my room, so I spread out all the papers on the table and a few on the couch. I grabbed a cup of hot tea and opened my laptop.

Where to start? At the beginning. I pulled out the original map my father had given me with the four town cemeteries shaded in. I hadn't looked at this one much in the past few weeks because I thought there was nothing more to see. There were family names spread out all over the map, likely corresponding to the landowners at the time.

Everything seemed to be about patterns. *Shingala* was everywhere, *shongos* too.

Something was still bugging me about the painting in Julianna's house, so I brought it up on the screen. I changed the contrast slightly, which made the picture a little easier to see. The *shongos* practically jumped off the screen. Patterns... everything had a pattern.

I read the image into a graphics application, then began to mark the location of the *shongos* on the painting. Then I stepped back and looked carefully at the screen full of green dots. Nothing—they were just dots... or were they?

I picked up the old cemetery map and held it next to the screen. *It could be.*

I found the electronic version of the map and sized it to that of the painting, then transferred the pattern of green dots from the painting to the map. They lined up perfectly with the family names on the map. There was a *shongo* for each landowner. *A gift from Komaket perhaps?* It appeared so.

After Tom helped me decipher the *shingala* pattern back in August, I had printed the image with all the lines drawn on it. I searched on the couch and found it. The entire town was based on this simple pattern. So was everything Komaket became involved in.

I placed the *shingala*-shaped maps and patterns in one pile, which left just a few scattered pages. The blank drawings were in a pile of their own, as were the town documents.

The only page left was the map of the cave-ins Russell had sent to me. They appeared to be random locations. I brought up the scanned image and compared it to the map with the family names. There was no match... not even close. I tried to match it with a few more patterns but to no avail.

I needed a break to rest my eyes, so I went to the kitchen to get more hot water for my tea. I drank half the cup, then gazed around the corner at the laptop screen. From there, the cave-in locations looked less random. I moved closer but kept my distance. The marks representing the cave-ins covered only part of the town, leaving the east side clean. The concentration of marks on three sides became clearer. *Spokes!*

This wasn't random; I was sure of it. I had been looking for a *shingala*-shaped pattern, but it was more complex. *Shingala* was just the frame.

I brought up the map that had the diagonal lines crossing in the center at the Fort New Dover site. I superimposed it on the cave-ins. *Bingo!* The cave-ins occurred directly on three of the four spokes on the map. Some were close to the edge, others toward the center.

What caused the cave-ins? We had the fort in the middle and four grass vaults on the outer points. Komaket had shown the founders how to protect the village. The Shadow Regiment defeated the British.

Then it came to me. It was the most logical solution of all. I laughed at my own cleverness. I laughed at my dad's cleverness.

It couldn't be.

It had to be.

There was still one piece missing, and the answer was on display in the Weaver College museum. Melody Tisdale Bancroft was the only person who could get me there.

Chapter 31

I paced and drank more tea. It seemed to help me focus on the drawings, the patterns, the problems and the answer... at least one of them.

Melody never told me when her workshop would end, so I had no idea when she'd call. I decided to risk calling and leaving her a message. This was just too important. I dialed her cell phone number and waited for her voice mail to kick in. Her message never seemed so long. Finally, I heard the beep.

"Hi. You want to know how the Shadow Regiment did it? Call me back and we'll meet at the museum. Bye."

To pass the time, I watched some TV, read a little, checked the internet for information on sinkholes and local geology. I even double-checked my maps and drawings. It was the slowest afternoon I could remember. My mom came home, followed closely by Stan. Oddly enough, I was happy to see him; that's how bored I was.

After we ate, I told my mom I'd be heading to the museum later that night. She gave me an uninterested look as she cleaned up.

Finally, my phone rang.

"Is this a joke, Dennis?"

"No. Can you get us into the museum tonight? It's very important."

"I suppose. You said something about how the Shadow Regiment did it. What did you mean?"

"You'll see. Meet me there at 7 p.m. or so?"

"I don't think so. How about I stop by your house a few minutes before and we go together. Oh, and sorry about the delay. The workshop went on forever: Pragmatics of Western Culture, if you're interested."

I wasn't.

True to her word, she was at the base of my driveway just before 7 p.m.

"Aren't you going to introduce me to your mom? I see other

cars in the driveway."

I hadn't thought about that and my heart sank. Mom hadn't liked anyone I'd brought home ever since I broke up with Darcy.

"I'm just kidding." She gave my arm a playful smack. "You said it was important, so let's go."

***

I parked as close as possible to the liberal arts building, but we still had a pretty good walk. At the side entrance, Melody called Frank in security so he could unlock the door for us. We headed up the stairs to the fourth floor, taking them two at a time. She unlocked the double doors to the museum, and I found the light switch.

"Okay," she said. "Want to tell me what this is all about?"

I escorted her to the Fort New Dover display and turned on the track lighting above it. "It's all right here."

"What is?"

"The answer to the mystery." I began to look around the display for a locking mechanism. "Can you open this?"

"Why?"

"This is an interactive demonstration. Trust me, you'll like it."

She gave me a stern look. "There's a key in the back room, but the door's locked. Let me see if I have my office key." She opened her pocketbook and brought out a small keychain. "Lucky you."

Melody disappeared through a back door, returning a moment later with a single key. "I have to call Frank to disable the alarm, so hang on."

She took out her phone and moved her hair out of the way to call. "Hi, Frank, it's Melody. We'll be doing a display switch-out this evening, so I need you to disable alarm three, please... Okay, thanks." She slipped it back in her pocket.

"This better be good." She twisted the key into the lock on her side, then tossed the key to me. "There's one on the opposite corner. Turn to the right and slide the lock off."

I unfastened it on my side. "Remember the cave-ins I was telling you about? The town had a slew of them starting back in the 40s. The same company, Tisdale Excavating, took care of filling them all in, no questions asked." It was not intended as a dig toward her or her family. She appeared to be okay with it.

"I remember."

"There is no known natural phenomenon that would cause that many sinkholes in this area. It's geologically impossible from what I've read and researched."

The display was about three feet by four feet, and the glass top slid out from one side. We eased it out, then leaned it against the closest wall. The fort was even more vivid without the glare on the display top.

"Okay, what do the sinkholes have to do with the fort?"

"The old town librarian, Kathleen Merryweather, told me that this is the only known scale model of the fort. Neil Hollinger as much as admitted that the Shadow Regiment used an alternate route to surprise the British, and, of course, Komaket showed them a unique way to defend the village. Put it all together, what do you have?"

In the display, near the exact center of the fort was a small building, perhaps a storage shed. I grabbed it and it came up cleanly.

"What are you doing? You can't take that apart."

I pointed to the void. There were miniature soldiers walking down a miniature flight of stairs.

"Tunnels, Melody. The soldiers slipped out under the fort and came up on the other side of the British. Komaket showed the town leaders how to defend their village by going underground."

"The sinkholes and cave-ins... they were collapsing tunnels, right?"

"That's the way it looks. The tunnels head out in all four directions toward the cemeteries."

She looked down at the display and pursed her lips. "I don't know. Maybe it's just a storage area. Small underground chambers were not uncommon back then."

There was only one way to find out. If this were, indeed, an authentic scale model of Fort New Dover, then all the details would be there. I looked closely at the display and noticed a slight separation that ran along the side of the model. It had to be.

The only handles were the walls of the fort. I grabbed opposite ends and yanked up as hard as I could. It came up, albeit slightly.

Melody began to slap my hands. "You're breaking it, Dennis.

Have you gone insane?"

"Trust me."

I spread my feet out and re-gripped the model. I pulled again. This time, the entire top layer separated. I placed it on the ground nearby.

On the lower layer were tunnels running in four directions from the center. Tiny soldiers walked along each tunnel, both entering and leaving the fort.

"Mystery solved, Melody. The Shadow Regiment drew the British toward the fort, then went under and surprised them from behind." I took out my phone and snapped off a few pictures as evidence of my find.

Melody walked around the model with a stunned look on her face. She reached in and touched one of the tiny soldiers, then ran her finger along the tunnel. "This is unbelievable. Do you have any idea what this means?"

"Besides the fact that the answer has been here all along, I'd say your dissertation will practically write itself."

She slowly shook her head. "This isn't about me, Dennis. It's about history. It's not as easy as you think to rewrite the history books."

"I thought this is what you wanted. You can prove once and for all how the Shadow Regiment pulled off the greatest upset of the Revolutionary War. I can't believe you're not doing backflips in the hallway."

"No one will believe me. I'll be a laughingstock—"

"You have proof, Melody. Komaket showed them how to do it." I waited a moment for a response but got none. "I get it now. *Shingala* means nothing. The shape is irrelevant. It's a big, fat red herring. The idea is to work in three dimensions when your enemy is working in two. God, this feels great. Tell you what; give me a few weeks to write it up and send it in. How hard can it be?"

She came around to my side of the display as I made my point. I prepared myself for a verbal lashing, but she put her arms around me and squeezed tight. "Thanks for showing me this. I've walked right past it 1,000 times without making the connection." She put her hands on my shoulders. "You'd make a great historian. You have the right mind for it."

"I've considered it. Now let's put this back together."

We gently placed the top layer onto the model, pressing it into place. It fit perfectly, as if it had never been taken apart. With the small building in the center, we slid the glass in and locked it up. Melody called Frank and asked him to set the alarm. Within minutes we were on the sidewalk, away from the liberal arts building.

It had turned dark and cold quickly, but I was prepared this time. I zipped up my jacket most of the way. I could tell by her look that Melody was deep in thought as we turned left toward the center of campus. She stopped for a second to make a point but continued walking. As we walked past a stone bench, she pulled me over and sat me down next to her. It was a dark area along the path, set back just slightly.

"This really doesn't prove that the soldiers used tunnels. It's just a model. It's just one artist's opinion. Without proof—"

"I can prove it. You'll just have to trust me."

"I do trust you."

She kissed me again and it was even better than last time. Then our hands started exploring, mine up the front of her shirt, hers along the front of my pants. It seemed like both of us were pleasantly surprised with what we found.

"We can't stay here, Dennis."

"What did you have in mind?"

"My place. It just so happens to be unoccupied." She peeked at her watch. "At least for another hour or so."

I took her by the hand and we practically ran to my car. This day was getting better and better.

Chapter 32

She lived on the second floor of a small apartment complex on a hill not too far from Weaver. She opened the door with her key and peeked in to see if anyone were around. Fortunately, no one else was. She pulled me in and pinned me against the front door. Her mouth was on mine before I could take a breath. Then, just as quickly, she pulled away before my hands could work any magic.

"How about a drink?"

"I'd love one."

"All I have is wine," she said from the kitchen. "I hope you don't mind."

"Perfect." I wasn't a fan of wine, but it would do in a pinch. It seemed like both our inhibitions were already trending downward.

We sat on the overstuffed couch and took our first drink. She practically downed all of hers in one gulp while I took a smaller amount. I didn't care how bad it tasted.

We put the glasses down. The clothes practically flew off. A few minutes later we made the short walk to her bedroom and I closed the door.

Our *quality time* was over in less than an hour, unfortunately. We moved back into the living room fully-clothed and sat on the couch.

"We have a strict rule about sex in the apartment when others are home. This is the first time I've had to use it, and I think we made it with a few minutes to spare."

Although I was still reveling in the afterglow, I took the opportunity to get a little more information from her. "You wouldn't happen to know about an art gallery around here, would you? Kathleen Merryweather told us the Hermillion Club sponsored the war monument, the Fort New Dover model and an art gallery at the college. She said it was a beauty."

She stopped watching the cooking show and faced me. "I've been here a long time and I've never seen an art gallery. There are some displays set up in the SUB, but they are changed twice a semester. The art department has a big studio but no gallery in the

191

traditional sense." Her face changed as her eyebrows went heavy. "Unless..."

"Unless what?"

"Well, there is the legend of the art wall. It's been floating around for years."

"What's an art wall? More importantly, where is it?"

"It's just an old Weaver College rumor, Dennis, so don't go crazy. It's been said that the greatest paintings in the area are on the art wall, but I don't know of anyone who has actually seen it. I've heard it's not easy to get to either."

"What building is it in? Can we get access?"

"It's not in any building. It's under the college. There are steam tunnels everywhere, in case you didn't know it. That's how they heat the sidewalks to keep the snow off."

I did know about the steam tunnels. The rectangular covers were all over the sidewalks. Most of them were welded shut.

The front door opened and in walked her female roommate, Kelly. After a short introduction, Kelly went into the kitchen and disappeared.

I stood up. "I should probably go."

"Yeah, I have some work to do. I'll see you tomorrow. Stay safe." She gave me another hug and kiss. "You never cease to amaze me."

I was thinking the same thing about her.

***

My phone rang on the drive back home. Tom and Jed were at O'Reardon's watching the baseball playoffs and wanted me to join them. It was still pretty early and I wanted to tell them the big news, but there was one person I had to call first.

Russell was on the highway heading back to New Dover when I rang him. He had been out on a business deal all day and truly sounded happy to hear from me.

"Can you meet us at O'Reardon's, Uncle Russell? Tom and Jed are already there. I have some interesting news for all of you."

He paused before answering. "O'Reardon's, huh? Did I mention I hate that dive?" I could hear in his voice that he wasn't really mad. "But you sound pretty excited about something, so I can stand it one more time. I'll be there in about twenty minutes, but it'll cost you a beer."

We were well into the first round when Russell arrived. He took off his leather jacket, tossed it in the corner of the booth and greeted me with his usual bear hug. Instead of sliding into the booth, he grabbed me by the arms and sniffed my head and shoulder area.

"Hmmm." He looked me over. "The unmistakable smell of perfume, red marks around the lips and neck, the classic dreamy look associated with post-coital glow; that can only mean one thing—penetration station."

"Koz, you stud puppet," Tom said.

Jed put his fist out and I bumped it. Then the others got theirs. It's what guys do. Nobody asked how she was or for any details. Russell slid in the booth and we moved on.

"I promised you a beer," I said as Tom slid it down from the end. "This dive is good for something, and you'll need one for this story."

I wasted no time telling them about my trip to the museum with Melody. "Once I saw the pattern from the cave-ins and matched them to another map, I knew what it had to be: tunnels." I pulled out my phone and displayed the pictures of the model with the lid popped.

Tom took it from my hand and examined it closely. "You mean to tell me that no one's been able to figure this stuff out for over 200 years until today? Koz, you're gonna get your own Wikipedia page for this, I'm sure of it." A waitress walked by and Tom stopped her. "Stacy, we are in the presence of greatness." He pointed at me with both index fingers. She gave him and us a crazy look, then walked on.

I shook my head and took another sip. "No. I'm not looking for glory or any of that stuff. Leave that to the real historians. My theory is that the tunnels were how the Hermillion Club members and later, the soldiers, got around. They went in through various entrances and likely had meetings somewhere down there. The tunnels could only last for so long before caving in, so they filled in the dangerous areas. Besides, it's still just a theory. I haven't really proven anything." I polished off what I had left, then wiped my mouth with my sleeve. "Which brings us to our next mystery:

finding the art gallery Kathleen Merryweather and Melody talked about. I know it's going to be a huge discovery. Unfortunately, it's not easily accessible."

"Where is it?" Jed asked.

"From what Melody said, it's under the college. She called it an 'art wall' and it's incredible, according to the legend."

Russell sat up straight at the mention of it. "You know, that rings a bell, now that you mention it. When I was at Weaver, there was talk of an art gallery down in the steam tunnels. My old friend, Steve Emerson, told me he saw it once. We didn't believe him because he was stoned to the gills most of the time, but the guy was half gopher. He used to go exploring down there all the time."

"So how do we get there? There must be an open cover somewhere."

"Don't count on it," said Jed. He gave his cap a 180-degree turn. "Security's a lot tighter than it was when Russell went there. I've never been down in them, but I also know someone who has. He said they started locking off parts to keep people away. Two guys got caught beneath the admin building last semester, and they brought the feds in. Since nine-eleven, that sort of trespassing is considered a terrorist act, and those two are looking at some possible jail time." Jed sat back, put his hands out at me and shook them. "Don't do it, Koz. I sure wouldn't."

Jed was always a bit too cautious, but he was probably right. There had to be another way. Then my wheels started turning. I grabbed a cocktail napkin from the table and a pen from my jacket. I began to draw the basic shape, the *shingala*. I marked the four cemeteries at each point and connected them to the Pelson gravesite in the middle. I made small circles along the spokes where the cave-ins occurred. Three of the spokes appeared to be useless; the fourth was clean.

"This tunnel is still active, I'm pretty sure." I tapped on the clean spoke with my pen. Then I drew a rectangle three-quarters of the way from the center point toward the endpoint at Oak Ridge Cemetery. "Anyone know what this is?"

Jed looked but didn't answer.

Tom gave it a shot. "The town museum is right around there."

"Close," I said, "but not quite."

"Weaver," said Russell. "The tunnel runs right along the college."

"That's right. My guess is that the art wall is in there." I put an X on the spot for effect.

Tom pulled the napkin a little closer. "If you went in through the center like the soldiers did, man, that's a long way to go underground. That can't be safe, Koz."

"I agree. That's why I have no intention of going that way. The Hermillion Club members needed other ways in; that's why the cemeteries are where they are." I made a big circle in the napkin. "The campus borders Oak Ridge cemetery. I'm going to pay a little visit to Syvanus Hartin's vault and see what's down there. So who's with me?"

No one at the table said a word. Tom nervously took a drink, then looked at me. "Assuming for a moment that you are not completely crazy, let's go with this. You're going to walk into the grave of a dude who's been dead for centuries, find a secret passage that leads to a tunnel that may or may not exist to find an art gallery that may or may not exist and you want an accomplice. Is that about it?"

Tom had given me his full support and invaluable help during this entire ordeal, so it was distressing, but understandable, to hear his tone.

"Come on, you guys," I said. "This is the big finish. I'll ask again: who's with me?"

Tom made a low mumbling sound, then cleared his throat and tried again. "I'm, uh, claustrophobic, Koz. I mean severely. If you need help above ground, I'm there for you, buddy."

Jed looked away. "Did I mention I really hate graveyards, Koz? With a passion. It's just... I don't—"

"I'm in," said Russell. "No one should go at it alone, Dennis. Hell, I'm kind of curious, truth be told. I don't know what sort of wild adventure Norm has created for you, but I'm sucked into it too." He polished off the last of his drink and placed the glass down with gusto. "I have to go back to my hotel room and make a few more phone calls; then my business is done in this town." He shook my hand hard, then pulled me in for a typical Russell hug. "I'll bring some bolt cutters and other tools. We'll get this done tomorrow." He shook hands with the others, then headed out.

"That's some uncle you have there, Koz," Tom said. And he was soon to be my partner in crime.

Chapter 33

I barely slept that night wondering about our trek the next day. I got up late because I had nothing better to do. As always, I immediately checked my email. I was surprised to find one from Ken Cordeiro from the planning and zoning board. He said he had some information about my father and wanted to meet me somewhere to discuss it. I called his cell phone and arranged to see him at his office just before noon.

Ken's full-time job was in the insurance business—a vice-president, according to the directory near the front counter. A young woman directed me to his office at the end of a long hallway. Based on the large size and plush furnishings, it appeared that vice-president was more than just a title.

"Dennis, great to see you again." Ken offered me a chair at a small table near the window. He sat on the other side.

"Thanks for calling me." I worked my way into the chair, trying hard not to slouch.

"First of all, I'm sorry I didn't get back to you sooner. I've been busy with the Founder's Day preparations, which, knock on wood, are all done and ready for tomorrow." He pulled a page from a folder and placed it on the table. "Back before we had emails, all town correspondence was done with memos. I found this memo written by your father and addressed to the members of the zoning board. It's rather strongly worded and states in no uncertain terms that he was not happy that the zoning board kept rejecting potential cemetery sites and they were violating several town ordinances for doing so. He planned on... how did he say it?" He picked up the memo briefly. "...taking action."

He turned it toward me, then slid it across the table.

"Your father signed it, but it never made it up the chain to the selectmen's office. It's a copy, but I don't know where the original is. Probably destroyed."

I stared at the words and the familiar signature of Norman J. Kozma at the bottom. My father was trying to do his job and they stopped him.

"There's something else." He took out another paper and placed it on the table. "According to this document, there never was any money missing from the town account. The sum of $9750 was temporarily misplaced and later accounted for a few months after Norm died. It seems that several cash payments were not processed properly by the clerical staff. It had the earmarks of fraud, but it was just an honest mistake. Your father took the fall for something that didn't happen, Dennis, and I'm not sure why. I have a reporter friend at *The Beacon*, and I'm going to make sure the truth is told. Your father deserves it."

I read the document... well, at least I tried to. My mind had trouble focusing because all I could think of was Dad. He knew he was innocent, but he never put up a fight and I couldn't figure out why. "Thanks, Ken. I'm not sure what to make of all this, but I'm relieved to know that his reputation is back, posthumously. I don't know; it's almost as if..." Then it hit me. My father gave me the town documents in the same file as the Komaket images. They were a package deal for a reason: he knew I would attempt to clear the Kozma name and that would keep me interested in Komaket, *shingala* and the "something big" that was about to happen. It was all about incentive.

"As if what?"

I gathered my thoughts and considered telling Ken, but it was too late in the game to bring someone else in. "Uh, nothing. Thanks again. I really appreciate everything you've done." I stood up to shake his hand.

"You're quite welcome. I'm just doing my duty as a town official." He gave me a firm shake. "Founder's Day is tomorrow. Are you going to join in the festivities?"

"I wouldn't miss it for anything."

***

Russell called later in the afternoon, and we arranged to meet at 9 p.m. I hadn't heard from Melody all day, so I assumed I had lost my shadow, which was fine with me. I had no intention of telling her about my plans to go subterranean.

I found some grubby clothes for the occasion, plus a water bottle, a flashlight and my fully-charged cell phone. Russell arrived on time but didn't come in. I went out through the garage without telling my mom or Stan where I was going. They didn't have a need to know either.

We sped toward the cemetery in silence. Russell reached for the radio volume, then pulled his hand back. "Ready for this?"

My mouth was dry. I wished I had brought some gum. "I think so."

"We can always bail if you want, Dennis. No shame in that."

I had never been a risk taker, so his offer was tempting. Fortunately, my overriding urge to know trumped everything. I even heard the voices of my mom and Gene Clausen telling me to finish this. "I'm good, really. Let's get this done."

We arrived at Oak Ridge Cemetery a few minutes later, parking on the street a block away in an unlit area. Russell opened his trunk to take out a pair of bolt cutters and a small bag of tools which I attached around my waist. It was a cool night, so we both wore dark sweatshirts to fight off the chill and blend in a bit better. We jumped the short stone wall in the corner of the cemetery, then headed to Syvanus Hartin's grass vault near the middle.

I was never a big fan of cemeteries during the daytime, but visiting one at night with only a flashlight beam and moonlight to guide us was pretty spooky. If Russell had not volunteered to come along, I would have chickened out for certain.

As we arrived at the vault, the moon went behind a large cloud, further adding to the eeriness. There was a small padlock on the door. I cast my light on it while Russell got out his bolt cutters. With little effort, he snipped off the lock and placed it nearby. He gave the door a slight push and it began to open.

"Here goes nothin'."

The smell hit me first. It wasn't the smell of dead bodies or anything morbid like that, fortunately. It was moist, moldy and earthy; I found myself nearly gagging. I took short breaths and it seemed to get a little better. Russell's flashlight was working the room. I could make out four tombs, two against each side wall.

"Love what they've done with the place." Russell focused on a large spider web in the corner. He squatted down and began to feel around on the dirt floor. "There has to be a passage way, Dennis. Look for a door or handle or something."

I got down and brushed handfuls of dirt away. I thought of

199

something and dug into the small tool kit for a screwdriver. I poked around in the front of the vault but found nothing. Russell saw what I was doing and did the same with his knife. Within seconds, his blade made contact with something.

"Over here." We both worked to scrape the dirt away, revealing a three-foot-square metal door. I shone my light and cleared the dirt around the edges and the hinge along the back. Russell worked his blade under the front edge and loosened it. We both used our fingers to pry it open. It was heavier than I expected, and the hinges complained as we worked it open. We shone our beams into the void and saw the bottom pretty far down.

Russell leaned into the hole. "Grab me by the belt while I check this out."

I steadied myself and grabbed his belt. His head, then his shoulders disappeared into the hole, and I felt his weight in my hands. He reversed out and sat back on his legs.

"There's definitely a tunnel heading east. There's a ladder down there too. It must've fallen down. One of us will have to jump down and retrieve it."

"I will."

He moved aside and I scrambled into the hole, feet first. I lowered myself down, then grabbed the front lip while he held his flashlight. It was only a few feet more, so I let go, landing softly on the dirt. I dusted off and retrieved the ladder, leaning it against the far wall. Russell came down into the surprisingly spacious tunnel, and we both shone our beams down its expanse. Thick timbers supported the sides every ten feet, so it appeared to be safe. There were no barriers for as far as we could see.

"We need more light." He pulled out what looked like a small LED lantern. It came on and illuminated the entire tunnel. "Much better."

I turned my flashlight off and secured it in my belt. I waited for him to go, but he motioned me forward and handed me the lantern. "It's your adventure, kid."

I gave him a playful slap on the shoulder. "Next stop: the art gallery."

Chapter 34

The tunnel followed a straight path, more or less, in the direction of Weaver College. The tunnel architects made sure to put in air shafts every few hundred yards so fresh air was not a problem, relatively speaking. I was curious about what covered the air shafts on the surface but not curious enough to investigate. We kept moving along at a quick pace until we came to a split. One section curved a bit to the right, the other kept going to the left.

"Which one do we take?" I held the lantern into each tunnel, but they were virtually identical. I had thought about bringing my portable GPS unit, but it wouldn't work underground.

Russell stared into both tunnels, then pointed left. "This one must go to Weaver."

I walked ahead with the lantern, then turned to see Russell standing at the crossroads. He was moving his index fingers around, drawing a map in the air. Satisfied with the visual image, he nodded and followed me.

The tunnel turned and maintained a parallel course to the other one. The air was sweeter for some reason, and the ground was firmer. About a twisting quarter-mile later, we came across a small branch to the right. I stuck the lantern in, and we were both shocked to see not a tunnel but a small room. There were several broken-down cots and mats on the floor along one wall, several chairs piled against the other.

"There's plenty of room at the inn." Russell examined the contents of the room.

"It's a perfect hiding place and a great spot for secret meetings. It's not like anyone would think to look down here." I remembered that I had my cell phone with me and snapped a picture of the room.

We exited and continued on toward Weaver. After a slight turn to the left, several crisscrossing wooden beams blocked the passage. I thought the journey was over. While I held the lantern, Russell examined the barricade. He grabbed a beam jammed into the lower corner and pulled, then pulled again. He was a lot stronger than he looked. It came out, nearly sending him tumbling back. The other beams came out easily, and he tossed them to the side.

"Just a minor setback, Dennis." He casually wiped his hands on his pants.

As we continued on, I noticed a difference in the tunnel wall and pointed it out to Russell. "Stone walls. We must be getting closer to civilization."

He pointed down. "Stone floor too."

On the left we saw a metal door with no handle. "I'll bet this connects to the Weaver steam tunnels, Dennis. We're close. I can feel it.

The art wall appeared out of the darkness on the left side of the tunnel. The ceiling became higher and the tunnel wider as we walked by it. The entire wall, about thirty feet, was covered in beautifully-drawn murals. We both noticed one of the murals at the same time.

"Komaket," we said. It was the portrait Dr. Ulysses Avila had drawn and the same one my dad left me. Komaket's face was a good five-feet tall.

I touched the wall… cold concrete. I took out my camera and captured the image.

"Dennis, this is absolutely amazing. I've never seen anything quite like it."

We slowly walked along, admiring the murals. There was something vaguely familiar about them. Then it came to me. "These aren't random images. They're sequential. It's the legend of Komaket drawn out. I'm sure of it."

Russell held the lantern while I got out my camera. I motioned him back to the beginning. I took pictures as I talked.

"Okay, number one, Komaket as a young man in the village. Number two, the smallpox epidemic strikes. Number three, Komaket leaves on a magical steed in search of a cure." The detail in each mural, especially the steed, was impressive.

By this time, the conditions in the tunnel had taken their toll on my throat, so we stopped for a quick water break while we admired the wall.

"Now, number four we both know," I continued. "Komaket returns, bringing with him the concept of *shingala,* the place where energy from all surrounding structures converges, and a magic staff. Number five, Komaket forms wolves in a pattern around the sick and raises his staff. The wolves breathe on them and everyone's cured." I had talked so much I forgot to take pictures. I backtracked and caught up.

"So, after curing his tribe, he next cured the villagers and showed them how to protect their village. In exchange, Komaket would one day return for what was rightly his." There was no mural to match the last statement, but I remembered Mr. Sellers telling me about it.

Russell recognized the next one. "The Battle of New Dover: the local militia defeat the Brits at Fort New Dover. Nice detail. You can even see the soldiers carrying the dead and wounded back to the fort."

We moved to the next mural, but its meaning was not clear. It appeared to be a large fire with people around it. "I don't get this one, Russell."

He placed the lantern close to it. "I'd say it's a bonfire." He moved to the other side of me and continued looking. "I see it now. It's at Komagansett Park. There's the stone archway and the arboretum in the background. Every Founder's Day they light a bonfire in the park. It's a tradition."

I saw something out of place in the lower right corner of the last mural and moved the lantern close to it. It was the initials HC. "Hermillion Club. Kathleen Merryweather told us they were responsible for the art gallery." The expanse between the bonfire and the end of the wall was blank. "It's not finished."

"TBD, Dennis. The final chapter has not been written. I guess we'll find out tomorrow."

I finished taking pictures of the mural and put my phone away. I went back for a second look to admire the artwork one more time. Just beyond the art wall was a small sign that said "ND MUSEUM —>" pointing in the direction of the New Dover Museum.

"I wonder how many other exits there are."

Russell took a flashlight and shone it down the tunnel, which seemed to be endless. "Well, this is no time to find out. You've got the information you wanted and I don't know about you, but I've just about had my fill of the spelunker's life." He gave the lantern a quick shake. "Besides, we're running low on light."

We headed back the way we came. The trek seemed to go quicker on the return. First, I replaced the beams that blocked the tunnel. Back under the cemetery, I went up the ladder first, then helped Russell into the vault. We closed the metal door and tried our best to cover it with dirt to make it look like we were never there. Once outside, Russell placed the broken lock back on the door so it looked uncompromised.

The air smelled great. I drew in several deep breaths as we quickly made it back across the cemetery. There was a sense of relief as we made it over the corner of the wall and onto the street.

"Nice work." Russell put his hand up, ready for a high-five. I came in low and gave him a huge bear hug, like he'd always given me.

We'd both earned it.

Chapter 35

Founder's Day finally arrived. It was a crisp October Saturday—sweatshirt weather, my mom liked to called it.

I had lived in New Dover my whole life but had never once attended Founder's Day, so it would be a new experience for me. I checked the town website for a list of events and locations. Most of the early stuff was for kids: face painting, pony rides, clowns. No thanks.

A section of Komagansett Park was declared "The Village." All the costumes, food and entertainment were authentic from the early 1700s. This included a short play written by a local playwright. That looked interesting, so I made a mental note to check it out later in the afternoon. The bonfire was scheduled for 8 p.m. I would definitely be there for it.

I spent most of the early afternoon at home looking at the pictures I took of the art wall. Some of the photos were darker than I had hoped due to the low output from the lantern, but I used some photo-enhancing software to brighten them up.

The blank area at the end of the art wall still bugged me. When would it be filled in and by whom? Thinking about it made my stomach tighten uncomfortably.

I showed the images on my laptop to Tom and Jed an hour later at Tom's place. He had to turn away after seeing some of the tunnel shots. "I get claustrophobic just looking at them, Koz; but, I must say, the drawings are pretty awesome."

My phone rang and I checked the caller ID. It was Russell. "Dennis, I have one last unforeseen loose end to tie up; then I'll meet you at the park."

"Sounds good. How about 4 p.m. at the arboretum?"

"Perfect. See you then."

Tom was fixated with the image of the bonfire from the art wall. He turned it back in my direction. "So, Koz, let's go back to your birthday in August when this Komaket dude's picture first arrived. All the experts have told us he's just a legend, but you're convinced he's coming back. If you believe the art wall, then

205

something's going to happen after the bonfire."

"Yeah," Jed said, "you've seen the wall. You've lived this for two months. What's going to happen?"

I started to speak but then halted. I honestly had no idea.

***

My two friends told me they'd meet up with me at the festivities later that night. I went home to change and rest up for Founder's Day, then sat quietly in a comfortable chair for a long while, thinking about the one constant through all of this—my father. Had he really foreseen the events as they played out the last two months? I wondered if he had ever seen the art wall in person during his college days or even later. He sent me on this wild ride, and tonight it may all possibly end.

An unusual noise interrupted my thoughts: my phone's ringtone. I couldn't remember where I left it, so I followed the sound to my sweatshirt hanging on the doorknob in my room. I got to it just before voice-mail kicked in. It was Melody.

"Do you need a ride to the bonfire tonight?"

"No thanks. I'm going early to check out some of the festivities."

She paused before answering. "So you're definitely going, right?"

"Of course. Wouldn't miss it."

There was another long pause. "That's great, Dennis. I can't wait to see you there."

Her tone sounded odd but that was typical for her. She said goodbye, then hung up.

***

I arrived at Komagansett Park alone and quickly mingled with the crowd. I had thirty minutes before Russell would show up at the arboretum, so I headed for The Village on the other side of the park. The path was lined with craftsmen and artisans selling their wares. There was everything from hand-made pottery to basket-weaving to gold and silver jewelry. The food court sold turkey legs and baked potatoes, as well as more traditional food. Most lines were several folks deep.

Just before the arboretum, I saw Neil Hollinger sitting at a table with a large poster of his book cover behind him. Several people were in line to get autographed copies. He saw me as I walked by, so I gave him a very animated wave, which caused him to turn away and continue signing his crappy books.

Everyone in The Village was dressed in authentic clothing from the 1700s. I watched a young girl in a very uncomfortable-looking dress engage in candle-making. She smiled politely as she went about dipping the candles into a vat of wax. Another was churning butter. It sure looked authentic. I checked out the play to pass the time.

I met Russell at the arboretum a few minutes later. He hustled me to the food court. "I'm starving. They have some great chowder and clam cakes, so let's go for it."

"Sounds good."

We grabbed our food, found an empty table and sat facing each other. He ate quietly and rarely made eye contact. I knew something was up.

"What's wrong, Uncle Russell?"

He finished chewing a clam cake. "I have to head back to Vermont. I've stayed as long as I can. There are contract issues to iron out, and I've been on the phone all afternoon. I have to be there or my business is in real jeopardy."

"So when are you leaving?"

"I should have left already, but I'll head out in a little while. I'm really sorry about this, Dennis. I know the timing sucks. It feels like I'm letting you down."

"No, really, that's okay. I mean, are you kidding me? These last few days have been great. Without your help, we never would have cleared Dad's name. Without you, we would've never figured out this whole Komaket mystery. Look around this park." I paused and moved my hand across the horizon. "Have many people here have set eyes upon the infamous art wall? As far as I know, only two. That kicks some serious ass."

He gave me that great big Kozma grin and put up his big, right paw. I wrapped my thumb around his and gave him a firm shake.

"You're a great kid, Dennis. Norm is doing freakin' cartwheels right now, he's so proud of you. I can guarantee that."

I laughed at the thought of my dad doing cartwheels. That was too funny.

We walked around the entire park, talking about nothing and everything. It didn't really matter. The sun was going down, and most of the booths began to close up. People were leaving the park by the dozens. Others headed past the entrance to the arboretum, as did we.

The logs for the bonfire were stacked about ten feet high in an open area near the end of the park. The fire department placed barricades around the logs to keep everyone back a safe distance, and a fire truck was parked over to the side, just in case.

I never realized exactly where we were until I looked toward the sunset. The park bordered the new cemetery, and I could clearly see a grass-covered vault a short distance away, Ralph Pelson's. Then it hit me: this was the big event everyone was waiting for. Komaket would come out from the center point during the bonfire and take what was rightly his. His followers had been preparing for this day for generations. I looked around to see if I could identify any. Hollinger was there, but he was a town official, so it would be expected. Everyone looked normal. Everyone fit right in.

An ancestor of one of the original town founders had the honor of lighting the bonfire. He dropped a torch at the base, and soon it was engulfed in flames. Everyone gathered as close as they could around the bonfire and clapped. I clapped too. I felt a tap on my shoulder and turned to see Tom and Jed behind me.

"What's the good word, Koz?" Tom said.

"Just enjoying the festivities," I said.

There was more applause as people dressed in wolf costumes began to surround the crowd. The sounds of bongo-like percussion filled the air.

I thought back to how wolves played a role in the Komaket legend. "Hey Tom, remember that meeting we had with Mr. Sellers at the museum?"

"Sure."

"What did he say about wolves?"

Tom thought for a moment. "I believe he said Komaket gathered the people in a circle, and ten wolves surrounded them and breathed on them." He looked all around the bonfire. "Kind of like now."

Jed did a quick count. "Yup, ten wolves. What does it mean?"

"Yeah, Koz," said Tom. "Should we move outside the circle? I'm kind of askeered."

Tom, as always, knew how to make me laugh. I put my arms around both my friends' shoulders and held on tight as a man-wolf danced behind us.

Nothing happened. There was no crazed native running from the Pelson vault, no fire or brimstone or flashing lights, no tormenting Tisdales—just a bonfire.

"Hey, Koz," Tom said, "shouldn't your uncle be here for this?"

"He is. He's right over—" I looked all around, but Russell was nowhere to be found. I backed up a bit, nearly running into a man-wolf. "He had to go back home. Something urgent came up."

I felt a stabbing pain when I realized he had left after all we'd been through. Maybe my mom was right about him all along. He could never finish anything. Maybe I couldn't either. My stomach sank just thinking about it.

The man-wolves left through a clearing in the arboretum, and the park grew quiet. The bonfire burned for another fifteen minutes or so. The fire chief put it out in just a few seconds. The smoldering mass drew a few more cheers as the crowd slowly drifted away.

Someone grabbed my arm and turned me around. It was Melody. She quickly put her arms around my neck and kissed me.

"Thank you very much, but what was that for?"

Tom and Jed saw her and stepped aside.

"Can you guys excuse us for a minute?"

"We'll be over there." Tom pointed to a clearing.

I craned to see where they went, but Melody turned me toward her. "I'm so glad you showed up. This is the most wonderful day, Dennis."

"Too bad nothing happened. I guess the Komaket legend remains just a legend. I'm sure Hermillions throughout the area are wondering what the hype was all about."

"You couldn't be more wrong, Dennis."

"How? I was here. I saw the whole thing and it was a dud. The story is over."

209

She let out a girlish laugh. "What did you expect to happen, Dennis? Thunder and lightning? Plagues of locusts?"

She touched my arm and her skin was smooth but cold. I shook it off and took a few steps back. I didn't like the way she was acting. In the moonlight, she had a look of quiet contentment. I had seen enough. I walked away.

"The story is not over yet, Dennis!" she yelled. "There is one more chapter to be written. Meet me at the Weaver history department at 9 p.m. if you want to know the ending. I'm betting you do."

I turned to respond, but she had disappeared into the twilight. No way was I going to indulge her again. The story was over. Of course, I wouldn't go. No chance.

What was I thinking? Of course I would. I needed to finish this, and I had thirty minutes to get there.

Chapter 36

The park was lined with lanterns that allowed people to safely exit the festivities. I followed one of the dimly-lit paths back to the parking lot and found my car. The traffic had died down so I exited without much of a wait.

I headed east toward the Weaver campus, fumbling for my phone as I drove. I speed-dialed Russell's number and put it on speaker phone. He had to know what happened and what was going to happen. After ten rings, I realized he was either ignoring me or had turned his phone off. Once again I was on my own.

The campus traffic was sparse because it was a Saturday night. The history department was in one of the older structures on campus, far away from any parking spots. I got as close as I could, then hoofed it the rest of the way. I still had time.

The front door was propped open, so I went into the lobby and leaned against a square pillar to rest.

"Dennis, I'm so glad you could make it." Melody emerged from the shadows behind me. "Come this way. Class is in session."

"Class?" It made no sense, but I followed her down the dimly-lit hall to the last classroom on the right. I had taken a class in here a few years ago. She gestured me over to have a seat near the front.

"What's this all about?"

"Sit down. You'll see." She still had that glassy-eyed look.

I sat in one of the uncomfortable chairs. "What class is this?"

A light came on near the front.

"It's a refresher course." It was not Melody. The voice came from a small door near the side. Dr. Jacob Overmann entered the classroom. "...A refresher course in local history, Dennis." He stopped in front of the podium.

"I thought you were—"

"Dead? Well, Melody, you were right. He doesn't read the papers or watch the news. Thank God for that. No, Dennis, I've just been away for a few days." He touched his chest and arms.

"I'm all here, perfectly fine."

"So what just happened at the park? Komaket never returned to fulfill the prophecy. I guess you were right about him being just a legend, Doctor."

"Quite the contrary, Dennis; he returned like clockwork."

I looked at Melody who sat a few seats down. "You're wrong. I've done the math."

"Let's work through it, and remember, it's all in the timeline. Recall for me, Dennis, the *mahica,* the cycle of the wolf and how it plays into all of this."

I took a breath, then let it out. I never figured there would be a test. "Ten wolves breathed upon the people and Komaket cured them. Then he said he would return in ten cycles, about three hundred years, right?"

"Very good. Now continue with that timeline."

"We went through this on our run, Doctor. It puts us back in the 80s."

"Again, the timeline is intact. He returned as promised. Give me more, Dennis?"

I threw my hands up. "Stop screwing with me. What the hell's going on here?"

Melody shot up. "Dennis, you're so dense." She got right in my face. "YOU are Komaket. Don't you get it?"

"What the…?"

"It's you, Dennis. It's been you all along. We're trying to tell you to do the math. You returned on the tenth *mahica.* Komaket cured the villagers when he was twenty-five. That's why your father waited until you were twenty-five. Now you must complete the cycle. You must fulfill the prophecy."

I had to laugh. It probably wasn't the best of timing, but I let out a good one. Besides the obvious fact that she had used me, the whole scenario was a joke. "You guys think I'm Komaket? That's just... that is seriously messed up. I mean, you two are really batshit crazy."

"I think you'll find that we're both quite sane," said Dr. Overmann.

I stood up quickly, knocking over the chair. "I've heard enough of this crap. You two certainly deserve each other, you know that?" I made it three steps before freezing. Dr. Overmann had a crossbow aimed right at me.

"This may not look like much, but…" He turned a few degrees and shot it at a large globe in the back of the classroom, splitting it in two. "…it is quite a useful weapon."

As I sat back down, Melody stood behind him as he reloaded.

"So what do you want with me? Really, you have my attention."

Melody opened a side door and propped it with a wedge. She stood near it and motioned like a model on "The Price Is Right." Then she said, "This way, Dennis; it's time to write the final chapter."

I had no choice. It was better to see what they were up to rather than end up shish kabob. Overmann was whacked enough to do it. Melody went first, then me, then Overmann. We turned right, then headed down a dimly-lit hallway. Melody opened a door that read "MAINTENANCE" and I followed. The room was filled with pipes, gauges and what appeared to be the heating system.

The silence was killing me, so I broke it. "I should have listened to my idiot friends, Melody. They told me you were just playing me, using me. I guess I just hoped it wasn't true. So tell me, have I been your mark all along?"

We walked past the furnace with Overmann keeping his distance, longbow still upright and ready.

"Dennis, to be honest, you are one of the nicest guys I have ever met, and therein lies your problem. Since I arranged to meet you at Roger's party, I knew this was going to be easy. It was just a matter of keeping you interested in Komaket and me, with no outside distractions. When I ratted out Roger, I knew you'd have to move home and keep digging."

"That was *your* doing?"

"Yes. Later, I called my aunt, Veronica Breezewood, and asked her to embellish your visit. When I had some friends report your lousy driving to your boss, I knew you would be fired, and that would sharpen your focus on the task at hand."

"Wow. Very thorough."

"My job was to get you interested, keep you interested and make sure you showed up for Founder's Day. I only had to bang you once to make it happen." She took a deep breath and smiled.

213

"My work is nearly done here."

There was a set of concrete stairs in the back corner. We stopped at the top step. Overmann threw Melody a key; she went down and unlocked the narrow door.

"May I ask where we're going?"

Melody turned on the lights, and Overmann nudged me down the stairs. He was uncomfortably quiet.

"It's about time you saw the art wall, Dennis," Melody said. "You've talked so much about it."

It appeared that my visit the previous day was unknown to them. At least I had that going for me.

"Speaking of tunnels," I said. "I'm guessing the two of you already knew about tunnels under the fort, right? And that the Shadow Regiment used them against the British?"

"Yes and yes, Dennis," Melody said. "Some secrets are harder to keep than others. My thesis will include all the details."

I had to hold back a smirk, thinking that I wouldn't get my Wikipedia page, after all. Tom would be so bummed.

The steam tunnels were much narrower than the others. They had concrete walls and large pipes running along the surface, forcing me to walk with a stoop to avoid banging my head every six feet. There were no side tunnels to escape down. We came to a gate. Melody unlocked it and ducked through. We took a left turn, then walked another hundred feet or so until we came to a metal door.

I took a quick look behind me. Overmann still had the longbow pointed at me.

"You still haven't told me what's going to happen. How do I fit into the final chapter?"

Melody unlocked the metal door and slid two bolts back. The door pulled open, free and easy. She reached above it for a large flashlight. Overmann donned a miner's helmet with a light on top.

"Get in the tunnel, Dennis," she said. "Now!"

I went in first. The smell immediately hit me. It was that dirty, musty smell I never got used to during my previous visit.

She slipped past me and shone the light around the tunnel. "This way."

I followed her and Overmann followed me, the light from his helmet casting giant shadows in front of me. There were others in

214

the tunnel; I could feel it. We came around a bend and there they were, lined up shoulder to shoulder against the wall. These had to be members of the Hermillion Club. I didn't recognize any of them until we got near the end. Neil Hollinger gave me the same wave I gave him earlier in the park. *What a douche whistle.*

"This is a most glorious day, everyone." Overmann's voice boomed through the tunnel. "Behold! The prophesy is fulfilled!"

The Hermillions remained silent and fell in behind Overmann.

"The story of Komaket has taken on many forms over the years, but the main chapters have always remained intact."

We came to the art wall, and he spotlighted the large picture of Komaket. We moved slowly along as he spoke, placing his light on each mural for effect.

"The arrival…"

"The outbreak…"

"The return…"

"The cure…"

"The battle…"

"The revival…"

"And finally…"

The last piece had filled in. It showed a lifeless-looking Komaket being taken away by two large eagles.

"The departure, Dennis. It is the final chapter. Komaket died at twenty-five and took with him the power of *jorva*… reincarnation. Many of his followers have already come back. He has come back. Now, many more await their turn." He motioned to the mob of followers behind him.

"Let me guess. The Hermillion Club?"

"Some have waited for centuries for your return, Dennis. Now they await your departure so that you may bestow new life on them and us. We come back as new members with new life and full memories of our previous selves. I, for example, was a soldier in the Shadow Regiment. I can remember it like it was yesterday."

Melody slipped behind me, stood by his side, then slipped an arm around him.

"Why don't you just kill me, doc, and be done with it?"

"That's not part of the legend, Dennis. Komaket dies alone and is carried away by eagles. Besides, I'm not a killer, at least not cold-blooded. You see, these tunnels are rigged with small

215

explosive devices that will cause them to cave in just like the other tunnels did when the club members didn't need them anymore. I have a friend in the geology department who will swear it's a natural phenomenon, just like the others were. I've already made arrangements to have the air vents covered."

They began walking backwards toward the metal door as the Hermillions began to file out. I ran toward them.

Overmann lifted his crossbow. "I never said I wouldn't wound you, Dennis."

They reached the door and stepped in.

Overmann stuck his head out. "The timeline is complete, Dennis. The prophecy shall be fulfilled."

Melody looked back at me. I wondered how much of it was an act and how much was real. Part of me thought she would change her mind, rescue me and declare her undying love.

"See you in the next life, Dennis."

Guess not.

The door slammed. I heard the bolts slide and lock. I was in total darkness.

"You'll all rot in hell!" I banged on the hard, steel door for effect.

This was no time for a pity party. I had to move. I knew if I followed the tunnel the other way it would take me to New Dover Cemetery and a chance for escape. I also needed light.

My cell phone. I dug it out of my pocket and turned it on. The light was enough to see where I was going, but I had to move quickly. Only one bar remained on the battery level, thanks to all the pictures I had taken. I mentally kicked myself for having such a crappy phone and not charging it.

I ran as fast as I could with the phone out in front. *How far was it? A half-mile?* It was difficult to tell underground.

The first explosion came. It was a low rumble that made the support beams crack and finally break. I stopped and pinned myself against the tunnel wall. Thirty feet ahead of me the tunnel was completely blocked.

I turned back and kept up the fast pace. My legs were aching from all the running, but I kept it up. I was nearly back to the art wall.

The second explosion happened just behind me. The

collapsing debris just missed me. I tripped over something on the path and tumbled forward, dropping the phone. It landed face down, putting the tunnel in total darkness. I panicked for a second, then began to look for the green LED on the side of the phone. I found it a few feet away and continued.

I arrived back to the art wall and stopped to rest. The soft light from the phone cast an eerie glow on the mural, especially the new entry at the far end. *How did it get there? Who drew it?*

My phone gave out a mild beep, then turned off. I was once again in darkness. If I kept going the same direction, what would I find? The Pelson vault? How long would that take? It didn't matter. I had to get moving and keep moving.

I used my right hand as a guide, keeping it in contact with the tunnel wall as I moved along. I felt the cold concrete of the art wall, then the rough stone just after it. Something unusual in the darkness made me stop.

Could it be light?

I turned and watched as a small beam of green light formed on the art wall. I went back to within ten feet of it. The light grew larger, spreading out over the first mural, then filling the tunnel with a flash.

Standing before me in a greenish glow was Komaket.

Chapter 37

Komaket had his staff in one hand and the *shingala*-shaped necklace around his neck. Was I dead already? Was this really happening?

"Komaket." I said his name again and he looked at me, or perhaps through me; it was hard to tell.

He began walking in my direction, casting a surreal glow in the tunnel, then stood a few feet away and held out his staff. It was a beautiful, fascinating combination of wood and light. The *shingala* at the top of the staff and the one on his necklace began to glow orange, then blue, red and back to green. I wanted to reach out for him, but I was frozen. He turned and walked past me, then picked up speed. I followed him.

The tunnel curved slightly to the right as Komaket continued running. Was he my guide? My savior? I certainly hoped so. I heard another explosion behind me, followed by cracking beams and the sound of another cave-in as Overmann systematically destroyed the underground structures. Komaket was unfazed and kept moving rapidly down the tunnel, casting a perfect glow as he went. I would soon be saved; I just knew it.

Komaket stopped and faced a metal door on the left: the New Dover Museum. I remember the sign on the wall pointing to it.

He was going to open the door and let me escape through the museum; I was sure of it. Instead, he touched his staff to the door. His light surrounded it, and with a flash he disappeared into the museum. My world faded to black.

"No, don't leave me! Come back!" I pounded on the door in the darkness until my fists were raw, then slid down and sat in front of it. It must have been a hallucination.

It seemed darker than before, if that were possible. God, I wished I had a flashlight or even a Bic lighter. I felt sorry for myself until another explosion got my attention. The Hermillion Club loonies would not defeat me. *Move it, Kozma.*

Using the right-hand method, I ran down the tunnel in the darkness. How far was it to the center point? I had no idea. I

218

tripped on something and sprawled out. My chin hit the ground and I felt like I had been punched. I got up, staggered and reached for the wall with my right hand, but nothing was there. I reached with my left and felt something. Had I gotten turned around? I couldn't tell. There was another explosion behind me so I ran in the opposite direction.

My face and chest felt cool from the blood running down my chin. I wiped it with my left hand, but it didn't seem to matter. I wasn't getting out. I was going to die in the darkness.

An explosion directly above me knocked me to the ground. I couldn't get up. My left arm was pinned under me, and I felt a tremendous weight on my back and upper parts of my legs. My face was still uncovered, so I could breathe but for how long?

This was the end. I was sure of it.

A million thoughts went through my mind, my final thoughts. I did what my dad wanted, and I ended up dying in a pile of dirt... underground.

What was your point, Dad? Why did I trust you?

Time seemed to stand still in the darkness. I had no idea how long I was trapped as I tried hard to keep breathing. Another explosion would seal me in for good and get this over with. I prayed for a swift ending.

Instead, I saw a light as far down as I could see. It was coming toward me. This wasn't the green glow of Komaket; it was a white light. My father!

"Dad! Dad, I'm here. Help me!"

I heard my name. It was faint at first, then grew stronger.

"Dad, hurry!"

The light was bobbing up and down. I could hear footsteps running toward me. "Dennis? Dennis!"

It sure sounded like my father's voice. I don't know how he pulled it off, but he was there for me. I looked up in the soft glow and saw his face. "Help me, Dad."

"I'm here, Dennis." He reached out and took my hand. The light shone back on his face. It was Uncle Russell. "Can you move your feet?"

"A little bit."

"Okay, I'm going to pull like a son-of-a-bitch, and I want you to push off if you can. On the count of three. One... two... three."

219

He yanked my right arm and I tried to wriggle my way out. I didn't move very much. He placed the flashlight down and shone it toward me.

"One more time. Come on, kid. You can do it!"

He dug in and pulled. This time I felt myself sliding out. My left hand came free. He grabbed it, then pulled again with a mighty grunt. I kicked free of the debris and landed on top of him.

When I stood up, all body parts seemed intact.

"You came back for me."

"I'll explain later, Dennis."

"We have to go. Overmann rigged the tunnel to cave in."

He picked up the flashlight and grabbed my hand. "Can you run?"

"Like the wind."

We sprinted down the tunnel as fast as we could. My legs hurt more than I let on, but I willed myself past the pain. The tunnel ahead was partly collapsed.

"If we stay to the right, we should be able get through it." Russell kicked a beam out of the way and squeezed past, then pulled me through just as another explosion rocked the tunnel, sealing it behind us.

I couldn't tell how long we had run... five minutes, perhaps ten. My lungs felt like they were on fire and both knees throbbed. Between my own gasping, I could hear Russell wheezing loudly.

After another explosion, we came to the end of the tunnel. The ladder had fallen and Russell reached for it with shaky hands. I grabbed it and placed it against the wall.

"Up the ladder, Dennis, and we're out of this hell hole."

"You first."

"No chance. Just go."

I went up as fast as I could, then braced myself to help Russell up. Another explosion forced the ladder out from under him, but I held him tight. Using all my strength, I pulled him through the opening and helped him to his feet. The door to the vault was open and we sprinted out just as the vault collapsed in on itself.

We both knelt in the grass to catch our breath. I switched to all fours and filled my lungs with pure, sweet air. That's when I left the contents of my stomach on the grass in front of me. Strangely enough, I felt better for it.

"You won't believe what... what happened down there. Komaket, he arrived... and..." I was too tired to talk. I breathed through it, but something crossed my mind. "The museum! Is your car nearby?"

"Yes, it's parked right over there." He pointed behind him.

"We have to go to the museum right now. I'll explain on the way." I got up and ran toward his car, somehow finding a second wind. He gave me a pissed-off look when he arrived. A moment later, we were heading west.

Russell's phone was on the console. I picked it up. "Okay if I use it? If I'm right, the others will want to witness this." Without waiting for his answer, I quickly texted Tom and told him to grab Jed, then get to the museum as quickly as possible.

Russell cleared his throat. "You mentioned something about Komaket."

"I saw him down there. He came out of the mural. I followed him to the door of the museum. Then he disappeared through it. He went there for something."

Russell pulled a bottle of water from a cup holder and poured it onto his handkerchief. "Wipe your face off. You know what? I should take you to the emergency room instead. You look like you lost a fight with a grizzly bear."

"No! There's no time for that." I continued to wipe, surprised by how much blood came out of my split chin. "Besides, it's just a scratch."

He pulled into the parking lot of the museum a few minutes later, and I barely waited for him to park. I ran up to the large glass window in front and peeked in. There was a green glow coming from the back, but I couldn't see much from there. Headlights approached behind us as Tom's car rolled in and parked next to Russell's truck. He and Jed sprinted over and ducked under the window with us.

"What the hell is going on, Koz?" Tom asked. "You look like hell."

"It's Komaket. He's in there. Let's check the side window."

We dashed around the corner and found the largest window. I could see some movement inside, but the angle was bad. I remembered from the tour that there was a window in the back. We cut through a hedgerow and went behind the museum. I peered over the sill and Komaket came clearly into view. He was looking into one of the display cases.

"What's he doing?" Jed asked.

"I'm not sure." Then I saw what was in the display. "Bones."

Russell lifted his head and peeked in. "What?"

"Not *what*, Uncle Russell. *Who*? That display has the remains of a Native American warrior from the early 1700s." I punched my fist into my left palm. "That's why Komaket returned."

We watched as Komaket placed his hands over the top of the glass display. He appeared to be saying something, but we couldn't hear. He took his staff and placed it on the display top, then again began to chant, lifting his hands up to the heavens and arching his back. In a flash of multi-colored light, bones rose from the display and disappeared into the staff. Komaket brought his hands down and the light stopped. He turned toward us and raised his staff above his head with two hands. He appeared to look right through me.

"What's he doing now?" Tom asked.

"He's fulfilling the prophecy."

With staff still high, he chanted. Another flash of brilliant light filled the room, and I felt it race through me. Then he was gone.

"Did you feel that?" I asked.

"Absolutely," Jed said. "Pretty wild."

Tom just nodded.

Russell grabbed my shoulder. "Dennis, what did we just see?"

Too startled to speak, I began to walk away from the building. It was another moment of clarity, even bigger than the last one. I finally got it. "He came back for what is rightly his. That's the key to the Komaket legend. It's not earthly possessions or reincarnation or anything like that. Tom, remember what Mr. Sellers told us? Komaket's tribe believed that you should never leave a man behind in battle. Komaket came back for one of his own..."

Tom clapped his hands once. "The very last one."

I barely had enough energy to make it to the car. Tom and Jed helped me into my seat; then Russell strapped me in.

"Let's get you home, kid."

Chapter 38

I don't remember falling asleep that night, but I woke with my face cleaned up and a butterfly bandage on my split chin. I was sore in places I didn't know I had. It was Sunday morning, which meant my mom and Stan would be off to church, then out to breakfast. I limped down the hall and enjoyed a hot shower. When I came out, someone was sitting in Stan's chair. It was Uncle Russell.

"Dennis, good morning. How ya feeling, today?"

"Like I was attacked by a grizzly bear."

He noticed my confused look. "We brought you home last night and cleaned you up the best we could. Your mother wasn't too happy to see you like this, but we explained that you had a little too much fun at Founder's Day."

"You didn't?"

"Sure, we did. Technically, it's true. Anyway, Tom and Jed left, I slept on the couch last night and here I am. After some convincing by yours truly that all was well, your mom and the bald guy left about twenty minutes ago." He took a quick look at his watch. "Your friends should be stopping by any minute."

As he spoke, I made it to the kitchen to get some tea. There was some Danish on a plate, so I grabbed one. "You want some?"

"No thanks, I'm good. So you want to tell me what happened after you left the park?"

A knock on the door startled me, then made me smile. It was the trademark knock of Tom Richcreek. I let him and Jed in and we quickly exchanged bro hugs.

Tom added an extra shoulder slap. "You still look like hell, Koz."

"Glad to see you're okay," Jed said with a laugh.

Russell came over to greet the guests as they made their way to the couch. "Good timing, gents. Dennis here is about to fill us in on what happened after he left the bonfire."

I sat in my favorite chair and told them everything. Tom put his hands over his face when I got to the part about being alone in the dark tunnel. It was probably a claustrophobic's worst nightmare. I had everyone's attention when I described my first encounter with Komaket.

"So he just appeared out of the painting," Jed asked.

"Yup, like a hologram."

"That is friggin' awesome." Tom slammed his fist on the table. "Your old man called that one."

I described how Russell came in from the center point and rescued me amid the explosions. This got him a fist bump from Tom and Jed. Ah, hell, I added one too.

"You really thought it was your dad?" Jed asked.

I replayed the scene in my head. "Same voice and everything."

They probably wouldn't have believed the Komaket part had they not seen the big finish for themselves.

"… And the rest," I said between bites, "well, you were there."

"So the femme fatale and the professor guy were in cahoots the whole time. Damn, I didn't see that one coming. To be honest, I never trusted Melody as much as you did, but I must say she was very convincing." Russell shook his head as he drank from a coffee cup.

Both Jed and Tom had I-told-you-so smirks when Melody's name came up. Neither one said anything. Neither one had to.

"They tried to kill you, Dennis," Russell said. "We should get the police involved."

"I don't think that will necessary. I'll find a way to make their lives miserable. Then again, I doubt we'll ever see them again."

Jed grabbed a Danish and used it to make a point. "This secret group… the Hermillion Club—what of them?"

"They're a complete farce. They spent generations waiting for something they could never have. The gravesite patterns, the *shingala, jorva*, all that crap was a myth perpetuated over 300 years." I polished off my Danish. "Okay, Uncle Russell, your turn."

He looked away from us to take a drink of coffee. "First of all, I'm sorry I left you like that, Dennis. I started to head back, well, because that's what I've always done. I turned off my phone and drove. Then the strangest thing happened. I heard a voice. It was my brother, your father. I haven't heard that voice in years, unfortunately. Anyway, Norm spoke to me and it wasn't really what he said, just the fact that he had something to say. I turned around immediately and came back."

"What about your business?"

"It'll be fine or it won't. I don't know. It became irrelevant very quickly. I switched my phone back on and tried to call you, but the voice on the other side said you were out of range. We're on the same plan, so I know that's impossible unless you're in a submarine or, more likely, underground. I knew you went back to see the art wall. I played a hunch and went in through the other entrance, the Ralph Pelson one in the new cemetery. The door wasn't even locked. When I heard the explosions, I thought I was too late. I never could've lived with myself if anything had happened to you."

The doorbell interrupted our conversation. I answered it and was surprised to see our old friend Gene Clausen, the attorney, standing there.

"Hello, Dennis."

I thought for a second about slamming the door in his face. "What do you want?"

"May I come in? I have something important to give you."

Last time I saw him, he spent most of the night telling me and my friends what a loser I had been. Maybe he was right after all.

"Sure." I led him in and introduced him to Russell. They remembered each other from years ago. He also shook hands with Tom and Jed.

"I know this may sound strange, Dennis, especially after our first encounter; but I made one other arrangement with your father before he died. He asked me to deliver a letter to you the day after Founder's Day of this year." He handed me an envelope with my name written in Dad's handwriting. "I have not seen the letter, but please know that I have completed my legal obligations to your father. He was a fine man. I miss him a great deal. Good day to all of you."

"Hey, Gene," Tom said with a smile, "you have no idea what you put this guy through."

"I think I do." He shook our hands, then let himself out.

I placed the envelope on the coffee table and went to get another cup of tea.

"Aren't you going to open it, Dennis?" Russell asked. "We'll leave if you want some privacy."

I sat back down with cup in hand. "No, we're all kind of in this together." I took another sip. "Of course, I'm going to open it." I lifted the flap, pulled out the hand-written letter and read it out loud.

Dear Dennis,

If all went according to plan, Gene presented you with several documents on your twenty-fifth birthday. What you did with them and what you discovered on your journey is something I'll never know. My goal for all of this was simple: seek the truth. Sometimes we know exactly what it looks like; other times we must break through the facade and cast away the debris to find it.

I wasn't sure if one truth were enough, so I gave you two to discover. The truth about me can finally be revealed. After I left the country during the last April of my life, Gene used his power-of-attorney privilege to transfer $9750 from a retirement fund to my savings account. This, not coincidentally, was exactly the amount of money I was accused of taking from the town. When the auditors discovered the deposit into my account, they concluded that I had bilked it. The game was on. I let everyone believe what they wanted to believe for the sole purpose of providing you with incentive for the discovery of Komaket's legend. I knew you could not discover one truth without the other.

I can't possibly know what you went through in your voyage toward the truth. It was my hope that you would get others involved. Your mother and your Uncle Russell have been and always will be special people. Please keep them in your life.

I hope you have found that truth is not just a discovery of facts. It's standing up for what is right and believing in yourself. It's about making and keeping really good friends. It's about family. Always seek the truth, Dennis.

Have a great life, son.

Love,
Norm

Chapter 39

As promised, I went back to school in January. I decided I wanted to be a teacher, a history teacher, to be exact. It would take me two more semesters, but I was determined to follow through with it. I could and I did finish something. I discovered that history—especially local history—was not boring. It was exciting and I wanted to pass that excitement on to others. I was incredibly focused, more so than at any other time in my life.

I never saw Dr. Overmann or Melody Bancroft again. Neither of them returned to New Dover or Weaver and, well, good riddance to both of them—out of sight, out of mind.

I moved out of The House of Stan a few months after I graduated and went to live with a guy who had just bought a house in New Dover: Russell Kozma. He moved his business, lock, stock and barrel, to the tri-town area. He even let me work for him on weekends and school breaks.

True to his word, Ken Cordeiro released the documents that proved my father was not a crook. I kept the headlines from *The Beacon*:

Kozma Vindicated

I never found out how my dad got involved in the whole Komaket legend other than because of the zoning documents we uncovered. Gene Clausen told us Norm was always the smartest guy in the room, and I had no reason to doubt it. Of course, the four of us never told anyone about our sighting of Komaket that October day... like anyone would believe us, anyway.

The three drawings Dad left me returned to full color. I had them framed and proudly displayed on my living-room wall. Were they magic? I suppose they were, but it really didn't matter.

Every so often I would walk past Komaket, and his eyes would follow me across the room. He knew the truth and, as my dad said, the truth is not always easy.

Dad was right about something else too. Something big did

happen on that incredible journey—the biggest. I discovered the truth about myself.

The End

Made in the USA
Middletown, DE
28 November 2022